MW00721081

BOOK ONE OF THE ARCANE VOLUMES

HIVE

HIVE

JEREMIAH UKPONREFE

Copyright © Jeremiah Ukponrefe

This book is a work of fiction. Any names characters, places, and events are products of the author's imagination, and any resemblance to actual events or places or persons, living or dead,is entirely coincidental.

All rights reserved. No part of this publication may be reproduced,distributed, or transmitted in any form or by any means, including photocopying, recording, or other electronic or mechanical methods, without the prior written permission of the publishers.

ISBN: 978-1-7773329-0-7 (paperback)

First printed edition 2020.

CONTENTS

CHAPTER ONE

THE MARKET

Alexander King stood tall while the citizens held whispered conversations along the muddy streets. He did not bother to eavesdrop; their words were nothing of importance. The snippets that he did catch portrayed nothing but complaint.

The common people's clothes bore no resemblance to cohesive style. Their variants of shirts, pants, and elder shoes were torn and marked with grime. Alex thought it a pathetic display compared to his pristine military outfit, which projected his position within the Collective. His sleek gray torso and pants were matching, while his boots were a harsh black, muddied with small specks of dirt. His face was protected by a black mask that hid his identity, with the exception of his brown eyes.

The market was built on dirt, its upper layer slowly decaying into mud caused by the light rain that conquered the sky. Carts and stands were made mostly of wood and were used for buying, selling, and trading goods that were needed for the common people. Food, clothing, liquids, trinkets, and other miscellaneous items dangled in view of all those who passed by, tempting them with a taste of remnants from the old world. The sellers got their merchandise using the same methods: thievery. Prior to Collective occupation of the dead city, the abandoned buildings had been raided, with the citizens then claiming that everything they had was their own.

"Guard duty. We have to get out of this soon," Alex said.

"Nothing wrong with it. It's what we've been asked to do," Takeo Oshiro countered. He stood a head taller and his muscular body mass nearly doubled Alex's. His clothing was the mark of a Collective soldier: a gray jumpsuit. He had narrow hazel eyes and buzzed black hair. The two men not only differed in size, but also in weaponry. Takeo held a pump action R-90 shotgun, Alex an AK-47, both weapons of the old world.

"I'm tired of doing nothing," Alex said.

"We have been given a great position."

Alex rolled his eyes. Takeo was never one to indulge in his valid complaints, never willing to speak an ill word against the Collective's inner workings.

Alex remained alert for illegal activity. As he scanned the busy market he caught a glimpse of the inner-city skylines; that was where he wanted to be, where gray clouds shrouded tall buildings.

His daydreaming was interrupted by the discovery of an act worthy of suspicion. A young boy in his mid-teens not far from Alex's own age handed a steel case to the first man in a long line of buyers.

"Three o'clock."

"We should call reinforcements," Takeo said.

"Just follow my lead."

"But ... protocol."

"Come on."

Takeo followed Alex as they marched towards the stand, leaving their designated spots and improvising a new position, forcing the common people to disperse.

Alex stepped into the line, cutting off the man whose hands were within inches of taking possession of the case. The young seller retracted the object with fearful eyes.

Two others stepped forward within the confines of the stand: a middle-aged man and woman, both just as frightened as the boy. The trio had the same loose brown hair and tan skin. A family.

"What are you selling?" Alex asked, deepening his voice in the hope that they would feel intimidated.

The citizens within the line scattered.

"Tell me," Alex demanded, confronting the boy.

The boy swallowed. "We are selling nothing but our own goods. Things that we own. Not stolen."

The father put his hand on the boy's shoulder, ushering him back to his mother.

"What's inside the briefcases?"

Within the family's stock Alex spotted six cases of similar caliber.

"They're guns!" Alex raised his weapon towards the boy's head, wishing that instead it was a plasma weapon.

"I'll call help!"

As Alex turned to tell Takeo that help would not be needed, he discovered a new threat: citizens with guns had their barrels pointed towards the Collective duo. Alex counted eight, all of them holding measly pistols with the exception of a BN-10, where a glowing blue plasma sphere within its barrel was ready to cause death.

"Drop your weapons!" a citizen demanded. His voice was shaky like his hands.

Alex spoke first. "If you do anything to harm us, I hope that you have a plan to leave the city because—"

"Drop!" Takeo warned him.

As Alex hit the dirt, an explosion drilled to core of the rebellion's forces. When he looked up the outline of a Mecha suit was hovering in the air, propelled by blue flames rising from its back, bullets shooting from its arms

Takeo and Alex quickly recovered. Takeo whirled to face the family of rebels while Alex released the safety on his AK-47 and sent a barrage of shots towards the rebel holding the BN-10. The man fell instantly without the chance to retaliate.

The remainder of those in opposition to the Collective attempted to disperse, but many of them were killed by the reign of plasma bullets. Alex shifted his priority towards the initiator of the conflict. The father had withdrawn a revolver, but with a quick shot from Takeo he was slain.

"Throw a grenade!" Alex screamed.

Takeo did as Alex suggested and tossed the black object within the tarp. A plume of white smoke came from the sphere, and Takeo heard the woman coughing. The boy made no sounds.

Alex pivoted and spotted that the adolescent had moved away from the stand. The opportunity to escape had presented itself in the chaos, but the boy did not take it. Instead, he stared at the body of his father.

"Stay there!" Alex yelled. He carried his voice for all the commoners to hear. To show who held true power: the Collective. Not small sprouts of rebels.

The boy started towards them but Alex lifted him by his shirt collar and slammed him against the silver metal of an alternative stand.

"I'm going to kill you!" the adolescent screamed, shoving his knee into Alex's stomach. Alex threw him to ground, deciding that he would tolerate nothing less than complete submission. He slammed his foot against the child's face, torso, and legs. The others would need to learn.

"Tell everybody you know what happened here."

"We just wanted to protect ourselves!" he screamed as tears began to fall down his cheeks and onto the floor.

"From who? You're safe here," Alex reminded him with annoyance.

"You're an idiot!"

Takeo added to his punishment and struck the boy with his foot, causing blood to stream from his nose. Takeo had the mother within his grasp, not bothering to struggle against his authority.

"Go or you will have the same fate your father," he told the boy.

"Son!" his mother screamed. "Let's go!"

The adolescent struggled to stand. It was clear that he wanted

to speak. As soon as he was able to rise his mother took him and the duo fled, showcasing their lack of bravery.

Those who were watching had returned to their previous activities, but it was disingenuous. They nervously kept their eyes on Alex and Takeo.

"That was awesome!" Patton yelled. Alex turned and found his unofficial protégé leaping towards him with boundless energy, his mop of orange hair bouncing with each movement. The boy, who had just turned eleven, had a smaller frame than others his age. His freckles were splashed across his nose and cheeks, and his deep green eyes looked upon Alex in awe.

"Another day on the job," Takeo said.

"That punk needed taken down."

"Needed *to be* taken down. Remember your proper grammar or nobody will respect you," Alex scolded, annoyed that a child of hisage still struggled with forming proper sentences.

Patton nodded eagerly to indicate his understanding. "Why not kill him?"

"Why does this kid ask so many questions?" Takeo wondered. "I don't know why I asked that," Patton said.

"What do you think we should do next?" Alex asked Patton. Patton pondered. His face morphed into that of a thinking man: his eyes crunched together, his teeth bit lightly into his lip, and his eyes narrowed.

"We should make sure we record what he looks like, and also write down everything he did."

"Why?" Alex asked.

"I guess it's because if anything bad was going to happen to us then he would get away with what he did."

Before he could evaluate the answer he was interrupted by their savior in the Mecha suit.

"Alexander, you are needed. Commander Ives would like to speak with you."

Alex became worried. He had either done something terribly wrong, or exceedingly right.

"Congratulations," Takeo said.

"Can you take care of this sector?" Alex asked Takeo.

"You're the one who needs help," Takeo jested.

"Take care of this old man," Alex demanded of Patton.

Alex then turned and headed towards Ives, rifling through his memories, searching for a moment when he had failed the Collective. All he was able to recall were the attacks he had made on citizens, increasing the city's already shaky tension, but each time had been a necessary act.

Guardians Gate separated the lives of the citizens and the Collective, comprised entirely of wood. Just tall enough so that no one could vault themselves over it with the sheer will of their body. It stretched as far as Alex's eyes could see, lacking proper defense, with signs which were hammered crudely onto the wall to say that it was off limits for those who had not been granted access. There were also two guardians who controlled the sliding gate.

Alex was granted entrance, and his senses were assaulted by the spectacle of the city. His feet left muddy ground and stepped onto hardened concrete road. The stands in the market were replaced with the skyscrapers of the old world where outbreaks of greenery interrupted the flow of gray ground. Vehicles with rusted bodies and broken windows had been pushed to the sides of the street, creating an open mid lane.

Along the barren street Alex could occasionally see a passing vehicle, or group of military occupants donning identical outfits to Alex, some having the privilege to leave the city's mammoth walls. When Alex arrived at the barracks he projected an image of servitude. He smoothed his uniform. Narrowed his eyes to remain watchful for suspicion, human or otherwise.

It was an old building with many floors used to bed guests of the city. When he first visited, he was shocked at the quality of the bedding. He had grown used to nothing but hard floors, finding slumber under the protection of a tent, but it did not bother him. Men of the Collective lived important lives fueled by purpose, not comfortable ones.

A pole stood in front of the building. On it was a white sheet with a blue circle: the mark of Collective territory, waving within the light wind.

Alex stepped into the building. It was illuminated by a flickering light which ran on the unreliable source of solar power. He reached room 108 and knocked.

"Come in!" Ives boomed. Alex entered.

Ives's gray hair had grown longer since Alex had last seen him. It was once buzzed like most men of the Collective, but it had now been styled so that his sides remained short, but along the middle it was spiked slightly. His once clean-shaven chin had sprung a coarse beard, and he had dark circles underneath his green eyes.

The room was bare except for a sleeping roll in the center, and two desks standing beside one another. The left one had stacks of paper jumbled messily in piles: maps, diagrams, and paper clippings. Relics of the ancients. The right showed the heights of the old world. A silver disk projected a blue hologram of a Hub, flickering and turning, its surface cracked with vile liquid dripping down its surface. The origin of the Hive's power.

"You're being promoted to commander," Ives declared.

Alex felt an instant surge of relief. He had finally been granted the position that he deserved.

"Here." Ives tossed a small flat hexagon towards him.

Alex caught the object and realized that it was a helmet. A gift all commanders received to cement their status.

"Try it," Ives urged.

Alex placed the hexagon on his neck, feeling a slight sting as its claws dug into his neck, bonding with him. He willed the helmet to take its true form. Black metal fiber sprung from the origin point and came to protect his entire head. The only part of his identity now visible was his brown eyes.

Ives pressed his finger on his gray earpiece as he joined another conversation. "The amount of radiation rises and falls all the time. I'm not a scientist. You figure it out." Ives then paused, his attention turning to Alex. "Who would you like for your squad?"

"Takeo. I would also like—"

Ives placed his hand in the air to silence Alex.

"You only get one choice. We have a new transfer for you from Zone 5."

Alex kept his facial expression tight so that his disappointment didn't show. Patton would have been the perfect subordinate. He had great potential, and with another commander the boy would be raised as nothing but fodder.

"Your new private's name is David Merlin. He's in the armory. Meet him. Tell him from now on you'll be hunting Hubs."

Alex was given a ride from the personal escort of Ives. She took unconventional roads to arrive at the armory with speed, probing Alex with questions about how he felt being promoted to Commander. He was both afraid and excited but chose to only share his excitement.

The armory was within the heart of the city where layers of the many occupancies within the environment were on display. The Collective took the forefront. Flags with their symbols were placed in strategic locations. They waved among buildings and checkpoints, acting as a reminder as to who held control. Some were transferred from the old world; many had been created anew. The new flags were made of looted ivory sheets where the blue circle of the Collective had been painted over. The flags of the old were created using the power of machines, pristine and accurate in their designs.

Heaps of hardened gray substance lurked in various areas, reminding all those who set their eyes on it of what had befallen the world. A failed invasion by an alien force.

The citizens had left nothing but chaos when they controlled the city. Corpses were left on the ground following petty squabbles. The citizens' only legacy.

The armory had three wings, two of which extended to the left and right, and the third stretched backwards. It was a single floor with a flat roof. A simple external design which did not match the greatness within.

The inside of the building had been cleared for Collective activities. Directly in front was research and development: Alex's destination.

Within the building were various compartments. Some had been boarded with wood. These were not watched by Collective military. The expansive weaponry of Zone 6 was guarded with lazy contempt.

Alex was annoyed. Then remembered he was a Commander.

He approached a man who slumbered in a chair. His torso was unbuttoned.

"Wake up!" Alex demanded. "Who-who are you?"

"A Commander. You would be dead if I were an enemy. Stay alert!" he warned.

From the corner of his eye Alex could see the others who had been sent to watch the weaponry perk up, shifting from laziness to awareness, making him wonder what else he could accomplish with his efforts.

Research and Development was the largest compartment in the armory. The theory of its existence was that the structure had not been completed when the world fell, leaving it empty prior to Collective reoccupation, a perfect state to create new weapons using remnants of old ones. Some who worked within it created inventions together; others acted independently. Sparks. Fires. Paper charts. Holographic images. Hustling bodies all played a role within the palace, centering around large tables which acted as bases where technology could be taken apart and reassembled, forging new creations. Most of them led to nothing important.

To find David, Alex had nothing but a physical description. He was told to find a middle-aged man with dark skin.

"I can help you with anything you need," said a high-pitched voice from behind. The man matched the description, but his skinny frame and old age left him worried. His brown eyes communicated kindness, a useless asset in their upcoming missions.

"In complete honesty I'm trying to get a minute off work and you looked lost," the man quietly claimed.

"I'm looking for David Merlin."

"That would be me." David extended a gloved right hand and shook Alex's with a limp grip.

"I'm Alexander King. A Commander. You're joining my squad."

"I didn't think that I would have to join one," David muttered.

"You're not military?" Alex asked with disappointment. He wanted the strength of Takeo on his side, not the uncertainty of a private.

"I ... well, yes. I technically work within it, but ... I came here to do this," David stated, pointing to the innovative events within the room. "I am best suited here."

"The Collective sees things differently."

"And I'm not questioning their judgment. I'm just conveying information," David stated.

"The amount of resources put into all this is a waste," Alex claimed with a scoff.

"I don't mean to offend, but you're incorrect," David said.

He led Alex down to a table with nothing on it but a blue circle, wrapped within the confines of metal claws. A useless artifact.

David's eyes darted around the room prior to pressing a button in the middle, supposedly activating the object. Nothing came from it but a spark.

"That's supposed to impress me?" Alex said.

"If I can develop it further I—"

"Forget about it," Alex interrupted.

"If you saw the next step—" David stuttered. His hands landed on a glowing blue crystal sticking out of an organized toolbox at the far end of the table. "An impulse crystal."

Alex looked at him, unimpressed.

"It's the source of power for EMPs."

"Focus on learning combat. That's all that matters now." "What makes you so sure?" a man asked. "The Collective
thinks human development is of importance."

Alex turned to see that the eavesdropper was an elderly man. His deep green eyes seemed to be projecting dangerous curiosity. Alex held his tongue. Speaking ill of the Collective may have him removed from his newfound position.

"My loyalty belongs to the Collective. I want what's best for us all."

"Should belong to yourself," the man replied.

"Who are you?" Alex pushed, needing to know the identity of one who would outwardly defy the Collective.

"An engineer. Innovator. Many things," he replied.

"I'm asking for your name."

The man paused. His face squinted and he coughed as a reaction to the simple question. "Connor East. Officer."

"Oh—I'm sorry I shouldn't have been—"

"See you soon," he promised. Connor turned away, coughing again, and returned to the sea of diverse workers in a rushed exit.

"How many times a week are you training?" Alex asked.

"I've spent the majority of my time here."

"Spend it there," Alex instructed.

"Noted," David said as his hand returned to his pathetic invention.

"What are you making?" Alex asked, irritated by David's lack of focus towards his message.

"Shields," David proudly proclaimed.

"That's it?"

"I believe mine will exceed anything that came before."

"You believe? So, it doesn't work then."

"No, but—"

"Your lack of progress will be reported."

"It would be best to wait."

"Why?"

"These impulse crystals. They're rare and it's not well known that I have one within my inventory. Once my invention's complete, nobody will be bothered by the fact that they were used."

"You not allowed to use these?"

"No but—"

Alex shot David a look of disgust, angered by the dishonest rat given to him as an underling. Noticing Alex's glare, David followed without further complaint.

Officer East had not gotten far as he walked between the lines of innovation on the tables, giving small compliments to the creators.

"Officer East!" Alex called.

"Yes?"

"Tell him of your crimes," Alex demanded, forcing David to confess.

David staggered with a reluctant stride. "I've been working on a secret project—but it's for the overall benefit of the Collective."

"Of course. How should he be punished?" Commander East asked. "Your subordinate. Your choice."

"I want you on the training ground seven days a week," Alex decided. "That's what will save us. Not your inventions."

CHAPTER TWO

THE OUTSKIRTS

"Why wasn't I a part of your team?" Patton whined.

"I did not get the choice," Alex replied.

"But Takeo is with you!"

"If it's a choice between Takeo and you, who would you pick?" Alex snapped.

Patton sulkily retracted his complaints.

The conversation took place between the market and the citizens' residency. Civilians lived in an endless stretch of tented homes. The people walked in varied directions except for north. Those moving to the left with water buckets and clothing traveled to the communal water supply, and to the right to harvest food. The largest group moved towards the city.

"Final check is done," Takeo informed Alex as he returned from his inspection of the M-ATV.

"Go back," Alex told Patton.

Patton complied, dashing back to the city without question.

While walking towards the vehicle behind him, Alex saw David sitting on a black chair which matched both the turret in his shaking hands and the vehicle's exterior.

"What's the most efficient way to operate this turret?" David asked.

"Figure it out."

David lacked restraint: the barrel swung from left to right with speed, causing him to recoil in shock.

"Are you excited to finally get some action?" Commander Green asked Alex, leaving his respective vehicles for reconnaissance.

"Of course."

"Which faction are we facing?" David asked.

"Anybody in our way."

"We could try to capture them. Find out why they remain so close to the city. What should I do if I see one?"

"Target practice," Green proposed.

Takeo warned the citizens of their incoming premise through the consistent belching of the vehicle's horn. Some were briefly defiant, but quickly moved when they realized that the trucks were not slowing. What followed was the scattering of citizens from the dirt road. A man carrying a pail full of water in both hands fell in avoidance of the trucks. Alex could not help but laugh, and Takeo laughed too.

Both trucks opted for the same set up. The team's Commander sat in the passenger seat, while one soldier took the occupation of gunner, the other as driver.

"How does it feel to be a Commander?" Takeo asked.

"It will happen for you soon. All it takes is hard work and dedication. You have both."

"I've been with the Collective the same amount of time as you," Takeo reminded him.

"You'll get there. I'll put in a good word for you."

"I don't need it. They always make the right choice."

Alex backed away from further speculation of the topic. Takeo's bitterness would not be smoothed with patronizing promises.

"I've heard the citizens are starting to think that the scientists can't control the radiation of the restricted zone. We should throw them outside the city if they can't be grateful."

Alex's thoughts flashed back to Ives's office. The possibility that rumors could hold a needle of truth within a pile of lies crossed his mind.

The citizens' dipped their bodies into the communal water supply. They had two duties: to bathe their bodies and whatever supplies they owned. Guards strolled along the sands at the lake and shouted at those who had exceeded their allotted time within the lake.

"This is the one post that I'll miss," Alex stated.

"What is there to miss?"

"Naked women all day."

"They're citizens," Takeo reminded him with disgust.

Takeo was partly correct. Most were nothing worthy, but occasionally full visual access was enough to spark interest in having one as an object for his pleasure. A reward for all that he had done. Takeo had joined him once; weeks ago when their former Commander died, they both took two for their own in grief.

The dirt path broke free of the congestion of Zone 6, taking them to the final gate of the city, comprising nothing but dry dirt on the ground. Human occupants were atop the city's walls. Soldiers paced alongside turrets, watching the land for reportable movements with sniper rifles that could spot what the human eye could not.

Most of the wall was a construction of the old world, circling Zone 6 in silver metal. Impenetrable except if attacked by plasma. The only part that was not protected was what Alex faced. Zone 6's main exterior weakness. A concrete construction.

A deep sense of worry clutched Alex, amplified by David's lack of control over the turret which he caught in his rearview mirror. His last time outside the city's walls ended in the death of his Commander, leaving him adrift, forced into the servitude of duties fit for a citizen. He made an internal promise that it would not happen again.

"What do you think of David?" Alex asked Takeo.

"He's smart."

"When we get back, help me get rid of him. Just make sure he is not fit for battle."

Takeo nodded, confirming his loyalty.

The main exit was made by metal cylinders at the edges of the gate, acting as catalysts for the plasma to work. Flickering purple plasma bars crossing into one another both horizontally and vertically created a pattern of perfect squares between them. They flickered on and off, showing clear deterioration. The four guards who protected it wore Mecha suits, over-prepared to defend the city.

Alex glanced down at his inferior AK-47, wishing for an upgrade of his weaponry. Takeo's R-90 shotgun was placed in his hands, and his battle knife handle was strapped to his hip.

The lack of David's battle experience corresponded with what he was given. His only weapon was a black Glock 20; he also had a flashlight strapped around his neck, and a small kit of medical supplies placed in his pocket.

Once Commander Green spoke to those ahead, the gates were lowered and the purple beams retracted back to their cylinders, clearing space for the trucks.

The truck surged forward, its wheels coming to meet with the dirt of the barren lands which only featured empty guard towers and a single trench being dug by citizens. It had only recently began, its construction needing days' worth of work to be worthy of combat. The citizens tiredly swung axes in downward strikes to break both dirt and rocks into smaller chunks. A second group lifted the debris into wheeled barrels and transported it to larger piles. They worked fast, but as the pair of vehicles drove by, their efforts were doubled.

The group rode forward for nearly an hour, when they were interrupted by a call from Green over the radio.

"Drifters!" Commander Green exclaimed.

Takeo's legs slammed on the brakes, halting the vehicle.

"Let's go!" Alex screamed as he sprang from the car, retreating to Takeo's side of the vehicle for cover. He searched the forest to discover an elk had been executed; an arrow was lodged in its neck. A poison from the weapon caused the animal's blood to turn thin and green. It twitched, whimpering for escape. Meters behind it two figures retreated.

"Should we engage?" Alex yelled over to Green. The advancement of Commander Green's body gave him his answer.

Alex and Takeo followed, but David had not yet moved. He remained glued to his chair, his hands clamped against the turret.

"Shouldn't one of us guard the supplies?" David nervously proposed.

"Let's go!"

With hesitance David jumped down from his position.

As Alex dashed into the forest adrenaline pumped through his body. A familiar grip of excitement.

The pattern of trees eventually ended, fading away into a downward slope of dirt. At the bottom of the slope was smooth rock, intersected by a plank that adopted the role of bridge between granite landmasses. On the other end were four black holes that were a possible means of escape. The camp was small, open to the morning sun, but those retreating were clearly not the only inhabitants.

The duo managed to cross the plank and attempted to remove the structure.

"Shoot them!" Green demanded.

Green's sniper lifted his weapon, and the man who'd heaved the plank suddenly fell to the floor, his head bursting with blood. The other deserter finished the task of his ally, pushing the plank into the abyss below. He turned and waved his hand to the left, then broke right. A stray bullet hit the ground, missing his leg.

Green sprinted towards the camp, and the others followed. It quickly became apparent that Green was planning to jump the gap. When he sprung upward Alex soared freely through the air in terror and landed on the hard surface without grace. The left side of his body crashed against the rock. A rush of pain ignited which he ignored.

The others followed behind him, surviving the jump.

"He went in there," Green stated, pointing at the cave to the right.

"We should stop and analyze what to do," David said as he dusted dirt off his knees, while Green's subordinates had already begun to move towards the escaping fugitive.

"Alex, take your men there. I'll take mine," Green instructed. "Let's go!" Alex shouted. When he moved, his foot kicked an empty bottle, one of many that were scattered across the rocky floor of the terrain.

"Get your light out!" Alex said as they approached the cave.

It took David a second to realize that Alex was speaking to him. When he did, he fumbled with the flashlight around his neck.

What light it gave them was pathetic: a small golden beam which gave the group very little in terms of a visual field.

"There is no need for us to enter. We have already driven them out," David said.

"Get in now or I will kill you myself."

The guiding dim light of the beam revealed that the interior of the cave was full of large boulders on the ground, a roof containing crystallized triangles, and bending walls. Alex saw it all as a possible danger. The boulders and walls would hinder their ability to chase, and the roof could cause great damage to their unprotected heads. As a precaution Alex withdrew his helmet from his shell.

After moving at a moderate pace through the twisting tunnels they gradually became acquainted with their new surroundings. The ground was turned flat. On the other end was an exit that sloped upwards. There were boulders across the reach of the landscape. Alex heard shuffling feet.

"Get cover!" Alex whispered.

Alex ducked behind a large rectangular slab and David joined him, holding his flashlight in one hand, his pistol in the other.

"What's happening?" David whispered.

As a response Alex urged him to shut off the light while he kept his ears sharp for any sounds. The shuffling continued. Takeo's large form was barely visible, but Alex could spot his dark outline, making it possible to convey instructions using his hands. He first pointed to David and motioned to the left, then to himself and drew a line down the middle before giving Takeo his instruction to flank right. Alex placed his fist upward to indicate a waiting period. The wait was torturous, casting doubt within his mind. He wondered if the sounds he had heard were the shuffling of animals instead of the enemy and if, through his caution, he had allowed them to escape.

A sudden smashing of glass came from the other side. Then a curse from human lips.

Alex clenched his fist and the three men moved into their respective positions until a burst of gunfire blasted near Alex's feet. He dashed to the nearest cover: a small slab which forced him to crouch in order to cover his body. The uncertainty of where the attack came from made his heart flutter.

A chip of rock that lay at Alex's stomach gave him an idea. He tossed it to the ground at the left, and the succession of gunshots that followed in that area confirmed his suspicion: his enemy was reckless. Untrained.

With a well-aimed shot, Alex managed to hit the outline of one of his enemies. He lowered himself before he would confirm the death of his victim, but then heard a howl of pain. At minimum the antagonist had been handicapped.

"Takeo, grenade!" Alex screamed.

The grenade landed at the mouth of the exit, capturing those who attempted to flee in the devastation of the explosion. It not only destroyed the enemy, but the environment as well. The rock from the roof rushed downward without mercy, crushing bodies, piling rocks high, blocking the exit.

"Forward, now!" Alex demanded. His rifle fire spread through the area of those who were not yet dead.

The lack of exit forced the enemy from a position of escape to into one of aggression. They rushed towards Alex, forcing him to return to his former cover.

Four enemies remained, forging their way close enough for Alex to strike an unsuspecting man with the butt of his AK-47, causing him to stagger to the ground. Alex stomped his boot down onto the man's face until he saw a pistol being swung in his direction, but before he could act the wielder caught the beam of a flashlight which made him squint and gave Alex the opportunity to end his life.

He was suddenly tackled to the ground. The surprise blow caused his weapon to slip from his hands, leaving him with nothing but the revolver in his side pocket. When he landed, his back skidded against the ground. A hard punch pounded his head, and blood spilt from his nose.

When a second punch was attempted, Alex quickly diverted his head to the left which made his enemy's swing connect with the ground. Alex used his remaining energy to wrap his fingers around the man's neck and throw him off. Alex dove his knee into the enemy, causing him to bend in pain. The man retaliated by attempting to throw Alex back to the ground.

Alex resisted, and used the opportunity to smash the enemy's head into a slab.

Relief took over him when he saw that both David and Takeo had left the skirmish unscathed.

"We have plenty to take back with us," David suggested. "Their weapons are shit," Takeo responded.

Fear took hold of Alex. In every mission he had been on, he always had a higher order commanding him where to go, what to look out for, and how to act.

"I surrender!" a slurred voice shouted from the enemies' side of the room. "I want to live!"

David dove behind cover. Takeo unclipped his final grenade and held it in his hand ready to throw, and Alex raised his firearm.

"If you have a weapon slide it across the floor now!" Alex screamed.

His request was fulfilled as the outline of a pistol clanged against the floor, creating echoes within the cave.

"Anything else?" Alex asked.

"No, that's all I have ... but my clothes. I want to keep my clothes."

"Put your hands behind your head and move forward."

"Just please don't kill me," the voice replied.

"Do what I say or we will kill you!"

A body rose from behind a boulder: the outline of a man with shoulder-length hair.

Alex could see that his request had not been met. In the man's hand was a mysterious triangle.

The defiance of his order ignited Alex's desire to kill him. "What's in your hands?"

"This is a piece of a Hub. I swear."

Alex's mind raced. An active Hub would bring great ramifications.

"What's in your other hand?"

"Just a bottle. I'll put it down carefully."

The object slipped from the man's hand and shattered on the ground.

"Pass me the Hub!"

"It's just a piece—not an actual Hub."

"Pass it!" Takeo demanded.

"Follow us outside," Alex interrupted.

They returned to the outside world. Their captive stumbled as he walked, tripping and muttering lackluster apologies. The material keeping him alive remained in his hand. The bottles, his slurred speech, and disoriented state was enough for Alex to deduce his drunkenness. It took double the time to leave the cave as it had to enter it.

Once outside the morning light provided the group with a proper view of their captor. He was in his late adolescence, handsome with deep blue eyes, blond hair, and sharp facial features. His cleanliness surprised Alex; he had always seen that those outside the cities had no preoccupation with cleanliness.

"Put it on the floor," Alex demanded.

The man did as he was told. The piece had a brown exterior with multiple deep cracks on its surface. From within the cracks, hard gray emerged. The man was not lying. It was from a Hub.

"What was your faction doing here?"

"Trying to have fun," he responded with a shrug. His eyes didn't meet Alex's as he spoke.

"Answer the question."

"We left a different place and came here."

"What's your name?"

"Reese," he responded.

"What place? What are your plans?"

"No plan," Reese said with a laugh.

Alex kicked Reese in the chest as a response to his arrogance. Most of the things about the man Alex disliked. His lack of proper answers was one of them.

"This is new," David blurted, causing the attention of the men to focus towards him. He stared at the specimen with curiosity.

"How do you know?" Alex asked.

"Look at the green."

With a second inspection Alex saw flecks of green within the chunks of gray. It rode the line between solid and liquid, dripping slowly. The mark of the Hive's substance.

"Where did you get this?" Alex asked.

"If I'm granted safety, I'll tell you."

Takeo rose his shotgun. Alex prepared himself to give the order.

"Oh, you're gonna need me. A person who discovered a piece of the Hub—come on."

"There are others in your camp that can replace you," Takeo said. This reminded Alex that the mission was not complete. They had no understanding of how many Reese had within his group, or if Green was in danger. "They kinda don't know I have this."

"Don't kill him," David interjected with desperation. "If it's eventually discovered by the Collective that we ended the life of a man who knew where an active Hub is we will be the ones at fault."

"How many of you are there?" Alex demanded.

"You kinda killed everybody."

"He does not have any reaction to his comrades dying. It's a lie," Takeo speculated.

"I didn't like them in the first place. Now I want to talk to whoever is actually in charge."

"I'm the only person you need to talk to," Alex stated firmly. "You're Collective; somebody's above you somewhere."

Alex felt trapped. No matter what he did, it would be a partway failure. If he ended Reese's life without finding out the Hub's location he would be a traitor to the Collective's greater will; if he allowed Reese to live, he would be playing right into his enemy's demands.

Alex smashed his fist into Reese's lip, a much lighter punishment than what Reese's comrades had to endure. He restrained himself from another hit, deciding that Reese was not worth the energy.

"What's this?" Green asked.

Alex saw that he was lacking his squad.

"He has a piece of the Hub," David blurted out.

"Why is he still alive?"

"He can show us where it is," Alex said.

"Is this the higher up that I want?" Reese asked.

"His people just killed ours. So I ask again: why is he still alive?"

"Are you forgetting who invaded who?"

Green picked up one of the bottles on the ground and smashed it. Its jagged edge proved to be an intimidating factor, forcing Reese into silence.

"I'm going to cut your throat open."

"We need him!" Alex reminded him, raising his voice with passion. Despite the fact that Reese had proved himself irritating, and unworthy of life, the fate of Zone 6 depended on the information that he held.

Due to his drunkenness, Reese consistently tripped as he walked through the forest.

"Get up," Alex seethed, tired of his antics delaying their journey. Reese vomited on the spot.

"Move forward!" Takeo placed his hand around Reese's neck with a harsh grip. Reese continued to puke, and a large portion of the liquid landed on Takeo's boots. "Are you serious!"

"I'm sorry, I'm sorry," Reese falsely apologized as Takeo shoved him away.

"We're hostiles. He might be more inclined to join us if we act nurturing," David suggested.

"I'm not his mother," Alex replied.

When the group arrived at Zone 6 they were immediately greeted by Ives. The citizens and gatekeepers continued their duties, but their eyes arched upwards towards his presence, as it was not a common occurrence that an officer found themselves at the city's gates.

Ives first spoke to Green for a few minutes, nodding his head as he took in information, sparingly looking towards Alex's truck. With each glance from Ives, Alex felt like he had done wrong. He had allowed Reese to fall fast asleep, giving their hostage a luxury that he barely gave himself.

"What happened?" Ives asked.

"Our captive. He has a piece of a Hub ... that was recently active."

"Take him to my office. Just you."

Both Reese and David withdrew from their positions at the vehicle as per Alex's request, allowing Alex to take hold of the wheel and have time alone with their hostage. Once they arrived at the barracks Alex woke Reese, taking him inside Ives's room.

"When you saw the Hub, how did you know what it was?" Ives asked Reese as he retrieved two nightsticks from his drawer, tossing one to Alex.

"I'm an educated person. Sorry but are those for me?"

"Not if you participate. I need a location."

"Can we make a deal?"

"Alex—"

Alex activated his stick, and a burst of blue electrical energy emanated from the black tip of the weapon.

"It was a lucky find," Reese sputtered, his confident demeanor gone. Alex felt a slight twinge of jealousy of Reese's eagerness to answer Ives.

"Where?"

"I can show you!"

"I know you will," Ives stated, looking back to the slab of Hub remnants on the table. "Alex, touch it."

"Isn't it dangerous?" Alex asked.

"It's a myth."

"How do you know it's a myth?"

"Because the Collective pushed it. Trust me."

"The Collective created the rumor?" Alex asked, needing additional confirmation. The idea did not seem real.

"To stop others from taking what we want for research. Nobody else in the world has the tech that we have for study. We did everybody a favor."

Alex exhaled and carefully placed his hand on the interior of the piece, allowing his finger to encounter both the hard and liquid layers of the object. His perspective suddenly shifted far away from his own. The room fell away. A series of loud bangs infiltrated his ears. His eyes caught a hundred white lights racing towards him. Once they hit, Alex snapped back to reality.

Alex swung his arm upwards in defense, and the slab left his hands, smashing against the wall.

"Sorry, I ..." Alex stuttered, surveying what he had done with shame. The piece had been broken into two, causing some of the liquid inside to streak down slowly.

"What did you see? Hear?" Ives inquired.

The memory of what he had seen had nearly vanished, but the pull of emotion that he had felt left a stronger imprint. Rage, sadness, happiness, and jealousy erupted inside of him, surprising Alex with the proximity to human feeling that the Hive had within its being.

"I felt emotions."

"Did you feel any intentions? Any inner thoughts of plans? Movements?"

"No."

A knock interrupted their stillness.

"Find him a place in the barracks," Ives demanded of Alex. "A man like this should be with the citizens. You heard me," Ives stated as he opened the door to discover two gruff soldiers harshly holding a woman. Her nose spewed blood and her eyes were blackened.

"A spy?" Ives guessed.

"A Libertarian spy," one of the soldiers responded.

The captured woman scanned the room; her eyes lingered on Reese first, then Alex, then Ives, before returning to Reese once again.

"Bring her in."

Alex wanted to find out more about the supposed spy but kept himself focused by leading his own prisoner outside the room, bouncing questions in his head of Reese's future. He was unfit to be a soldier, and too brash to be a citizen. For a man like him the best option was the mercy of exile.

"What do you think of Libertarians?" Reese questioned.

Alex kept silent. Spies came in many forms. Some amassed power over a long period of time, carefully crafting a view of themselves as trustworthy. Some were like Reese, acting as fools so their true intelligent intentions remained hidden.

"Do you know who Libertarians are?" Reese continued.

"I doubt you do," Alex snapped.

"It's just a question."

"Stop talking."

"I guess you don't know the answer."

Instead of a direct strike Alex threw Reese against the wall. "You're a drunk, an idiot, and a fool."

"Pretty sure idiot and fool are the same thing," Reese replied.

"I'm a Commander of the Collective. You will respect me."

"Should I throw you a party? Have you heard of birthday cake? It's from the old world made for these times like this … fake accomplishments."

Alex stopped himself from harming Reese further, seething as he led him towards the barracks, hating his decision to follow the rules, and subsequently angry at himself for wanting to break them.

CHAPTER THREE

THE HERO

While Alex waited for the aftermath of their trip to the outskirts, the days crawled. The potential of a small group of Hive, whispers of spies, the fate of Reese, and the recent increase of radioactive activity within the city were all left as dormant questions, while Alex performed his new duties. Rather than his body submerging within the water of the lake, his feet briefly remained on the sand. He no longer changed the bedsheets in the barracks but walked its halls, making sure the operation ran smoothly. When the days drew to an end his hands did not ache, but his eyes grew tired from remaining watchful.

Alex found himself bored while standing on the only guard tower in the area, watching an expansive field being plucked for weeds. The area had been ignored for so long that it was no longer a viable source of food until it had been cleared. A job for citizens who had misbehaved.

Alex and Commander Hazel were sat beneath a flat wooden roof. Her eyes matched the bleak gray of the clouds and were framed by a pair of binoculars.

The majority of the citizens pulled weeds with their hands, forced to use what little strength their malnourished bodies could offer. Some had the luxury of curved axes, rakes, and shovels to uproot the tiresome greens.

"After all that we did we're still in the fields," Alex complained.

"Wait. What did you guys do?" Hazel prodded.

"Nothing."

"Can I have a hint?"

Alex ignored her.

The citizens worked quietly as Alex and Commander Hazel had brief bursts of conversation until a lunch break was provided, delivered to them by Runners: citizen children a little younger than Patton. The Collective personnel ate a can of fruit and a slab of freshly roasted meat each. The citizens' bounty was a small bowl of oats, manipulating them into producing less output in the afternoon.

"Everybody come to the guard tower!" Alex screamed. His message was only received by a few who looked to him with disinterest. "Come here now!" Alex added with a raised voice, confirming that there was power in visible rage.

The citizens dropped their work and sauntered towards Alex. He did not have a proper agenda of what he would say to motivate the tired workers. His only hope was that his inner knowing would lead him towards a victorious speech. Once the people had gathered, Alex spoke.

"Thank you. I know that it's been hard working here day in and day out but there is something that you're working for. Eventually this city will be close or even equal to what we had in the old world." Alex hoped that his words would inspire. Instead most frowned, bored of his words.

"What I'm saying is these weeds are just a start. The people of the future who you have helped will appreciate it, and if you work hard enough, you can be on the tower watching people work …" Alex's final words generated an even greater negative response amongst the crowd. Angered at the group's response, Alex ushered them back to work, but Hazel quickly stepped forward.

"You have a quota to fill, and if you don't fill it you'll learn that there are worse things than picking weeds." The people moved back to their work with haste.

Embarrassment took hold of Alex. His face turned red and his throat dry. He internally replayed the speech, rethinking the various ways that he could have inspired the people, becoming fixated on whether he was too harsh or too soft.

Alex's gripes were interrupted by the radio ingrained within his helmet. A bell rang three times: the harsh tone of an emergency.

A rumbling formed in the distance. Alex looked to the skyline to discover three black aircraft figures making their way towards him.

"President Ye is inbound," a voice informed him through the radio.

The reveal relieved Alex, but his relief was immediately followed by a wave of stress. President Ye's presence meant that the life course of the Collective personnel would change.

The field workers pointed at the helicopters in awe. The vehicles had a bulky exterior used for defense, and a black hue to navigate the night undetected. As a means for offense there was a measly cache of missiles attached to its wings.

Alex traveled with Commander Hazel to the city's midpoint where both Commanders and Officers stood together. They stood in silence, eager to hear the commands from President Ye.

The edge of the restricted area had not changed since Alex last saw it. Heavy green smoke continued to dance within the air, preventing human eyes from seeing past the border. For some, discovering the nature of its existence was enough to pull them towards entry. Those who returned experienced premature death. Alex became pestered with occasional thoughts of curiosity. He knew from old world maps that the opposite side of the city matched what was already occupied, but the Hive's previous ownership of it, as well as its growing presence, gave him the terrifying thought that the Hive's toxic remnants may one day take the rest of Zone 6.

"Each of you is a hero. Fighting against great evils. History will remember you," Ye proposed as he turned, revealing his brown eyes. He appeared to be slightly younger than Ives, with a full smile of white teeth. His pants and jacket were made of black silk. His shirt was white and buttoned, his shoes brown and polished. A way of dress in the old world.

The crowd cheered at the notion, caught in the prospect that their lives had great meaning. As they were enthralled in celebration Alex spotted a small translucent hexagon appear behind Ye.

"President Ye, look!" a man shouted, revealing that Alex was not the only one who had seen something suspicious.

As the President turned the diversion within the restricted area disappeared.

"I know about the restricted area, private," Ye responded mockingly. Laughs came from the crowd. Alex remained silent.

"I saw something behind the—"

"We're here to discuss higher matters." Ye's statement quickly quenched the semblance of laugher.

From the emerald smoke a body suddenly emerged. The visitor was covered in rubber, preventing their skin from coming into direct contact with the earth. A clear plastic over their eyes enabled them to see. They wore silver boots which gifted the user with movement beyond natural ability. Their clothing was suitable to enter the treacherous hands of radiation.

"Your journey was not authorized," Ye stated.

The explorer looked upward in confusion. "It was authorized by—"

"No person is allowed in the restricted Zone unless given permission by me," Ye claimed. Despite the implication of betrayal he remained calm. Ye's words brought worry to Alex, for if they were true it meant that all those who had entered before under the command of Ives had done so illegally. "Who here would be willing to perform an execution?"

Several hands shot up. Alex reluctantly included his own.

The deserter suddenly got up and attempted to return to the green smoke. The journey was cut short by accurate shots from Collective guns.

"I know that you have all heard rumors of the Hive's return. The Hive is spreading, but not for long. The years spent trying to find the Hive's heart have ended in success. We found the central Hub. When it's destroyed, the entire Hive falls. It is close. Very close. It was us that drove it back. It will be the Collective that will end it."

Alex felt elevated by Ye's words, wondering if he was wise enough to be just like him. He had already become Commander. Having Ye's position was not too far out of the realm of possibility.

"None of this would be possible without heroes. Heroes such as Reese Minnet," Ye finished.

Alex's joy fell away as Reese appeared from the crowd, waving his hands at the people.

"Reese was part of the faction called the Chained. He chose to leave. They were men without merit. They found the Hive's heart and wanted to keep it a secret. Reese thought differently. That it would be best to share knowledge with the Collective. Knowing that we would be able to defeat it. We should all strive to be like Reese."

Alex's mouth went dry. His spirit was crushed by the unjust lie. He deserved to be a symbol. He had braved the caves. Engaged in a firefight. Spared the life of one who did not deserve it who was now being uplifted, while Alex blended in with the crowd.

While a series of claps burst forth from the group, a fire of hatred took hold of Alex's heart. The praise should have been for him. He looked to Ives who stared at him with an expression of warning. Alex justified that the lie must have purpose if Ives was going along with it.

"Reese is one of us now. Along with his Commander King he will lead you to the Hive's heart. You must protect him." Ye looked directly at Alex while he spoke. The acknowledgment made Alex freeze in intimidation.

"If the mission fails your prestigious ranks have earned you a place in the Haven. A safe zone within Peddlers Lake. It's a cave at the end of a ravine. This information is not for your subordinates."

CHAPTER FOUR

THE FAREWELL

Ye entered as he left: with haste, making an impact on those who had been graced by his presence. The effects of his visit were prevalent amongst all of Zone 6; stemming from the lowest citizens to the highest officers.

"What's the President like?" Patton asked Alex.

"He's fine," Alex replied. "I am going to tell you something that needs to remain a secret. This is for you. Nobody else."

"Okay?" Patton stated with sarcasm.

"Look at me," Alex demanded with a harsh undertone. "Peddlers Lake. The Ravine. If anything goes wrong, go there."

"Something wrong is going to happen at Peddlers Lake?" Patton screamed with confusion.

"Keep your voice down," Alex warned.

"Peddlers Lake," Patton whispered.

Alex nodded, looking around. Final checks of vehicles were being made; new soldiers' hands shook with fear as they listened to their Commanders' detailed plans.

"Watch the citizens. Protect them."

"I'll do my best."

"I want better than your best."

"Are you scared?" Patton asked.

"No."

Patton nodded with reassurance and wrapped him in an unexpected embrace. Alex awkwardly patted his back. He did not push him away, as there was a possibility that they would never see each other again.

"I'll see you soon," Alex promised as he stepped forward. "Don't die!" Patton cried out.

"Maybe I'll join the Hive instead," Alex joked. The duo laughed.

Alex moved towards the other vehicles which were idly waiting for combat. M-ATVs were paired with sole motorcyclists who were given the advantage of agility, trading it for protection. Their group was made up of over fifty vehicles, showcasing the Collective's strength.

Alex gripped his gun, thankful for what he had been given: an LZ-100 rifle, marked with gray tint. In his pockets he held two caches of stock. The Smith and Weston remained in his holster.

Neither David nor Takeo's weaponry had changed. Takeo kept his R-90 in his hands, David had only Pistol. Takeo took the wheel of the M-ATV, Alex the passenger seat, David at gunner.

Reese entered the back seat. He had been granted an SNH- 21 sniper rifle. The scope was hidden in the moment, but if it was needed it would emerge.

"Long time no see," Reese stated with a smile. He appeared happy. His breath smelled of liquor. His teeth sucked on what appeared to be a small white protein pill.

"You've been drinking! I'm reporting you," Alex declared. "You can't report a hero."

Before Alex could act they were commanded to remain still in their positions. Alex fantasized that he would be the one to take out the Hive and return a hero. It would be his chance to be loved by both the citizens of the city as well as the military. He would be donned with countless medals, and he would no longer have to spend his days exposed to the elements, but instead would likely be offered a position in Zone 1, a comfortable one that had been blooming for a decade and remained untouched by war.

"When are we going?" Reese asked, sighing, clearly bored. "When we are all ready," Alex replied.

"You don't know? What a surprise."

"You must be an idiot if you think that this way of acting is going to get you anywhere."

A beep sounded from the internal radio, signifying movement forward. The group of cars moved together through the city's gates, forming a destructive force.

The city disappeared from the rear-view mirrors. Its large walls slowly lost their visibility as they entered unfamiliar terrain. They passed bridges, lakes, streams, keeping their eyes open for anything foolish enough to attack their forces.

"How long until this shit is done?" Reese asked.

"If you're not interested in helping us, then die," Alex answered.

"This makes me wish I was a part of the old world."

"You don't know what it was like," Alex replied.

"I've done extensive research on the topic. People were fed well, there was a lack of conflict—" David said.

"You believe that? Then why would there be so many weapons around?" Reese asked.

"To keep people like you in line," Takeo said.

"Real peaceful."

"Quiet," Alex said, hushing the three bickering men. "Would you know what to do if we were attacked right now?" Alex challenged.

"Why do I have to keep reminding you that I'm a hero?" "You're a disgrace," Alex said.

"You don't deserve to fight by my side," Takeo added.

"I'm fine with that. Are you aware that every skirmish that you've fought has been based on bullshit?"

"We have purpose," Takeo answered.

"Your purpose is to do what somebody tells you to do."

"I fight for what I believe in."

"Ya. Somebody else's orders."

"If the others fail we need to be the ones to destroy the Hub." "Okay." Reese's casual tone was unsettling, but Alex decided

to let it go. He had greater things to focus on.

"I'm for sure going to be the one to kill it because I am—"

"Delusional," Alex said.

"Dreaming," Takeo said.

"A hero," Reese finished. "But wouldn't that be disrespecting our orders? What are the consequences?" he asked with false sincerity.

"Execution, or exile," Takeo informed.

"Wow! I just love the Collective."

"Enough!" Alex shouted.

"The Hive stole my family. It stole the world from us. The Collective wants to bring it back, and whatever they want me to do I'll do it. If you don't want that, then you're the idiot," Takeo proposed.

"What do you have against us?" Alex asked.

"You take things that aren't yours. Small things like … cities," Reese replied.

"We are helping the world in ways that you're too foolish to comprehend."

"You own slaves. You're also a slave. Ives told me—"

"If it's between you and Ives, we should not know," Takeo stated.

"I'm not interested," Alex lied.

The position that Alex found himself in was not one he had ever imagined to be in. He had a man who lacked complete enthusiasm for their mission, and one who had no battle experience.

"You're lucky to be allowed with us," Alex continued.

"My old group was pretty fun. We didn't even own slaves." "You didn't even mourn when they died," Takeo said.

"I said they were fun. Not that I cared about them." "Everybody stop," a message from the radio commanded.

Ahead a blockade had taken a grip on their path in the form of fallen trees.

"This is where we get out. Delta squad remain back and watch the vehicles." Alex had hoped that gamma squad would also have been called, but they were not so Alex urged the others to step out.

They stepped outside. The sun was beginning to set.

"Commander King, bring your squad up front," Officer Mint commanded through the radio.

"Let's go." Both Takeo and David began to move, but Reese just stared, his eyes filled with regret. "Now!" Alex continued.

"We're close," Reese replied.

"This blockade looks intentional," David said.

Officer Mint stood in a Mecha suit. A sandy brown coat of paint covered his armor with the exception of a dark brown pallet at his joints. Three cylinders on his back would produce flame when called for. His face was hidden by tinted glass. A holographic map projected from his wrist, providing a vague view of the area.

"What took so goddamn long?" Mint asked.

"It was me. I had forgotten my weapon, and it held the others back," David lied. Alex had no interest in correcting him.

"That's not true. We're sorry, we should have ran," Takeo said. "Reese. Can we get to the Hub from here?" Mint asked. "Sure," Reese said, pointing directly to the left.

"Move out! We're close!"

The group moved as instructed, reveling in the thought of a venture into the forest. Mint appointed his second-in-command to lead while he remained in the back with Alex's squad, citing that if Reese was incorrect he would be the one to cultivate the execution. Eventually the group stepped upon a rocky cliff. Reese's claim was true: the large Hub existed. Its exterior was etched with cracks where drips of green poured out. The dome breathed in small increments, rising and falling slowly. Circling the Hub were dispatched Hive bodies. Hardened gray came from their mouths.

"See now this looks familiar," Reese stated.

"Delta squad, remain back," Mint commanded. He blasted in the airspace along with the few others who donned Mecha suits. Those without descended down the rocky slope manually without the aid of technology.

"I always believed that the central Hub would be bigger," David said.

"Don't complain," Alex said.

"Hubs correlate to the amount of the Hive that they control. If this is the main Hub, it should be larger."

"Where did you hear that?"

"Old Collective files."

Alex wondered whether this could be another cultivated myth. He didn't say anything, but the possibility nagged at him.

"And there is an incredible lack of defense," David added.

"There was some," Takeo said as he pointed to the Hive's failed guards in the form of corpses scattered upon the earth below.

"They weren't around when I was here," Reese mentioned.

The ground forces landed at their destination. The lower elevation had been cleared of trees within a long radius; the only attraction was the Hub.

"It's not in the Hive's nature to leave itself unguarded," David mentioned.

"It tried," Takeo said as he pointed to the cluster of bodies.

"Deploying explosives," Mint stated through his radio.

The ground forces stepped onto the deceased, throwing sticky bombs onto the Hub: the first phase of ending the Hive's reign.

"We won," Alex said.

Suddenly a set of stray hands came from below the ground forces. They wielded plasma melee weapons which struck the members of the Collective down. The Hive was active.

Within seconds the Hive's trick had come into focus. The bodies on the ground revealed their true nature: some of the dead bodies had been used as a distraction, while others rose from their dead state. The ground forces aimed their weapons downward, pumping bullets into the enemy.

Alex acted quickly. "Sniper fire, now!"

The elevated group sprang into action, raising their weapons towards the Hive with precise shots. Alex decided not to join the group. His LZ-100 did not have far range. He would have to descend.

"Behind!" a call warned.

Alex turned to find four Mecha suits flying towards the group.

"Spread then shoot!" Alex warned.

The Mechas proved themselves effective. The lasers that came from their weapons crossed over one another, slicing limbs off Collective soldiers, and making escape nearly impossible.

Alex turned his attention to the sky and unloaded a shot from his LZ-100. He made a direct hit, slicing through the chest of an enemy. The trio within the air pulled themselves away in ascension, avoiding bullet fire with synchronized circular movement. Alex was unable to make another direct shot. The inaccuracy of the Collective increased as the Mechas flew higher.

"Let them come to us!" Alex warned, but his suggestion was ignored, drowned out by the calls of others with differing agendas.

"What?" David shouted. His handgun followed the air forces, but he refused to shoot.

"Help them!" Alex shouted, pointing his head towards the Hub. His comrades were engaged in tense battle, struggling against their enemy. The Hive bodies moved swiftly, using melee weapons to cut down the Collective.

"Snipers, attack!" an officer yelled.

Alex spotted the long hair of Reese, who foolishly shot in a straight line instead of downward.

"Shit," Reese said with a giggle. His eyes left the scope and Alex noticed that his pupils had grown. His smile made Alex boil with rage: others were dying, and Reese somehow found enjoyment.

Alex ripped the weapon from his hand and firmly placed his own rifle into Reese's unsuspecting grip.

"What the hell, man?" Reese lazily complained as he stumbled backward, coming close to the cliff's edge.

Alex took a step closer, deciding that Reese's death would mean a lesser burden for them all.

"They're coming!" Takeo warned, detracting Alex from his new objective.

The trio of Mechas attacked once again at the reduced Collective forces.

The red lasers swiped from left to right, scorching the earth. The Hive moved with its expected synchronism. Every movement of one Mecha matched the next, until one fell due to a blue ball of plasma wedging its way into the suit's stomach. The Mechas turned away again.

"Don't waste your ammo!" Alex warned. His words were meant for the privates who would shoot at anything deemed an enemy, including David who fired his pistol aimlessly below. "What are you doi—"

Alex found his answer as he peeked over the edge and found the Hive forces scurrying its way up the rocky cliff. The ground forces had ceased in their defenses. Only one surviving member wielded a flame thrower. Harnessed to his back was a tank connected to two hoses where columns of flames forged his immediate surroundings. He surged towards the Hive's heart; the Collective's last hope. The man was a few feet away from the Hub when suddenly his stream of fire was directed upwards courtesy of a thrown knife that lodged within his neck.

A firm hand gripped his leg. With an automatic jolt Alex's foot hit the enemy's face directly. The Hive had reached the top of the cliff. The Collective was a few; the Hive was many. The Collective turned, running away, choosing to avoid conflict instead of staying loyal to their vows. Alex saw that David and Reese were doing the same. Alex planned to kill them until he saw each body retreating. He could not stand alone.

Alex caught up with them and was relived to find Takeo had followed. They ran with the others until Alex spotted one of the Mechas dash to the left. It was damaged and slower in its flight pattern than usual.

"To the left!" Alex shouted.

Alex did not grant himself the luxury of looking back, and within a few minutes Alex realized that they had separated from the majority of the group.

"Give me my weapon back!" Alex demanded as he took his PLZ from Reese.

"What now, genius?" Reese asked.

Alex looked to Reese. His fate would be grim.

"Killing your own is against the Collective philosophy," David said, predicting what Alex was about to do.

Suddenly a burst of laser light headed towards them. The four of them broke their position, finding themselves lucky to be unharmed.

Alex responded by taking a shot at the Mecha which narrowly missed. Takeo's shot hit. It hit the Mecha's back, and he fell from the sky.

"Keep your hands down or I will kill you!" Alex shouted towards the fallen.

The Mecha spewed dual laser beams from his hands, ignoring Alex's warning. The red line blasted through the air in a frantic mix of horizontal and vertical directions. Alex dove behind a tree, preparing himself for pain.

But the laser had been weakened. It passed through Alex's cover, but was unable to slice the bark, giving Alex the chance to emerge and release the trigger of his rifle. Alex's laser cleanly hit the Mecha's bicep.

The being did not shout as green liquid flew from the ventral point. Takeo provided a second attack through his R-90. It burned into the enemy's chest, making him fall for the final time.

Alex sprinted towards the Mecha. His left laser shot wildly as a desperate act of defense. Takeo jumped from his cover with his machete hilt in hand.

"Al—"

"Wait!" Alex yelled.

His command went unheard. Takeo activated the machete. A rectangle of red plasma jumped from the hilt which plunged into the spot where the shotgun pellets had been entrenched.

"The Am—have … when … Tech—treat—" a voice from the man's helmet projected. Alex focused on it. Then nothing came from it. They had been cut off from possible information.

"We have to get back to the city," Alex decided.

"Is anybody else really tired?" Reese asked.

"You have a radio. For safety purposes shouldn't we call in?" David suggested, ignoring Reese's question.

"The Hive's here. It's probably listening in," Alex explained as he stepped forward.

"Did anybody hear that I'm tired?" Reese asked.

"Let's move!" Alex said.

The group sprinted to the blockade. They reached it to find that the group who had stayed back had been cursed with a dark fate.

Deceased Collective bodies had been piled at the side of the road. Some had been left alive. They dropped to their knees, begging for their lives to be spared. Those who were spared were stripped of their weapons by the Hive forces.

Alex's hand gripped his buzzed black hair. He had failed. He had nothing left.

"We're going back to Zone 6," Alex decided.

"Nope," Reese argued.

"We do have to warn them," Takeo reminded them.

"To get back without a vehicle, the journey will take days," David said.

"It's our responsibility to warn the others. We're men of the Collective. We don't cower."

"It looks like there is no Collective anymore," Reese stated with a laugh.

Takeo grabbed Reese by his shirt collar and shoved him directly into the hilt of his machete.

"Okay, the Collective exists … God," Reese reluctantly acknowledged.

Alex turned back to the taken area, knowing that the criticisms he had heard held merit.

"There are alternative factions," David said.

"Where are you from, Reese?" Alex asked.

"That's classified."

"I don't have to, or indeed want to, threaten you again. You claimed to be nearby. Tell me where it is."

"Are you admitting that the Collective does not know everything?" Reese teased.

"You're a deserter. I don't know if you're a technician deserter, Amish-fuck, maybe even a Loyalist, but you left your people. Tell me who they are."

"The Libertarians."

CHAPTER FIVE

THE RIVERSIDE

"The Libertarians," Alex echoed.

"It must be fake," Takeo decided.

"What, are we not on some Collective registry?" Reese asked. "They exist. A smaller group, but I have heard whispers of their existence," David stated.

"I know they exist," Alex replied.

"This could be a trap," Takeo proposed.

"Good, let's not go," Reese said.

"Show us the way," Alex instructed.

"I just showed you the Hub. Can I have a break?"

"We will rest when the Hive is dead."

The men trudged through the forest until night fell. Due to exhaustion Reese got his requested break. The slow breakdown of Alex's body had caused him to consider the idea. They rested next to a river, using its water as their primary source of nutrients. Lacking the luxury of Zone 6, Alex's empty belly ached with starvation. He internally replayed the failure of the Hub attack. He agonizingly pondered the ways that he could have acted differently to turn it into a success, making it his greatest desire to change his actions in a way that would destroy the Hub.

"We should hurry," Takeo said.

"We'll be back soon," Alex promised.

"The Hive might have taken Zone 6 by now—it takes everything. Both of our birth families. Our friends. Now it's coming for our home. Whatever you want to do, I'm right behind you. Do you think they are?" Takeo asked, tilting his head towards David and Reese.

"They will be."

"In battle they might hold us back."

"They somehow survived the first attack," Alex said. "They're not fighters. I don't want to die because of them."

Alex noticed that Reese had fallen into slumber, broken by a harsh shake from Takeo.

Reese mumbled as his eyes fluttered open. Dark circles shrouded his glassy eyes.

"We need to keep going," Alex said.

"What happened to taking a break? We're almost there anyway." Reese's speech was slurred.

"Get up," Alex said. Red hot anger rose within him: the people of Zone 6 were in danger, and Reese was wasting the precious seconds that they had to save them.

"Just … follow the river … let me sleep."

"Takeo," Alex said.

Takeo punished Reese for his disobedience with a harsh strike. "Ow!" Reese protested.

"Is there a specific reason why you don't want to go back?" David asked.

"They're super controlling," Reese stated, reluctantly standing up.

"What have you heard about them?" Alex asked David.

"I am unsure of their nature."

"You have a lot in common," Reese said.

The group followed the river. Alex took the lead with David trailing closely behind and Takeo holding Reese within his grasp. Reese kept his mouth free of reckless comments, replacing them with unwelcome sleep patterns which would be broken by a vicious shake from Takeo.

A bend in the river changed the landscape. The remainder of the water stream was blocked by a wall, similar to that of Zone 6. The white gate comprised of bars which began in the middle of the river and spread across the trees. It lacked the width to support a guard, and as an alternative defense mechanism, white spikes extended from it.

Within the water there were two guards, each using a pair of binoculars to search for activity.

"Move back," Alex warned. In a fluid motion they lowered themselves to the ground.

The guards bobbed within a curved boat large enough to fit the two of them. On the sides of the boat were two paddles with a wire connection embedded into the legs of the measly defenders.

"If there is a trap, let me be the first one to walk into it. I'll take Reese with me. You two stay back," Alex decided.

"Portray him as prisoner. The Libertarians may offer whatever communication system in exchange for his return," David suggested.

"This won't work," Reese said.

Alex ignored him and marched forward.

The two men caught sight of Alex, dropped their binoculars and raised their pistols.

"Hold on!"

"I'm his prisoner. He thinks I'm a good hostage," Reese stated. "Shut up," Alex seethed.

"And who are you—" but the guard answered for himself. "Reese."

"I expect a homecoming party," Reese joked.

"I am ... Officer ... Alexander King of the Collective. Reese Minnet is my hostage."

The man's boat propelled forward through the paddles which splashed through the water in a continued circular motion, courtesy of the connecting string strapped onto his legs. "The Collective. That's what you left for?"

"I'm an officer," Alex lied. "If I don't get what I want, others will find you and kill you."

"I'll call Sheila—"

"No, call Lonnie," the other guard argued.

"Is he back?"

"He said he would be this morning."

"Is he really that accurate?"

"Get your leader! Whoever they are!" Alex demanded.

"Neither of them will care if Reese dies," the guard said.

"If I don't get what I want right now I'll kill him—"

"What?" Reese asked lazily.

"But I'll also make sure the Collective comes for you. We owned the old world. This place will be ours too if you don't listen."

The guard withdrew a small yellow radio from his hand, placed his thumb onto its side and spoke. "Get Sheila. We have an Officer of the Collective with us. He threatens to bring the Collective to us if she doesn't come now."

He received a response quickly, but Alex couldn't quite catch it.

"She's coming."

"No need, look who's here," the guard stated.

Alex saw a rumble coming from the river. A cohort of triangular boats was coming towards him which differed greatly from the river guards. They were a great deal larger, able to fit multiple bodies on each along with mysterious boxed cargo. They glided across the water without the need for paddles, jumping at great speed, propelled by its inner workings.

Alex tightened his grip around Reese's neck. Reese did not bother to struggle against it, as he had somehow almost returned to sleeping.

"If you run, Lonnie's going to find you," the guard warned.

"If I die the Collective will come."

The group of boats slowed as they reached Alex. At the front of the first vehicle a man became distracted from steering, staring at Alex with curiosity.

"Lonnie. These men approached. He claims to be an officer of the Collective. Reese is his prisoner."

"An officer? Do you have any proof?"

"I ... no."

"What do you want?" Lonnie asked.

"To speak with the leader of the Libertarians."

The vulnerability that Alex felt cast a heavy shadow within his mind. There were turrets attached to boats, ready to shred his body

apart. As a distraction Alex set his eyes on the cargo, some of which had the tips of plasma weapons poking through the top.

"We just raided an enemy with greater numbers than us. Yet we still won. Go ahead, bring the Collective," Lonnie boasted.

"You're making a mistake," Alex warned.

"What's an officer doing out by himself in the middle of nowhere?"

"I need communication with Zone 6."

"Oh, is something wrong?"

"I'll discuss terms in private."

"You will do as I ask."

As Lonnie finished his sentence, the gate opened to reveal a woman approaching on an identical boat to the guardsmen. She was in the beginning stages of old age. The skin at the sides of her eyes and mouth was wrinkled and she had graying braided hair, and a slim lean body.

"Whoever this is, is he worth our time?" she asked Lonnie. They both had the same facial structure with sharp features, olive skin, and green eyes.

"This is Alexander, an Officer of the Collective. He wants to use our radio."

"What do you think we should do? Bring him in to see what he can—"

"Why ask me if all you're going to do is give ideas?" Lonnie accused.

"It was a suggestion," the woman said.

"You always do this."

"Focus," she warned.

Lonnie huffed and, retracting his leaning body, crossed his arms and turned back towards Alex.

"I was thinking about killing them."

Alex gripped Reese tighter than before, his heart racing. He desperately tried to think of ways to keep himself alive.

"Sheila—I'll tell you anything you want to know about the Collective," Reese pleaded. His words had more energy than anything that had been seen from him in the past hours.

"What do you have that I can use?" Lonnie asked.

Alex knew he would rather accept death than to bow down to the weak forces of the Libertarians. But the danger of the Hive was far more important than his personal feelings.

"Military experience. Lots of it."

"Good. I'll need some."

"What for?"

"We have another mission. They're going to be a part of it. Him and his two scared friends."

"What friends?" Reese asked.

"Come out!" Alex called.

David and Takeo both withdrew from hiding.

"Do you all have military experience?" Lonnie asked.

"Yes," Takeo said.

"A sufficient amount," David said.

"Alex, let go of Reese," Lonnie requested.

Alex loosened his grip, but did not let go. He figured that since Reese had witnessed the Hub attack, he needed to be kept alive in order to relay the story.

"It is my duty to keep him alive," Alex said.

"He will betray you," Lonnie claimed.

Sheila propelled the boat to the shore so that Alex did not have to plunge himself deep into the murky depth below.

"Just you," Sheila clarified, as Takeo attempted to follow.

As they entered the gate the Libertarians' base was revealed. The river led to a lake which was bordered by a circular shore. Countless boats were docked, floating side by side.

Warships were wedged beside canoes, spaced by the occasional wooden dock. Houses lined the steep hill.

"Welcome to Riverside," Sheila greeted.

"Save the courtesy," Alex said.

"What would the Collective do if they came across a wandering traveler asking for aid?"

"An interrogation."

"Followed by?"

"This conversation is a waste of time," Alex said with angst.

Sheila did not formulate a reply. She steered the boat into a dock that was nearly empty except a military boat similar to the one Lonnie rode in. The external was made of an entirely gray shell, interrupted by sleek black windows on its front and sides.

Alex stepped onto the wooden dock to look up at the house that stood before him. It was much simpler than the others. Its outside was comprised of simple logs. They were cut within the same size, stacked atop one another, only breaking where there was the door and window. The roof was gabled in a triangle and looked like it was made of tough brown straw.

"Let's go talk to your people," Sheila said.

Each of the walls within the building contained a painted photograph. One showed a smiling family, another showcased guns, another was a man in a boardroom. The last was a blond girl with white wings spreading from her back.

"I don't have time to waste. Is your radio strong enough to connect with Zone 6?" Alex asked.

"It is."

"Let me use it. The Hive has returned. I need to warn the Collective."

"It never truly died. I understand that you want to fight, but I am not the one to decide if you can use my radio or not. I can only advise. I advise against it."

"Why?"

"You faced a weakened version of the Hive, and look at what it did to you. I just want to see if the Hive will grow or die before making rash decisions."

"You're waiting to pick sides." Sheila nodded without shame.

"The time to pick is now," Alex declared.

"You make many demands of me, but there is no incentive to follow."

"What is it that he wants?" Lonnie asked as he entered the room.

"To use our radio. Send a message to Zone 6 that the Hive is growing."

"They just found out?"

"You've known!" Alex called.

"For a while," Lonnie answered.

"You didn't do anything to warn us," Alex said.

"If we had the Collective's attention, Riverside would be claimed as Zone 7."

"How can you be such cowards?" Alex accused.

"Cowards? That cargo I have is stolen from Technicians."

The words bit into Alex's ego. Lonnie was right, he should have remained fighting to his dying breath.

"He can be used. We still have the EMP," Lonnie said.

"We have others that can be used," Sheila stated.

"I'll be with him. I don't want to sit around all day giving speeches."

"The people need to see you as their leader."

"You want me to steal?" Alex interrupted.

"The EMP was ours first. Stolen by the Amish. Your journey will take a day."

"It was taken just last night."

"We have to get going. Get this thing. Get these idiots to have faith in us again," Lonnie stated.

"They do have faith in you," Sheila said.

"No, they had faith in my father."

"If you want the people to believe in you, show them your strength," Alex advised.

"I don't need your help. My mother is a better adviser than you and she has never seen battle."

"I'll be sure to ask of it when I see her."

"Ask away," Sheila stated.

Alex was not surprised that they were mother and son due to their similar facial features.

"You were born into leadership. That's why you don't understand," Alex said.

"Our family is the best choice to lead the Libertarians."

"You need democracy."

"Democracy was always nothing more than a lie. In the old world, and the new," Sheila said.

"President Ye was voted in. He was chosen."

"Did you count the votes yourself?"

"No," Alex said defensively.

"The last Collective election was twelve years ago. Does that sound right to you?"

"Show me evidence of your radio," Alex demanded, ignoring her attempt to shake his faith. "We need to move, but I need to see what I'm working for."

Sheila led Alex to the south end of the cabin where a painting depicting four men signing a treaty was present. Upon closer inspection Alex could see that in the center of the table was the Collective's blue circle. It was a depiction of the unification of the Collective. Each of their names were visible on the treaty paper: John Umber, Kin Terra, Mamet Kupar, and Conrad Westwick. Sheila placed her hand on the painting and the wall in front of them slid open, slowly teasing the communication system.

A black bar was at the top. At the bottom was a maze of varied buttons. The top had a gray box where a headset dangled, connected to coiled wire. Embedded within the paint were the words Westwick Enterprises.

Sheila withdrew the headset from its original place, her hands furiously tapping away at the buttons, and on the black bar coordinates began to show up: the known coordinates for Zone 6.

"Hello?" a voice called from the speaker. A voice Alex recognized: Private Tine. A friend of Patton's.

Sheila placed her finger on the blue button below, cutting off further communication.

"No!"

Alex's hands came for Sheila but were blocked when Lonnie stepped in, pushing him away with a powerful shove.

"If you want to use it, then help me. I'll get the boat ready," Lonnie stated, leaving Sheila and Alex alone.

"When you're on this mission, protect him," Sheila said.

"If he dies, it's his fault," Alex replied.

A beep came from the radio, followed by a feminine voice. "Libertarian. Speak."

"I can't right now!" Sheila desperately informed, rushing to the wall.

"Sheila," the voice said, recognizing her voice, "defiance. What I'm—" The words were cut off as Sheila rapidly disbanded the radio.

"Who was that?" Alex asked.

"One of our possible allies if negotiations go well. Don't worry about it. I'm sure they would like you."

"Who?"

"Technicians," she answered.

"Your son just stole from them."

"Eventually everything is forgiven."

"Oh—would you forgive me if your son died?"

"If he dies, you die."

Despite knowing his words had hurt her, Sheila's veiled threat propelled Alex to challenge her. "I just wouldn't come back here."

"We'll track you down. I've done it before."

"You would just waste your resources … I can't believe you're in charge. You and your son would never last in the Collective."

"Are you always this rude to people helping you?"

"I won't need you after this mission and you won't need me. We can be honest with each other."

"It must be refreshing to speak your mind."

"I can talk all I want."

"Save your words for when they're important," Sheila said as her fingers pointed towards the radio that stood behind her, winking with various lights, broadcasting its availability. As she drew attention towards it the temptation to overpower her and contact the Collective on his own was almost overwhelming.

"I'm not afraid of any Libertarian."

"What if they're helping take Zone 6 right now?" Sheila bitterly replied.

Alex laughed at the notion, for he knew Zone 6 would not fall to a human army, especially such a weak link as the Libertarians. The Hive was the only thing that could topple their walls and take control of the city.

"You shouldn't be laughing. Taking the EMP will be extremely dangerous."

"It will be nothing. I've been on real missions before. Not hiding away from the world."

"Like what? I still don't know that you're qualified to protect Lonnie."

"Countless," he boasted.

"No direct answer? That's not a good sign."

Sheila's annoying insults and the alluring hum of the radio propelled Alex to take another step.

"What don't you want me to see?" Alex questioned.

Sheila's eyes pivoted towards the black bar, the white line within it lifting in small hills. The signal that whoever was on the other end continued to listen.

"Why don't you go to the docks?"

"I'm calling Zone 6," Alex decided, tired of hearing orders from one below him. Her vulnerable position made her an easy hostage.

"No," Sheila seethed.

Alex took a third step. Sheila's position did not change, confirming her false threat.

"Who is that?" the voice within the radio called.

"My name is Alexander King. Are you Sheila's son?"

"Go now," Sheila demanded.

"I could kill her if I wanted to. Tell her to let me use the radio or she won't make it to the end of the day."

"Bold, but rash," the voice declared. "Did you hear what I said?"

"If you kill me, you die," Sheila threatened.

"I'm okay with that as long as—"

"The rest of your squad dies too." Sheila's hand briskly moved towards a downward switch, then the radio went black and moved backwards into the wall.

"Bring it back!" Alex shouted.

As Alex sprinted to the radio wall Sheila flung her hand towards a bare spot on the wall. From within it a turret emerged. The prospect of death took hold, forcing Alex to stop.

Alex moved left, and the turret followed. From the turret a pellet emerged and struck the floor beneath Alex's feet, crafting a permanent indent within the cabin floor.

Alex backed down. The beady eyes of the barrel seemed to be taunting him, laughing at his failure. He rattled with curiosity, speculating about the location of Sheila's ally and if he played a role within the coming conflict. As Alex unlocked the door he reminded himself that the Libertarians would only be a brief encounter within his existence and that his focus should remain on the actions that would save Zone 6.

CHAPTER SIX

THE BOAT

Before departing, the group nourished their bodies by eating a stew primarily made with potatoes and a broth that tasted more like water than any meat-based flavor.

"They're taking a long time. We should depart as soon as possible to achieve our goal," David said.

Alex agreed but remained silent. He did not want to jeopardize his prospect with petty complaints. The prod from David made his mind wander to antagonistic possibilities of getting quicker access to communication. He considered sneaking back into Sheila's base as soon as Takeo, Sheila, and Lonnie departed from their mysterious meeting. Alex guessed that Takeo was being interrogated on all aspects of the Collective, making him tense at the possibility that Takeo had forgotten his lie about holding the title of Officer.

"They're probably picking matching outfits," Reese suggested. "If they ask you anything about the Collective make sure that

you both keep your mouth shut," Alex said.

"What about morsels of information that we can grant in case they begin the torture process?"

"My answer is the same."

"Maybe we could cultivate a false story together."

"Great idea," Reese said. "Let's start with how my real name is Alexander King."

Alex let out a tense breath. As tedious as it was, he decided it would be beneficial to consider the possibility that they may all be prodded for information.

"If you ever get captured focus on questions about yourself. Never give anybody else up. Whoever captures you will make sure that you're miserable. They will do their worst to hurt you, but they'll keep you alive long enough for somebody or something willing to save you."

"Get in the boat," Lonnie suddenly requested. He was flanked by a duo Alex was reluctant to share the battlefield with: an elderly man alongside a young girl blooming into adolescence. Takeo followed closely behind.

"This is Andy and Gianna. They're joining us," Lonnie explained.

"Why?" Alex asked.

"They did some bad things. Same reason why Reese is coming," Lonnie said.

"They're not up to the standards of a soldier," Alex quietly suggested.

"We're fighting Amishmen. Gianna could take ten of them herself," Lonnie said.

"We didn't expect the Hive to attack when we searched for the Hub. We should consider the best defensive strategy," David said in support of Alex.

"Let's leave you here then," Reese proposed.

"The Amish are weak. They will be easily crushed," Takeo insisted.

With a wave of Lonnie's hand, the door to the boat opened. The red carpeted floor within was untouched by the withering decay that spread its hands throughout the outside world. It was made visible through the bright lights on the inside roof. Despite the blackened windows on the exterior, the calm waters were clearly visible from the inside. Underneath the front window a dashboard awakened, sharing statistics. The steering wheel was within the front-center with two red buttons to the sides. Along the entire cabin was a silver holding bar. Chairs were placed at the wheel, facing the back, and two at the side, all of which had joy sticks for turrets.

Lonnie took steering. Takeo occupied the rear, Gianna found herself seated on the left, and David the right, leaving Reese, Andy and Alex to grip the holding bar.

"Do you know how to operate a gunner?" Alex asked Gianna.

"It's straightforward."

Alex instantly knew she was lying.

"The gun is connected to your thoughts If you panic, so will your weapon."

Gianna nodded, but her demeanor remained timid. A character that was easy to manipulate.

"I can take over," Alex offered.

"Lonnie is watching. I have to do my best."

"Do you trust him?" Alex whispered.

"Ya."

"Why?"

"He brings us food and stuff we need all the time."

"Why is that enough?"

"Because it is."

Alex backed away, knowing that he was wasting his time on the immature girl not yet equipped with a critical mind.

"You should try the upper deck. Play lookout!" Lonnie shouted.

Alex turned to move away but stopped when he realized that they had not addressed David's worries of moving into battle without precaution.

"Once we encounter the Amish, push for surrender!" Alex stated to the whole group as he stepped upwards.

"Forget about that. Kill them all!" Lonnie countered. Alex heard the words only when he had reached the top deck with Andy. Both men placed their hands on the bar which pulled them both with a tight electronic grip, ensuring their safety. The boat began to move, making it too late for Alex to acknowledge Lonnie's disrespect.

Alex took the opportunity and turned to Andy, asking the same questions that he had asked Gianna.

"Of course I trust him. Why are you asking? Planning a coup?" Andy questioned, laughing at his lackluster cleverness.

"I'm making sure that I won't be betrayed in battle."

"Lonnie is the best goddamn fighter in our group. I've seen it myself. Sometimes he gets into trouble with his reckless behavior, but hey! He was born into leadership. I guess that means he deserves his place, wouldn't you say?"

Alex took a break from speaking to figure out the subtext of Andy's words. Being so close to Lonnie meant that unfiltered thoughts would not be shared, but Andy's comment about recklessness made Alex believe that his words harbored an agenda.

"In the Collective we earn our place. The way it should be."

"Some Libertarians would love that! Myself included. Can you

believe that even I have supporters who think I would be a good fit as leader? Me of all people! Tell me: if there was an election between the family who has ruled for decades or a man who knows what it's like to be born without anything, who would you pick?"

"Myself."

Andy projected a smile which revealed his lack of teeth. "If you're with us for long, it's a question you'll have to answer."

"I won't be. Not for long."

"Let you in on a secret. People born at the top. They think that good guys like us aren't worth keeping promises to."

"I saw evidence of what I want."

"Are you sure that it's not half a story?"

"My men and I will not play into your Libertarian politics."

"You already are."

"What you're doing would be treason in Zone 6."

"I want you on the winning side."

Alex remained silent. Within the Collective, rebelling against the leader of one's company was an instant report, but they were not in Zone 6. He was free to choose his own code.

As hours passed night quickly descended. Their pace remained smooth until the vehicle stopped, followed by the immediate shutdown of the searchlight.

"Alex, Andy!" Gianna desperately called, waving them inside. When they entered Alex found that the internal cabin was draped in darkness. The lights from the dashboards turned to black state.

"This is my favorite part," Lonnie revealed.

Alex turned his head to the front where he saw that three small boats inched ahead: the Amish.

"Which one has the EMP?" Alex asked.

"How should I know? They all look the same," Lonnie said. The top of each boat had a chimney, a strange choice for the Amish, and wooden boxes within the back that shared the cargo that had been hauled to Riverside. No defenders were visible within the vessels.

"What's the mass of the EMP?" David wondered.

"Big," Reese answered.

"Look closer at the left shipment."

It was the only boat that held priority of large crates over smaller material.

"Let's destroy the other two," Takeo proposed.

"I'm all for it," Lonnie said.

"Recklessness is not the way to do things, people," Andy said.

"What about my opinion?" Reese asked.

"You can do what you want. I'm fighting," Lonnie decided.

"It has to happen," Takeo acknowledged.

"One foul shot can destroy the EMP," David informed.

"Then we'll intimidate. Look at our boat. Swords and bows are nothing against it."

"Fine, but if anything goes wrong, have my back," Lonnie demanded.

The boat moved onward upon the silent ocean, moving close enough for Lonnie to speak.

"Amishmen! Surrender and you will not be harmed!" Lonnie shouted into the dashboard. The message was amplified by speakers that projected through the exterior.

"No answer," Takeo said.

"No shit," Reese retorted.

"Surrender and you won't be harmed! If you don't then you will all die," Alex offered.

A white shirt popped from the front of the Amishmen's vessel, acting as a beacon that battle would be avoided.

"Show yourself!" Lonnie exclaimed. The shadow of a man emerged.

A knock came from the upper deck of the Libertarian vessel.

Alex called forth the presence of his helmet. "Takeo. Let's go!" Alex said.

"I need you on gunner. Andy is free," Lonnie interrupted.

"Happy to help in whatever way I can," Andy informed.

Deciding he did not have time to argue Alex turned to the upper deck, followed by Andy who had a rifle of the old world in hand. Takeo arrived seconds later.

"You're not staying?" Alex asked. Takeo shook his head.

Alex pushed the door open, then sensing a threat of an attack, withdrew back into the cabin. His correct hypothesis yielded a swordsman who slashed downward at Alex's foot, missing it by a few inches. Alex's weapon sliced through the enemy's body, and he fell backwards into death.

Takeo rushed to the upper deck. "Get ready!" Lonnie said.

"Oh my fucking god," Gianna squealed.

Alex followed Takeo to the unknown dangers of the surface.

Takeo was crouched at the back deck. His back was pressed against the right side of the blockade that separated the deck and the cabin. Alex was thankful for Takeo's swiftness and grateful that they were on one another's teams instead of facing against each other in the battlefield.

Alex took the left side and peeked around the corner, spotting legs surging towards him. Alex sent a laser to his feet but the man jumped, managing to avoid the attack. He retaliated by slashing his sword. Alex pivoted backwards. The swordsman swiftly swung for Alex's neck, missing only because Alex was able to burn a hole through his chest, ending the attack. His body stumbled backwards and fell into the water below.

"These aren't Amish! They have guns!" Andy exclaimed as he looked over the edge.

Takeo dashed towards Andy and gripped his neck, attempting to pull him back.

"Get back!" Takeo yelled.

"Let me g—"

As soon as Takeo let go a grappling hook punctured its way through Andy's head, clawing from the front to the back of his cranium, claiming his body, and his life.

Alex carefully leaned over the edge to get a proper view of the occurrence. Andy was correct. Their enemy was not Amish. They used technology to climb forth onto the boat by moving upwards through the use of glowing blue gloves. Andy's body fell freely into the sea while the grappling hook returned to its owner. Alex took a sweeping shot below, killing two more men.

From the Libertarian vessel came a continued patter of lead bullets, splintering the Amishmen's center boat. People on board were screaming as others attempted to escape by jumping offboard into the sea.

A grappling claw penetrated its way onto the deck. Its user soared through the air before Alex could sever the connection. The enemy's second grappling hook was aiming for the front deck, pulling him forward before Alex could make a direct hit.

Takeo threw a grenade into the inner cabin. "What are you doing?"

A puff of gray smoke wafted from Takeo's explosive, sending the others outside. The only ones who remained inside the boat were Gianna and Lonnie.

"What the hell!" Reese complained. The clouds billowed outward from the cabin, dancing in the open air.

Alex took David to the left side, and Takeo led the right assault with Reese.

"They faked a surrender. They don't deserve mercy," Takeo proclaimed as he released a bullet from his shotgun.

Alex jumped to the top of the cabin, aided by David who pushed his feet upwards. The vantage point gave him a proper understanding of the predicament. A group of antagonists swam towards them. The duo of remaining boats attempted escape.

A pair of arms began to climb up the left side of the boat and had almost reached the surface. Alex prepared for an attack when the vessel suddenly launched forward, the surprise knocking him back below, his rifle flying from his hand.

Shield-wielding enemies clashed directly into Takeo. The first delivered a direct stunting blow to Takeo. Reese retaliated by using his rifle as a blunt object and smashed it against the enemy's skull until they begged for mercy.

As the second shield wielder attempted to rise, Alex withdrew his revolver.

"Stop!"

He rejected his offer and crafted a purple shield around him.

Alex followed through with his threat. The first two bullets splintered the shield, the third shattered it, the fourth penetrated the enemy, killing him instantly.

The first shield wielder begged for his life. Without prompting, Takeo activated his machete and separated the pleader's head from his body.

The boat picked up speed, chasing the vessel that contained the smaller cargo, and not the hypothesized EMP.

"Stop him!" Alex instructed to no one in particular, as he journeyed along the boat's edge for observation.

Once he made it to the front end Alex was startled when he found a man at the front on his knees. His breathing was heavy. His eyes were closed. Alex released his pistol, but nothing came from the empty chamber.

"Shit!"

The man woke. When he attempted to stand a desperate gurgle came from his mouth. His arm raised in preparation of a grappling attack which Alex denied by tackling his body to the ground. The man writhed in a lackluster struggle.

"He's a potential hostage," David reminded them, "and if we kill them all it is unknown what repercussions it will yield."

Alex's eyes turned to the man who was pinned to the ground. His head slammed against the wooden floor, still no words of protest or pleas for forgiveness being spoken.

"What faction are you from?"

David began to speak for him. "Wait, he's—"

Before David could finish the boat took another sudden increase in speed. The group was sent backwards, all four of their bodies slamming against the upper deck.

The man used his grappling hook, sent it forth against the metal railing, and set himself free by vaulting into the ocean. The drifters within the water were crushed.

"No!" David pleaded, as Lonnie was seemingly set on a direct course to smash into the vessel ahead.

"He's going to kill us!" Takeo screamed.

Alex considered jumping into the water as an alternative to Lonnie having control over his fate.

To Alex's relief, the boat slowed. The group killed the few men who were on it with ease.

"It's all clear!" Takeo shouted as the quartet jumped onto the final boat.

Takeo withdrew his machete, carefully using it to peel off a part of a box.

"It's the EMP!" David exclaimed.

Alex looked to the object with awe. Its internal organs were shown. An intricate web of wires crossing into one another, and long clear circular tubes which extended vertically. At the top was a great antenna.

"It's not complete. It's missing its crystal. It can't be used," David revealed.

"They probably knew about this," Reese said.

"Let's get going," Lonnie called as he emerged from the cabin.

"These parts are valuable," David revealed.

"Surrender!" a chorus of voices called from the water below.

Alex investigated the source. The blinking lights of sticky bombs had been attached to the boat. Stoic bodies bobbed within the water.

"Surrender!" they called again.

The bodies shared a blank expression. They voiced their demands at the exact same time. The Hive had returned.

"What do we do?" Gianna panicked.

The Hive's sudden emergence of forces tripled the Alliance.

They slowly clambered onto the boat. "Drop your weapons," Alex instructed.

"What? We can't! It will take us!" Takeo argued.

"I'm going to negotiate."

With the exception of Lonnie and Takeo the group gave up their weapons.

Lonnie attempted to retaliate, but his hope was ended when he was subdued by a Hive which came from behind, knocking him unconscious.

"Why attack Amishmen?" the Hive asked.

Alex stood frozen in terror, not yet ready to die. "We-w-wanted to get the EMP."

"Your origin is of the Collective," the bodies replied.

The fact that the Hive knew where his true loyalty lay filled Alex with fear. The answer was obvious when he glanced down at his uniform.

"We're not here for a Collective mission. If it's a body you want, take mine, but let the rest of my men go!"

"I am interested. Potential—you have it. The marks of succession."

Alex's hatred for the Hive burned. He had watched the entity that stood before him slaughter without mercy. It was the reason for man's downfall. Its mocking tone pushed Alex further towards rage. He wanted nothing more than to permanently end its words.

"You have questions. I have answers. Join me. If you don't, you die. I will not take your body."

Alex saw the offer as an opportunity: he had been given the chance to watch the inner workings of the Hive. It would be best to infiltrate, escape when necessary, and bring the information to the remaining Collective, using it to end the Hive's uprising. His only other option was death.

"Why keep us as Loyalists?"

The bodies remained blank.

"Potential for you. I will see the rest," the bodies replied.

"We'll join. We are now loyal to your will," Alex lied.

CHAPTER SEVEN

THE INTERROGATION

A blindfold stole Alex's vision. His positive feelings on temporarily joining the Hive had wavered as he fantasized how significant it would be to die in a blaze of courage. He was stripped of everything but his clothing. Reese had been placed beside him, made obvious through his fidgeting and gratuitous groans. The negative aftermath of his pill was taking effect. The Hive did not speak. The only sounds were breathing and the boat's mechanisms. Alex was led outside by firm hands. He detected the scent of seawater. His boots submerged within it, before transferring to what felt like incredibly small grains.

"Every question I ask, I want honesty. I always see the truth. The Collective. You've been with them long?" the Hive who led Alex asked.

"A few years."

"Before?"

"I was with my family. They're all gone."

"Killed by who … me?"

"Yes. I escaped the attack."

"You are strong. It shows. I remember. Your face. Seen it in many places. Last was when you struck my heart. Why fight?"

"I protect people."

"So do I."

"If my bodies were yours. What would you do?"

69

"Rebuild what you destroyed," Alex answered without hesitation.

"A formidable task. Requires courage. Decisiveness."

"I have both."

"Alexander King." Alex was taken aback by the knowing of his name. "Why is a Collective man with a Libertarian?" the alien asked.

"I've promised not to speak of it."

"You claim loyalty. Yet you falter. I admire courage. Now show true courage."

Alex's blindfold retracted. In front of him was a sword. Next to it was Commander Hamish, his former leader. He had been confirmed dead. His current presence proved it to be a lie.

His loss of weight was a small physical change compared to the significance of the black W inked onto his forehead. The mark of a willing Loyalist.

"Alex—" Hamish shrieked, regret beaming through his voice.

"A traitor to you."

Hamish did not deny the allegation. Alex gripped the steel sword.

"A traitor to me. Kill him."

"Alex, don't join. It's dyi—"

Hamish's pleading ceased once Alex plunged the blade into his chest. Alex was torn; he immediately felt guilty. Hamish did not deserve death at the hand of his subordinate. In an attempt to relieve his guilt, Alex theorized that Hamish had been taken by the Hive. The red pouring from his wound disapproved the theory.

Alex withdrew the sword and caught the body of his Commander. "I-I'm sorry," Alex admitted.

"Prove yourself," Hamish said as a last command, its meaning vague.

As Hamish perished, the Hive body stood blankly. For more than a minute it did not speak nor move. Alex saw the hiccup as a chance to escape, but he knew nothing of his landscape or the location of the others, dashing away his hopes.

"Hello?" Alex asked.

There was no reply from the Hive.

"Good choice," a woman from behind stated.

Alex turned to find that in her left hand was a skinny metal stick, and in her right was a vial filled with thin black liquid.

"What about the Hive, it's—"

"It's nothing to worry about," she claimed, dipping the metal tip into the liquid. The substance did not drip when she withdrew it.

"My hand," Alex requested.

"Others choose the forehead. Makes their loyalty visible."

"I'm not like other people."

The black tip torched his hand, and he groaned in pain. He looked away as the marking was etched into his skin, reminding himself that he was betraying the Collective only in appearance, that he would come to them with enough information to justify the choice. He had already discovered the existence of its island, and more would be coming.

"Come on," she said once she lifted the needle.

The W etched onto Alex's hand was the identification of a Loyalist.

Alex looked to the water, briefly wondering whether it could wash away his blasphemy, knowing that it wouldn't and that he would never be welcomed back into Zone 6 with open arms.

A line of guardsmen took the coastline, comprised of both Hive and Loyalist bodies. The distinction between the two was obvious: the Hive stood with solid stoicism; the Loyalists were identifiable by their black markings and servitude to human nature, unable to stand still without shifting feet or craning heads. The Loyalist bodies outnumbered the Hive, subverting Alex's expectations. The line did not have a visible end, making the prospect of an escape route more difficult than he'd imagined.

A man stood at the beach, alone. Alex was relieved when he saw it was Takeo, but when he realized that both Reese and David were missing, he was immediately concerned and it prompted dark thoughts within him that they had perished, but he pushed them away by guessing that they were in the same position: isolated and forced to answer questions about who they were.

Takeo caught Alex's eyes and looked downward in shame. His forehead had been branded. He would not be allowed within the Collective without excessive political backing. To console him,

Alex flashed his right hand, showing that they had both taken a fall in status.

"You are mine. Former titles. Now gone," the Hive informed.

"Where are the others?" Takeo asked.

Alex tightened, immediately questioning whether their temporary leader was a fool's gambit.

"Alive," the Hive responded.

Takeo almost spoke again, but Alex sent him a harsh look, sending him to silence.

"Follow," the Hive continued.

The Hive walked them through a jungle of trees that Alex had only seen in relic photographs from the old world. Every few feet along the brown base, the bark stemmed outwards. The leaves were in the shape of green triangles. They walked along the only solid path.

"Your role. Protect me. Protect my stock. If you succeed. Rewards. Great ones. The—"

The Hive stopped moving. Its bodies coughed at uneven moments. For the first time Alex saw the Hive lack cohesion.

"I leave. You stay," some of the bodies announced, but they all ran away.

"There's something wrong," Alex said. He had been left alone twice in an hour. The Hive's state was not a coincidence.

"We can't talk. It's going to be back soon," Takeo warned. "We need to find the others."

"This place is crawling with guards. I don't think that—"

"I am so sorry that you had to wait," a woman said. She was young with a slender figure. Time had been put into crafting her beauty. Her nose was thin, black hair straight. Clean white teeth. As an alternative to military garments she wore a short black dress. Despite the environment there was not a single particle of dirt on it. The only ugly part about her were the inked W's that covered her body in more than one place. Her stomach was round, indicating pregnancy.

"I'm Raina. Has your role been explained?" Raina asked.

"We are protectors of the Hive. This island," Alex stated.

"You're in one of the best places you can be. Some others aren't so lucky."

Her positive view of the island was odd. Alex hoped that all the people of the Hive's island were like her. If they weren't it would mean a lonely existence.

"What are the others doing?" Alex asked.

"They have a mission, you have yours."

They reached a fork in the path where there was a path straight ahead, one going to the right, and another to the left. The woman moved them to the left, and after a couple minutes the woman began to speak.

"You're from the Collective?" the woman asked both Alex and Takeo.

They nodded in response, curious as to what else she would want to know.

"What do people even do all day?"

Alex found the question stupid. She was clearly not a woman of the world. If she was, she would have known that there was no time for leisure. All communities focused on the survival of their people which meant time spent farming, hunting, and building infrastructure.

"Try to survive," Takeo answered.

"Like us."

"We're not the same," he defended.

Alex wanted to shush him, but Raina's prying ears restricted him from doing so.

"How so?"

"You might even be a little better," Takeo clarified.

"I would hope so."

"We'll do whatever we can to pay the Hive back for its generosity," Alex claimed, making sure to appear interested in its will.

"Anything? That may not be the right way to live … Stick to your morals."

"To protect something, sometimes one has to change them."

"What did you tell the Hive of your identity?" Raina asked.

"That I defend people who can't defend themselves," Takeo revealed.

"You're not the first of the Collective to come. I've heard those words countless times before, from people who left us. I expect you have the same independent spirit."

"I do," Takeo said.

"Good. We'll need it."

"Who was it that left?" Alex asked. His thoughts drifted to the many Officers and Commanders who had departed on perimeter missions, and never returned. It was assumed that they had died, but Alex doubted that was the endpoint of many of their stories.

"Their names don't matter. They shared the same fate. They tried to leave, and when they were caught, they begged for mercy."

"It gave him the chance to leave?" Alex asked, unable to hide the excitement in his voice.

"It used to let some go."

"Why?" Alex tried to calm himself, keeping his voice neutral.

"Many different reasons," Raina vaguely stated, leaving Alex struggling to uncover the meaning in her answer, "but keep your focus on what's important."

The end of the dirt path was shrouded by two large leaves. Raina lifted both and uncovered an alternative landscape. It was flat ground which had been cleared of trees. Replacing them were multiple small shelters next to one another. The entire north grounds of the houses were being operated by beautiful women, all of them wearing the same outfit: a black dress.

The north side of the grounds was filled with the homes while the back end was of an entirely different nature. It was an armory, stocked full of guns, and melee weapons of the new world. All being handled by children, none of them over the age of twelve.

"This is what you're here to protect," the woman continued.

Alex looked to the children's faces; just when he thought he didn't recognize any of them, a familiar one stood out. It was Patton.

Alex chose to restrain himself from approaching Patton, as he was unsure of the identity that Patton had crafted for himself within the island. If he had not revealed that he belonged to the Collective, Alex's recognition of him would place the child in danger.

All other thoughts fell away from Alex as he focused on Patton's nearly impossible reemergence. He toyed with the horrendous idea that the child had somehow been a spy of the Hive, but it was dashed away when he saw that Patton lacked the marks of a Loyalist. The realization then dawned on him that if Patton was within the island, he had left Zone 6. The reason why would need to be explained.

Watching the training yard, Alex saw for the first time that the enemy did not exemplify evil. The children showed joyful smiles as they learned, and the Hive present bent down to their height level while teaching. Correcting their body position when one could take an incorrect shot, some leaned forwards as the Hive spoke words of encouragement, while Patton and a few others backed away.

"Your quarters are this way," Raina said, interrupting Alex's speculation.

"Who are the kids?" Alex asked.

"Our master's children. Made only of the strongest genetic material," Raina answered as her hand rested on her flowering belly.

"All of them?"

"No. Some are from opposing factions. We bring them here. Rehabilitate them from their old ways and raise them right."

"What do you do with people who don't … line up with the way you think?" Takeo asked.

"Nobody is ever wasted by our leader. They all serve a purpose. What does the Collective do?"

"Kill them."

Alex reluctantly walked up the hill, hoping that he would be given the chance to see Patton once again.

A tight squeeze gripped Alex's wrist. It was not strong, but the intention was clear: the Hive was trying to take him. He quickly lifted his hand to try to save himself, but when he turned, he saw it was Patton.

"Alex!" He gripped Alex in a tight embrace. "You're here!"

"You know each other?" Raina asked.

"My mentee," Alex answered.

"You should have told me. I don't appreciate being lied to," Raina said, killing the moment between them.

"Nobody does," Takeo said.

"Takeo, you're here too!" Patton broke free of Alex and embraced Takeo.

"He has training to do. Try your best not to disturb him," Raina reminded them.

"Of course," Alex stated.

Alex was led to his sleeping quarters which was nothing more than a hut that he would be sharing with Takeo. All that was inside were two cots.

"It's not what I thought it would be," Takeo said.

Alex circled his finger to indicate that they check their surroundings first. He stepped outside to search for any lurking bodies, before conducting an internal search for any advanced technology used for spying.

"What isn't?"

"The Hive."

"Nothing ever really is."

"It showed us mercy."

"We don't know if that's true for the others. We need to find them. Now."

"Soon," Takeo said.

Alex knew that Takeo was right.

"I can't believe that it has kids," Takeo continued. "From using bodies that is not its own."

"The two of you must be hungry. Come with me," Raina said as she stepped through the purple curtain that acted as a door.

"We're both fine," Alex decided.

"I am," Takeo said.

Alex realized that Takeo was probably right; rejecting a generous offer may be an insult to the Hive's giving nature.

The men followed Raina and were taken into the forest with a few others standing in a single file line, moving to a fork in the road that split into four paths.

"Don't go further north than this point," Raina warned. "It is off limits except for those who are chosen."

Alex knew that at the first opportunity available it would be the first place that he would go to find David, Reese, Lonnie, and Gianna.

"What's over there?" Alex asked.

"Precious cargo."

Alex held off on further verbal investigation, as it might arouse suspicion to ask too many questions at one time. He wondered whether cargo meant human bodies.

The group moved further left until they found another open field, where a great feast was lain before the Loyalists. There were various thick slabs of meat, vegetables and fruits of vivid colors, and some foods that Alex did not recognize.

When he sat down Alex took a portion of food from a wooden bowl ahead of him. It was a white paste put together in lumps. It was soft on his tongue and tasted like a rare delicacy. Another delicacy was put in front of Alex when he was almost full: a few slices of fruit, cut in triangular shapes that had pink filling embedded with black seeds and green crusts.

Alex ate only a small amount thinking that it may be poison, but Takeo indulged in both the food and the alcohol that came after. After spending the rest of their day in a state of leisure Alex walked back into his hut speculating about the future. The landscape was free of moving bodies which meant that the island's guards would not be a great hindrance. On clear nights Alex decided that along with Takeo he would sneak out and discover where David and Reese had gone.

As he stumbled into bed the horrifying thought that the food he had ingested could be an assassination method entered his mind, but the speculation quickly vanished, for if the Hive desired his death, it would be done in a direct manner. A manner that Alex would encounter if he was caught betraying the Hive, an act that would make him wish for death by poison.

CHAPTER EIGHT

THE HUNT

Alex was woken with a shake. His hand gripped the skinny wrist of a child. Emerald eyes stared back at Alex. At first he thought it was one of the Hive's offspring, but a second of clarity made him realize it was Patton.

"Sorry," Patton said.

Patton reached over to Takeo, but Takeo was already awake.

"What do you want?" Takeo asked.

"I'm here to serve. First you need ..." Patton paused and rubbed his head, trying to remember the correct word. "Breakfast."

From the floor Patton picked up two bowls filled to the brim with murky brown cooked oats, mixed with a heaping of berries. Alex was grateful for the nutrients. Luxurious silver spoons extended from its depths.

"How did you get here?" Alex asked.

Patton was wary to answer the question, as his eyes investigated the inside of the hut. But the only things in it were the two beds and aimless flies overhead.

"Zone 6 got taken over," Patton sadly revealed.

Alex did not believe him. With the strong defenses of the city there was no enemy that could penetrate their walls. Even though the Hive was strong, it was much weaker than before.

"This can't be true," Alex claimed, defensively crossing his arms.

"How did you get out?" Takeo shouted. He gripped Patton by the collar and pulled him close.

"A few hours pretty much after you left. Bunch of Hive and Loyalists came in. They had all kinds of stuff. Aircraft. We could not win."

"In all that you managed to escape?"

"Let him finish," Alex said.

"Don't let emotions blind you from traitors."

"I was allowed life because I got out. That's it. That's when the Hive came. Said I was strong," Patton revealed.

"Is anybody that we know alive? What about Ives?"

"Nobody ... important."

The revelation stung. It meant that their entire journey had been useless. If Alex had chosen to return to the city instead of traveling to Riverside he would have been able to defend it and warn the Collective of what was to come. Instead, they were now stuck in an environment that they may not be able to escape for years to come, and Zone 6 had fallen. An event that Alex considered to be his fault.

"But the city is there. The citizens joined the Hive. It's really bad."

"Alex, this kid joined the Hive. Don't talk to him about anything."

"So did we."

"We're doing it to—I'm not even going to say it. I just want to know what good a kid can do in the world's biggest army."

Once he posed the question Alex realized that he had not asked Takeo the same thing.

"I told you. It liked how we escaped. Said we're strong."

"Bullshit. Where were you escaping to?"

"Quiet down," Alex warned.

"We are the only two people left in our group. I'm not having myself killed, or you, by this kid leaking our secrets."

"The rest are alive."

"Not by now," Takeo said.

"How can you say that?" Alex asked in disgust.

"The kid is old enough to hear how harsh the world is. He is also old enough to be a spy."

"David and Reese being dead is not truth, and Patton is not a spy," Alex said as he separated the two.

Takeo shook his head. "You can't let him leave. Not until we've interrogated him. It's the way that we do things."

Alex began to doubt Patton's loyalty to him until Patton backed behind him. As he gripped his wrist, his fear was evident. He was still the same boy.

"I want to get out too," Patton said. "I don't like it here. I feel sick sometimes. I'm tired. It's terrible. I'll help you do it, Takeo."

"Not yet," Alex said as he leaned down to his level, "but we will."

Alex felt great sorrow. He no longer cared about his own safety; all he wanted was for Patton to be okay.

"Why didn't you go to Peddlers Lake?" Alex asked.

"Why does Peddlers Lake matter?" Takeo asked.

"It was a rendezvous point. A place to escape if anything goes wrong. Commanders were told about it."

"You told him this, but not me?" Takeo hastily asked.

"I knew that no matter what happened, you would be able to survive."

"If I die, it's your fault." Takeo stomped outside in righteous anger.

"I'm sorry. I shouldn't said that," Patton said.

"It's have said that, and he's right. He should have known. Everybody should have known."

"Everybody? Is there space?"

"I don't know, but I would give up my spot for you," Alex said as he walked outside seeing that the compound was alive with movement. Takeo had not gone far as Raina had gotten in his way, and he was only a mere minute away from their living space. Once Raina spotted him, she waved Alex over.

"The three of you have been chosen for a mission. Come along," Raina stated proudly.

"What mission?" Alex asked.

"A great honor."

"I'm asking what we are going to be doing."

"The food you eat does not come from thin air. You have been chosen as hunters. A great honor."

"You already said that," Patton said.

"Aren't you insightful."

A duo of bodies flanked their group. Both of them being Hive, identifiable by their synchronized movements.

"Each of them has worthy skills," the Hive said. They weren't close enough to hear Raina's words.

"Are you coming with us?" Takeo asked the bodies.

"No. I wanted to speak."

Alex tensed as he wondered whether the Hive had overheard their traitorous conversation.

"Any questions for me?" the Hive continued.

"Why am I coming?" Patton asked.

"Be grateful," Raina hushed.

"Coming? I want to see your strength. The strength of your crop. I want to see everything."

"What are we hunting?" Takeo asked.

"Different question."

"Question. How can we hunt? We don't have weapons," Patton mentioned.

"You will receive another question."

"Why do you need children? You are already so powerful," Alex said, hoping that the stroking of the alien's ego would result in an answer.

"I need a follower. Might be them," the Hive answered prior to departing without another word.

"Why would the Hive need followers? It already has so many."

"Humans are not loyal, but when a person is the Hive's descendant, that's a different story," Raina answered prior to leading the group to the east beach. Another area with Loyalist guards around the edges.

"That island. A deer is preferred," Raina stated as she pointed to a piece of land in the distance.

"How is one deer going to be dinner for everybody?" Alex snapped.

"I'm telling you only because I like you. This is not just about food."

"Then what's it about?" Takeo asked.

"Of course, I can't tell you," she teased as a Loyalist came forward and gave each of the men a bow, a quiver of arrows, and a grenade.

"A bow," Takeo said with disappointment.

"Takeo, I need to speak with you."

"Is saying 'a bow' forbidden?" Patton asked fearfully.

"It's not that," Raina said.

The trio looked to one another with suspicion until Takeo heeded the request. As they spoke, Takeo consistently glanced over to Alex, and Alex's hands gripped his bow, prepared to fire at Raina if Takeo gave him a sign to do so.

"What are they talking about?" Patton asked.

"I don't know," Alex snapped.

Raina withdrew Takeo's machete hilt, along with two glimmering silver rectangles. He took the gifts without reservation.

When Takeo approached he gave both Alex and Patton one of the rectangles each. Seeing them close up Alex recognized the material. It was what he was given when he had first become a Loyalist.

"Why do I have to wear a blindfold?" Alex asked.

"Just put it on," Takeo urged.

Patton placed the silver block to his eye, and it quickly expanded around the circumference of his head, blocking the child's vision.

"Answer me. I am your Commander."

"Not anymore."

Alex had to restrain himself from striking Takeo. The fact that he would rather take instructions from the Hive angered him. Even with Zone 6 gone, the Collective was not yet lost. Once the other Zones came to their aid Alex fantasized that dolling out Takeo's punishment would be the first thing he would do.

"When does this thing get off?" Patton complained.

"It comes off when we get there," Takeo replied.

Alex snatched the silver strip and placed it over his eyes. Not only could he not see, but he also couldn't hear, giving him a sense of empathy for Patton's reaction.

Takeo acted as an anchor for Alex's direction, steering him towards the small vessel that would take them towards the island. The boat swayed as they journeyed across the water. Once they reached the shore Alex's silver blindfold was withdrawn, and in that moment he turned to Takeo.

"You're not coming back to the Collective with me."

"They won't let us back in. Not with this," Takeo countered, pointing to the marking on his skin.

"Let's kill this animal," Alex said, ignoring Takeo's argument.

"Do you know what these weapons do?"

"Arrows and a grenade," Patton answered.

"They mean more than that. These three are to make a fire," Takeo said as he held up three arrows with red tips. His hands then switched focus to the arrows with blue tips. "These ones make ice. I don't know about the others."

"None of these were in the Collective," Alex said.

"Raina told me what everything does. Our grenades explode at the moment of impact."

"Then none of us will use it. It could be a danger to ourselves," Alex decided.

Takeo did not argue. A small victory for Alex, as it showed that despite their equality in the Hive's eyes, Takeo was still somewhat loyal to the Collective hierarchy.

"How do you use this again?" Patton asked as he ran behind the others. His trembling hands tried to save the arrow that tilted to the ground.

"Back straight first of all," Alex said.

As Alex turned to ensure that Patton had followed his instruction, he saw that the Hive's island was gone.

"Where are we?"

"The island is over there, somewhere. It's camouflaged," Takeo said as he waved his hand to the unending stretch of sky and sea. Rescue seemed even more unlikely.

Patton attempted to string his bow once again, which resulted in an embarrassing failure when his arrow fell to the sand. "Shit."

"Just keep your feet shoulder-width apart."

"What?"

"Move your feet so they line up with your shoulder," Takeo added.

Patton followed the simplified instructions.

"Clip the back of the arrow into the string. Then put the pointy end where that block lies," Takeo said.

Patton struggled, but after a few tries he completed the task.

"You're preferred by the Hive," Alex accused, interrupting Patton's lesson.

"We need to use it. Learn about the Hive. Everything about it."

Alex was denied a reply when Patton foolishly released an arrow. Alex went to scold him but discovered that it was not an accident. His weapon soared through the air and hit a tree beside a new enemy.

From the depth of the green, a bear three times Takeo's size emerged. Its composition was not of the natural world. It had four eyes, six limbs, and a belching roar that produced visible sound waves.

"Shit! Shit! Shit!" Patton screamed.

Once the beast's circular sound waves came into contact with the ground, it manifested a tunnel of sand that came barreling towards the group. Alex gripped Patton and flung him behind while the dread that came paired with battle wrenched him. He had felt it when his family was attacked by bandits. His heart raced, while the remainder of his body tightened.

"We only have a few arrows! Make it count!" Alex commanded, but his message was drowned by the deafening scream of the beast.

He shot a red arrow, having no concern for preserving the mission. His purpose hadn't changed: it was still to survive.

His shot was meant for the animal's chest, but instead it lodged itself within its arm rather than the expected pillar of flame. Its top right arm became entrenched in a thick layer of ice.

Takeo and Alex nodded; the non-verbal promise that they would support each other.

"Let's see what this does!" Takeo said as he withdrew a blue arrow.

"Patton, provide cover! If we die get in the boat and go north!" Alex said.

The bear charged. The ice that Alex had placed within its upper arm forced it to heed its way on two hind legs.

"Cover me!" Alex yelled as he approached doom.

"Wait!"

But it was too late. Alex had no time to consider his words. He had made a decision and Takeo was to comply with it.

A cylinder of fire exploded from Takeo's blue arrow which landed a few feet ahead of the animal. Its fur peeled off from the flame's licks, slowly unveiling silver beneath.

Takeo, with an activated blade, rushed past Alex. The hilt had produced a bar of purple plasma larger than his previously owned machete. But he forged to meet the bear head-on and the animal's sharp claws swung in defense to tear Takeo to shreds.

Its inaccurate swipe at Takeo's head gave him the opening to swing his sword upwards. The purple plasma connected with the arm, revealing the animal's insides, but did not slice through. From the wound a tangle of multicolored wires, displaced motherboards, and red blood spilled below in a shower of sparks.

The bear took another strike at Takeo. He diverted most of the animal's power with his blade, but not enough to prevent its claws from reaching Takeo's skin.

He screamed as he dragged the sword forward with might, managing to tear off the limb. First came a shamble of intricate technology. Then a flow of blood.

"Get out!" Alex screamed.

Takeo ducked out, and Alex's purple arrow traveled into the enemy's stomach. Purple electricity encased itself around its body, glitching its movements.

Takeo hacked at the left arm until he was backhanded. The sword slipped from his hands, landing near the bear's legs. Alex recovered it, managing to duck beneath the animal's vertical swing, and retaliated by stabbing the sword into the bear's neck. When his strike did not slow the animal, he attempted to withdraw, but it came out tediously. Alex dropped the hilt and backed away to safety, until the animal's claws connected with his flesh. Both his clothing and stomach were narrowly skimmed.

Alex ran. An act he despised. "Now!" Alex called.

The animal's life was terminated courtesy of Takeo's grenade. Patton took off his shirt and rushed to place it on Alex's wound. Blood soaked through the cloth, painting the material with red splotches. The scratch was not deep enough to kill, but it did cause throbbing pain.

Alex looked to the animal's corpse. Its remains of fleshy organs, chopped wires, dead bulbs, wet blood, and charred fur were scattered across the beach; the result of Takeo's wise defiance.

"Thanks for not listening to me."

"We need to get you back," Takeo said.

"The Hive was controlling the animal. Look at the blood," Alex realized.

Takeo and Patton both investigated with squinted eyes, quickly registering that within pools of red, the animal's blood contained flecks of green.

"It controls animals too?" Patton asked.

"Maybe more," Takeo theorized.

"It's changing. It's weaker than it has ever been, but it's still advancing. This needs to be known. We find the others, and we leave tonight," Alex decided.

"Maybe leave me here. When you come back with the Collective, I could tell you its secrets," Takeo suggested.

"We go together. As a team."

Takeo did not argue further.

The trio waltzed into the boat without the silver blinds that blocked their senses, allowing Patton to propel the oars. At the journey's midpoint the atmosphere shimmered. Reality broke. The Hive's island became visible. The impressive display stirred up fear within Alex. It became clear that they would not be saved as any search for them would only be complete with specific coordinates.

"That's amazing!" Patton exclaimed.

"Did Raina tell you if it can be destroyed?" Alex asked Takeo.

"All she told me was that I should not go back to the Collective. That I'm valuable here."

"We're not beating it," Patton sulked. His enthusiasm for rowing began to wane. "I didn't do anything during fight."

"*The* fight, and I wanted you safe," Alex replied.

"I felt frozen. I'll never beat it."

"If you think that way, it will come true."

"What if it kills us? We didn't listen. We've brought no deer."

"Sometimes you have to make your own rules," Takeo said as the boat came to shore, where three Hive waited.

"The blindfolds. Takeo did not place them," the Hive stated.

"We finished what you asked. We deserve to see where we are," Alex said.

"Men of the Collective. A simple battle does not mean reward. No deer meat was returned."

"We can go back," Takeo offered.

Alex agreed, as it would give them a chance to speak without uninvited listeners.

"Unnecessary."

"The bear was controlled by you. You saw us. What did you think?" Alex accused.

"You proved yourself. Through bravery. What I search for." Alex and Patton remained silent.

"Thank you," Takeo said. "Patton. With me. Training."

"Which one?"

"Me." The words came from all three bodies.

CHAPTER NINE

THE FEAST

When Alex woke from his deep slumber he saw that the Hive had placed Raina at the foot of their doorstep, bringing Alex to a hyper aware state of suspicion.

"Why are you here?" Alex asked.

"The Hive has won a great victory. We're celebrating with a feast."

"What victory?"

"You'll see."

The words worried him, as in Loyalist eyes a victory could mean the Collective's failure.

From behind Raina, a skinny frame of a young woman emerged: Gianna. Alex restricted himself from acting in recognition of the girl.

"A new generation is coming," Raina claimed.

Gianna looked ashamed. A blossoming of tears formed around her crimson eyes. All the questions that Alex had were tortuously postponed.

"I live on the restricted side of the island," Gianna blurted. "If you see animals—"

"Quiet," Raina warned.

"Shouldn't she be with the other kids?"

"She chose to serve."

Gianna nodded in agreement. Alex guessed that she only did so because of Raina's prying senses that would report any misgivings back to their new master.

"You seem confused," Raina noticed.

"I'm happy with my role here," Alex lied. "I was a soldier before so it's not much of a change. I'm just wondering about the people who are forced to become something that they don't want to be."

"What was she before coming here?" Raina asked.

The question posed made Alex realize that he knew next to nothing about Gianna's life before the mission. His extended silence pushed Gianna to answer for herself.

"I did nothing. I was nothing. I would have been nothing if I had stayed."

"It's the story of us all. If you want to keep your life preserved, don't spill your location at unnecessary times."

"She's young. She didn't know any better," Alex said.

"That goes for both of you."

"You're right. I'm sorry," Alex stated. Gianna looked to him with heavy desperation, clearly wanting him to break her free from the Hive's grip.

"Is something happening to the Hive?" Alex asked as a bid to free himself from compliance.

"In what way?"

"It had to leave us twice when I came here. If any extra help is needed, I want to do everything I can to protect it."

"It has adopted customs from our world. That includes needing its own space to meditate. Nothing that should be of concern," Raina claimed.

Raina's unsatisfactory answer led Alex into a heightened state of suspicion; a monstrous alien needing to meditate seemed like a rushed lie.

"How much time?"

"Sometimes minutes. Sometimes hours. Our only concern is following the place that it gives you. Focusing on doing so is what saved me."

"Us," Gianna echoed convincingly.

"You don't miss your old place?" Alex asked.

"Her people didn't care about her."

"They were horrible," Gianna admitted.

"Do you know what happened?" Raina asked.

"No," Alex said.

"I'm the person who told Sheila about Andy. He wanted to lead an election. I reported him to Sheila the day right after he told me. She said that it took me too long to say anything about it."

"You're not wrong about them," Alex said. "They don't matter now. You can choose your own path."

Raina dismissed Gianna and took Alex to the dining quarters. Hive bodies did not exist within the environment of Loyalists being serviced with alcoholic drinks paired with mysterious foods. The bustling landscape showcased an alternative side to the Loyalists. They laughed with one another, a contrast to their reputations as cold-blooded killers. Alex hoped that when the war came they would lay down their arms peacefully.

Alex crouched down to Takeo. "This is our chance. Everybody's here."

"The Hive is still on the island."

"We'll find out where it went. Get the others and get out."

"You're being too hopeful."

"Do I have to turn for Patton for help?"

"He won't be much of one."

Alex spotted Patton seated at a table far away from his own, ingesting his first helping of alcohol. Alex began to rise.

"He's growing up. Nothing you can really do to stop it," Takeo warned.

"He needs to be in peak condition."

"Alex, I really want to leave too. It's just—"

"I'll do it myself," Alex decided as he prepared to venture into the unknown.

"Silence!" multiple voices harshly demanded from the greenery.

Alex remained in his seat.

The Hive slithered forward in the greatest sum that Alex had seen together. Two hostages were bound together in a single file line by a rope chain.

The first was a woman unmarked by tattoos. The other Alex instantly recognized: Reese sauntered forward with tired eyes.

Alex's fists tightened. His desire was to rise, cut Reese from the chain, and flee. An impossible act without death following for both men. Takeo shared the sentiment as he leaned forward with a harsh frown, showcasing similar aggression.

"Victory! It is ours to withhold! Kneel!"

The hostages fell with compliance. Alex's mind burned with reckless ideas to save Reese.

"Your identity," the Hive asked as one of its bodies withdrew a needle.

"I'm Tina. I used to be a part of the unifiers."

The woman was independent in her speech. Free from the Hive's true grasp.

The vial was injected into her neck. The woman flinched and closed her defeated eyes. Her body went limp. Within seconds the woman's eyes opened. They had changed from brown to green. She had been taken. The Hive had cultivated a way to steal a body within seconds. A dangerous turn from the hours it once took.

"She is mine." The message came from the bodies of the Hive, the woman included.

Reese shuddered in fear while cheers of applause came from the Loyalists.

"Enough," the Hive said.

The body of the taken woman was given a knife, which she used to plunge into her stomach. Green did not come from the stab. Instead a river of red came from the taken woman, yielding horrifying implications. The Hive's green blood was what made it distinct from free men. The saving grace of humanity. With it gone, the Hive could lurk anywhere.

"This has to be a trick," Alex stated in horror.

A second booming wave of approval came from the crowd.

"Silence!" the Hive demanded again as it approached Reese.

Alex had to look away in order to avoid watching a man who did not deserve it have his body taken in a petty demonstration.

"Your identity?" the Hive asked.

"Reese. From the Libertarians, and you can go fuck yourself."

"Another example."

"Wait!" Alex interjected "Take my body instead!"

All heads turned towards him. The Hive. Loyalists. Reese.

Takeo.

"Why?"

"It's my fault he's here. I should take his place."

"True bravery."

"I was doing fine!" Reese insisted as he clenched his fist in a firm pattern. A circular blue beam came from his hand, which enraptured the surrounding area.

All those loyal to the Hive rose to quickly aid their masters, holding onto the bodies that flailed with unrestricted chaos.

"Kill them! Destroy the castle! Take out the aircraft," random commands rose from the Hives' mouths, not meant for those present. The Hive had lost its cohesiveness. The bodies no longer spoke in a chorus, but instead a tangled mess of commands.

The Loyalists attempted to absorb the change. Some held the bodies with soft grazes and shouted for the Hive to remember its origin. The Loyalists were in dire fear. Alex saw opportunity.

"Now we go."

"It's too dangerous. This could be a trick," Takeo replied.

"You're a coward!" Alex insulted.

Alex ran to Patton only to discover that the boy had passed out. Circling his head were six finished bottles of alcohol: the cause of his slumber. He turned to Reese as an ally. Alex sliced the rope, picked him up and headed towards the restricted Zone. While doing so the Hive bodies emanated solid gray from their mouths and eyes, rendering a cohort of unusable corpses.

When the Hive ceased speaking, Loyalists accused one another of treason. Confrontations that resulted in physical brawls, granting Alex the avenue to dash into the forest. He surged for a few minutes, before placing Reese's body against a tree.

"What?" Reese asked. "Where have you been?"

"Alex, David's here. He made this." Reese opened his hand, revealing a small gray disk with a dim blue glow in the center. "I stole it."

"Where were you?"

"Take a guess."

"What do I need to watch out for in the restricted Zone?"

"Alex, I ..." Reese turned to slumber once again. Alex shook him, then hit him, but received nothing.

Before leaving Reese, Alex instinctively came close to cutting his skin to check if had been taken, but opted out. It was no longer a useful act.

Alex rushed down the main path. Hive bodies were scattered throughout, sharing the same fate as those within the dining hall. Dead, unable to fight. A grim fate for the host who had occupied it. Gianna's words rang true, as Alex discovered a field full of various foods which had just begun growing in the form of small stalks and trees.

In front of the open field was a large gray building. A representation of the old world. It had three wings. A large cylinder within the center point of the building that extended high, a shocking lack of security defending the perimeter. Only three held the line by continuously circling the building.

Alex exhaled from the weight of his heavy decision. If he continued towards the facility, he could retrieve David, Reese, and possibly Lonnie with Gianna. They had the chance to escape that night. If he returned then it meant there may not be another prospect to escape again.

A hand brushed Alex's shoulder. His natural training took over and he attacked, almost striking the source, stopping himself when he saw it was Takeo.

In his hand was a CR-99 rifle. Its stock was a red cache of liquid that released corrosive material.

"Take it," Takeo offered.

Both men turned their attention to the guards. Once the guard at the front end was halfway through its distance, Takeo came up from behind and impaled his throat with his sword. The blood that spewed painted the gray walls red.

Takeo recovered his weapon, a seeking shotgun that allowed the user to control where its shots went. Alex crouched along the right wall with perked ears prepared to meet the enemy searching for the source of the disturbance. The moment the enemy turned the corner, Takeo sliced his arm. The scream that followed defeated the prospect of further stealth.

"What's in the building?" Alex asked.

His question went unanswered as Takeo beheaded the enemy.

"Why?"

"He was too loud."

The third enemy emerged from the sky. He was equipped with maneuverability from his jet pack which contained two wings and four jets of flame. A long hose attached to his back extended into his hand.

Alex sent a shot upwards. The red liquid of his rifle was unable to reach the enemy.

The enemy released the trigger, and from his barrel a flame of fire was released downward. Alex jumped away, avoiding the brunt of the attack, but a small lick of fire came into contact with his pants, then his flesh.

While Alex extinguished the flame by rolling through the ground, the enemy was distracted by a shot that came from Takeo. Even with the capability to seek its body, the man managed to evade them by spinning, leading Takeo's bullets to smash against one another.

"Who are you?" the antagonist demanded. He hovered high enough so that neither Alex nor Takeo could make an accurate assault.

"Come here and find out!" Takeo taunted.

The enemy shot a series of fireballs directly towards Alex, changing his strategy from streamlined flames. Alex jumped away swiftly at first in avoidance, but as they continued he was forced into a panicked run.

Takeo released desperate shots towards the enemy who dodged them by dashing a few feet away once they came near him. Lacking forward momentum in their position, Alex opted to travel towards the facility's front entrance, luring the antagonist closer. As the flamecaster lowered their position, Takeo was able to shoot one bullet into its shoulder, and the other into its right leg.

Neither penetrated the armor, but the enemy reacted with an enraged scream and a blast of fire towards the door.

The incoming heat rushed towards Alex. His heart pounded with fury as the environment's humidity rose. In the last moments before the combustion reached the door Alex hauled himself right, avoiding the attack.

Its twirling smorgasbord of red, orange, and yellow contrasted the night sky as it smashed against the entrance. The flames spread in altered directions and evaporated in a puff of smoke. Alex stumbled away from it, as the remnants of fire reached their hands towards his legs.

The flames oddly did not cause a fire within the grass. They instead painted black marks within the earth in the form of twisted lines and circular splotches.

The enemy's attack against him briefly ceased. Alex turned to discover why. They had chosen to attack Takeo, returning to cascading fireballs. Takeo jumped, rolled, and sidestepped. After doing so he lifted his shotgun but was not given enough time to release a shot.

With the flamecaster distracted Alex released a cache of his corrosive liquid which smashed against the jet pack's right wing, instantly throwing off its flight pattern. They sputtered upwards, then unintentionally nosedived. Before harshly hitting the dirt below, they regained a semblance of control by dimming the working jets, and digging their heels into the earth, managing to stay upright as a trail of grass was uprooted through their backwards momentum.

Alex and Takeo subsequently attacked the enemy. Alex missed, the crimson liquid from his weapon adding a bubbling red into the brown soil. Both of Takeo's bullets embedded within a different shoulder; blood spit from the wounds and the antagonist fell.

"Again!" Alex shouted.

But their second opportunity didn't come to fruition, as they were cut short by the mountain of fire that came from the flame-caster, eating their attacks and shrouding its position.

"You take the right, I'll—"

Before Alex could finish his command, Takeo had dashed to the right side, completely sidelining Alex's plans. Alex huffed and moved left. His run was ended when a sphere of fire rushed towards him. He collapsed to the ground in avoidance. During the evasion Alex's weapon slipped from his fingers, leaving him vulnerable.

The flamecaster stood behind circles of smoke that danced within the air, cementing itself in one spot as a final stand. It altered between casting fireballs between Alex and Takeo. Takeo had made it a few feet ahead. Whenever the enemy's assault came towards him he used it as an opportunity to dodge and spring forward.

Alex copied his style of movement, becoming desperate as he weaved through the consistent onslaught of flames, when he realized that he was without a weapon.

"Takeo, save your ammo!" he warned.

Takeo was already practicing frugality when Alex spoke, rendering Alex's words a useless distraction.

The flamecaster responded to Takeo's patterns, as he focused more of its inferno towards him, backing away slowly. After a large fireball, Takeo dove and released two of his shots which directly landed into the enemy's chest. The shock that came from it caught him off guard, and he fell backwards into the ground.

Alex and Takeo ran towards him. The enemy spoke. "Father would be impressed."

"Who's that?" Takeo asked.

From the man's wounds, green mixed with red then turned into concentrated gray, answering Takeo's question: the man was one of the Hive's children.

"Back away," Alex instructed, hoping that the man had not seen their faces.

"Why?" Takeo asked, stepping closer.

"He wants people like you," the enemy wheezed.

The man popped upwards. Alex turned away, hastily hiding his identity, and marched towards his fallen CR-99. Takeo remained still.

"Don't try to hide. You'll be found out eventually."

Alex marched back with a downturned head, and fired a trio of corrosive shots into the flamecaster. The first hit his stomach, and he screamed with pain. The second landed on his mouth, stifling his scream. The third struck further into his exposed skull, ending his life.

"He would have revealed us to Conrad," Alex explained.

"Maybe he already knows," Takeo suggested.

"Let's hope not."

Alex and Takeo entered the facility with the use of a grenade. The hallway was black and silent. The only light provided was the purple glow of Takeo's sword.

As the light only covered a few feet in front of them, it was a sudden shock to see a corpse on the ground. Crystallized gray oozed from its mouth. Another dead host. Upon further inspection they found the hall was crowded with bodies that shared the same fate. The Hive had failed in its power; the hope that it was dead spread through Alex's mind.

There were three hallways ahead, providing three diverging paths.

"To the right," Alex decided.

At the end of the corpse-filled hallway was a room. Within the room a meeting of active technology took place, more than Alex had seen in one setting before. The walls had active screens beaming with energy, displaying different scenes. Maps littered with green dots, historic texts of ancient news, and weapons from the new and old worlds were showcased on the walls. The light from the screens whitened the room, contrasting the darkness outside.

"We should go," Takeo said.

"We have time, we could find—"

"I'm here to look for David."

This reminded Alex of his original purpose.

"Let's hope it's dead," Alex said as he stepped over a corpse.

"Maybe. How would you know?"

"The coughing. It's barely around, now a bunch of its bodies are dying at random."

"Then we could avoid fighting and come to terms."

"Terms?"

"The Collective is gone. Who will fight?"

"Zone 6 is gone," Alex corrected.

"I won't go back to fighting for them."

"Why not?"

"They won't accept me with this," Takeo said as he pointed to his forehead marking.

"If we achieve something, they won't mind," Alex said.

Within the back end of the room they found a miniature Hub nowhere near a healthy state. There was no green within its cracks which were instead sealed by hard gray. Its rising breath was cut. The left side of the dome was sinking.

Seeing how the intimidating enemy was being brought down to its knees did not fulfill Alex as he'd expected. All he could think about was the loss of the Hive's children, and how each body belonged to a host with a stolen life.

Alex touched the Hub and felt nothing. It was truly dead. The item of the island that Alex thought was possibly the Hive's heart ended up being useless.

Chattering voices came from the hall, urgency pushing through their voices. Takeo disengaged his sword.

"Time to go," Takeo said.

Alex agreed and both men fled back to the mainland.

CHAPTER TEN

THE SHORE

When they escaped the facility and returned to the fields, Alex discovered the small stalks had sprouted to a harvestable length, the origin of their food source. Alex's initial reaction to the near impossibility was to accept it. He went to find Reese, discovering that he had wondered elsewhere, forcing him to return to the compound. The composition of the area had been flipped. The tables were decorated with the spilling of alcohol and leftover food. The celebration that had ended last night failed as Loyalists were in a state of grief.

The Hive corpses remained untouched. The Loyalists simmered in mourning. It was undeserved as Loyalists soldiers had many similarities to those within Zone 6, and just happened to fight for the wrong side.

The state of the children varied. Some barley held onto life; some were healthy. Those who were dead remained in the trembling hands of their mothers. They died the same way that the Hive bodies scattered around had. A corpse without blood, and an abundance of hard gray.

"You were supposed to protect us!" Raina claimed directly to Alex. She cradled an infant daughter, both of them sharing the same black hair and dimples. Alex felt guilty that he had never asked if she had other children.

"I will," Alex promised.

"That doesn't mean anything! My daughter is dead!" she screamed. Alex wanted to strike her, but stopped himself; she had already suffered enough.

Alex, along with Takeo, sat on a rock and ignored his need for nourishment. Reese and Patton approached him together. Patton's smile was gone. The essence of trauma crossed his somber eyes.

"Alcohol is terrible," Patton informed.

"Good in medium doses," Reese countered.

"I'm never having it again."

"Then you're one of the lucky ones."

"Where's David?" Alex asked Reese.

"You missed a wing, didn't you? This one slow you down?" Reese joked, tapping Takeo's shoulder.

"Act somber," Alex redirected.

"We don't have a reason to. We won today," Takeo said, pointing to the distance.

David walked towards them with a small group behind him. His exhausted eyes wandered. Within a few days he had lost weight and gained enough facial hair to represent a beard's shadow.

"David!" Alex shouted, waving his arms.

David, the final member of their original squad, approached.

"Now we can finally get out of here," Reese said.

"You didn't save me," David said.

"We couldn't. The Hive was around the entire island."

"Did you complete a perimeter check?"

"It couldn't be done. Where's Lonnie?" Takeo cut in.

"He escaped, a while ago."

The sting of betrayal wedged into Alex's thoughts. "How?" Alex questioned with great interest.

"There was no perimeter on my side of the island," David answered.

"Everybody! Come to the beach!" a repeated shout bellowed from Loyalists, inspiring those who were still to begin their movement, dwindling the amount of people within the compound.

"Now we should go," Takeo said.

"What about Gianna?" Patton asked.

"There's plenty just like her."

It became clear that the beach was the expected destination for all Loyalists, as they were approached by a group of Loyalists with great fire power, inquiring as to why they had not moved yet.

"Where did you pick for the tattoo?" Alex asked David in an attempt to make conversation.

"I was never offered."

"Thank God. You're going to regret the forehead," Reese said to Takeo, laughing.

"Maybe," Takeo answered.

Alex scanned the environment twice before repeating a previous question.

"What did you do in the facility?"

"I was a test subject," Reese answered.

"It was his composition. He had a body full of substances.

Meant he could take some more," David explained.

"Have you seen what it can do with its blood now? It used some of my blood to make it," Reese claimed.

"I did whatever I could to slow production while simultaneously making it seem like progress was being made, but we could not keep it up forever. To survive we almost perfected it. It still remains submissive to EMPs. If we are able to get our hands on one, events could turn in our favor," David said.

"You gave one to Reese," Alex reminded him.

"Firstly, that was not an EMP. If he was going to be sacrificed, it would happen in front of Loyalists. When my device worked, I thought that it would end in my rescue, but we were fine with saving ourselves."

When they arrived at the beach the next actions of the Loyalists were unclear. They lacked leadership to give them purpose. Alex decided to give them some.

"You have all lost something you love!" Alex projected his voice without the guidance of technology, or a social structure that put him in a position of status. "It is not the fault of anybody here, or present." Alex almost ceased speaking when he realized he had said the same statement twice, but he continued quickly after. "We share the same pain. We were given a glimpse of the Hive's greatness. It deserves a proper burial. Then we will get revenge against whoever caused this!"

Some heads nodded while tears were wiped away. Others stared forth with suspicion, regardless of opinion. Unmarked graves were formed. They were dug with the use of shovels made by stripped materials from the boats, both metal and wood working towards a common goal. Completing the task stole the day. Alex was drenched in sweat and his hands swelled with calluses. While his body was tortured his mind worked towards preparing convincing words to push the Loyalists off the island. He traded glances with his team at various points. It did not bother him as an explanation would be provided, but it just had to wait.

Once the bodies had been buried Raina was the first to pay respects. "He was the same to all of us. The rest of the world won't understand. He gave us hope. He did it all for the good of the world—" She bit her lip, her eyes streaked with tears. "Now that's all going to change."

"It won't change," Alex said. "I can—"

"Thank you, Alexander, for your leadership in the burial," a Loyalist interrupted. "I am Nero and it's good to know that even a man from the Collective can change. Now that our master is gone, many of you are asking what to do. I have heard horrid suggestions of abandoning the home the Hive had created for us."

"We should turn it to the people. See what most people want," Alex suggested, treading his words carefully.

"What is it that you want? To go back to the Collective? You have been plotting. Staying away from our group. Only speaking to each other."

"People will want different things."

"I am taking over."

"Was that responsibility given to you by the Hive?"

"Your time is over."

106

"Nero's right," Raina stated. "We have been betrayed by too many spies before."

"I gave my loyalty!" Takeo spat, pointing to the W on his forehead.

"Speaking out of turn without being told to. That is bold," Nero accused.

"We should communicate with other Loyalists' branches. Through them we will see what the Hive wants to do with us," Alex proposed.

"You're trying to—"

"Where should we contact?" Alex asked. "The other Loyalists need to know what happened here. They need to know that the Hive is sick."

"Sick?" Nero asked. "This was done because of an attack to one of our beloved Hubs."

"It is simply a theory cultivated because of its dwindling presence. If it is in a weakened state we must do whatever we can to aid it," David said.

"None of you should trust this man!" Nero's sway over the others had slipped. Heads did not nod to his statement.

"He helped us build these graves," a Loyalist within the crowd brought up.

"This is between them," Raina claimed.

"You're standing with Nero?" Alex asked.

"I stand with our master."

"Then you would know that suspicion should not be directed towards us. I am the one who aided in amplifying the power in the Hive's blood. You watched it. I choose to make a difference within all of our lives. I am not your enemy. Neither are those I came with," David said with a heap of false anger.

"I may have misjudged you, but the people you came with cannot be trusted."

"Then you will have to kill me, Nero," Takeo said, dropping his weapons. "A duel. Only with our fists."

"That is not how we conduct ourselves," Raina said.

"I am the Hive's right hand. I deserve to be next in line, and you are all considering—"

"It doesn't need a right-hand man. It has thousands of left hands too. You weren't picked for anything and you're getting emotional because of it," Reese mocked.

"You're all going to listen to this?" Nero raged. "They say Collective fighters are the greatest in the world. I will show you what a real soldier looks like! The Collective is weak."

"See, too emotional!"

"Ya, go cry or something," Patton called.

"Is this for some kind of Collective honor?" Reese asked.

"For mine," Takeo revealed.

Alex patted Takeo's back in encouragement, for if Nero was defeated he would be cast down from leadership candidacy.

As the gap between the opponents closed Nero hurled insults.

"I'll bury you!"

Takeo remained silent. His pace was steady. Nero's quickened.

"Who will join me?" Nero asked.

The indecisive Loyalists remained torn by the presented opportunity. It became clear that the victor would receive the gift of their malleable minds.

"Cowards!" Nero accused. He broke his walk and transitioned into a sprint. Takeo's reaction opposed it. He cemented himself in a still position. His right hand gripped a handful of sand and once Nero was close enough Takeo pitched the grains into his unsuspecting eyes.

Nero swatted it away, but the smokescreen managed to make a disturbance within his path. It gave Takeo the opportunity to hit Nero with a right strike to his jaw, then a left; in the aftermath Nero grasped Takeo's shirt collar and spurned him into the ground.

Alex took a step forward, wanting to help Takeo. He was stopped when David gripped his shoulder. "They'll need to see how he is on his own."

In Takeo's struggle to break free he landed three strikes against Nero's ribs, none of which stopped Nero's body from pressing against Takeo, paired with mocking words.

"This is what the Collective is. They're weak and—"

Nero's enthralling speech was interrupted as Takeo brought his head upward. The expected clashing of their foreheads never came as Takeo soared past Nero's hairline, and sunk his jagged teeth into the enemy's ears.

Nero screamed as his body shifted, releasing pressure, allowing Takeo to push the body off, stand up, and back away.

"Look at him running away!" Nero claimed.

Takeo bent downward; his hand reached into the material below.

"Sand won't work again!"

Takeo stood. From the sands he had withdrawn a stick so large that it took both of his hands to handle it. Born from the earth, the stick was crude in nature, for it contained various small dents and twigs that detracted from its frame.

Takeo used it to garner a direct strike against Nero's upper torso. He followed with a spiteful jab towards his stomach which was caught halfway through its destination. The duo struggled for control until the wood broke in two parts.

Both men slipped backwards, refusing to fall, and picked up one end of the fractured pieces and threateningly raised their crude swords.

Takeo rushed forward. He jumped and struck below. The two pieces clashed, and the crack from the conflict orchestrated across the quiet battlefield showcasing the power that lay within their strikes.

The wood was detracted first by Nero. He slid backward, leaving Takeo stumbling forward awkwardly.

Nero used the opportunity to land two successive strikes against Takeo's back. Takeo cried out in pain from the first, unsuccessfully tried to dodge the second, and stopped the third by landing a hit against Nero's lower stomach.

The next assault from both men had their swords meeting each other once again, both snapped in two. Their shortened weapons ended up the size of a dagger.

Nero charged. Takeo stabbed the wood into his right eye. It forced him to the ground. Blood burst from the impact. He lost the will to fight, opting to squirm in torturous pain from the injury.

"We will continue the Hive's legacy!" Takeo falsely claimed.

The people looked to him with approval. They had chosen who deserved the respect. Alex walked forward, ensuring that he received the same praise as he took control of his new subordinates.

"If you stand with anybody but us this is what you'll become!"

Takeo's hands pointed to Nero. He bathed within the sand. His blood produced dotted markings within the material.

"They're liars!" Nero shouted.

"Takeo and I trained together. We can teach you how to be like us," Alex offered. "Powerful. Unable to be stopped, but if anybody here thinks that they can do a better job than us, then step forward."

A few faces within the crowd appeared to be in consideration.

Alex kicked Nero upward to turn their minds. The blood that left his eyes was such a grotesque image that nobody stepped forward.

"We will bring glory to this island. The Hive's strength lives in all of us. Our enemies will be crushed. If anybody ever comes to our shore with evil intentions, they will regret the decision," Alex claimed. Using fear had gained their attention, but for him to leave an everlasting impression they would need confidence that he was there to help them, an idea that was entrenched in lies.

Alex was bombarded by questions from his new followers, curious as to what roles they should be designated. He dispersed the Loyalists and the remaining children, giving them tasks tailored to their presented skills. Those with a passion for battle acted as watchmen for the island alongside Patton. Others were sent to cultivate meals from the genetically modified fields. Reese was allowed the privilege of relaxation. Raina stood by Alex watching his every move, backing his decisions every time there was protest. When all was done Alex spoke to David while he walked towards the facility.

"How long until we depart?" David asked.

"We're in a tight spot. If we leave right away it will only make Nero's accusations look true. They'll kill us. If we can guide for a short while, then I will have their trust."

"And what happens after that?"

"Get these people to a better place, find the boats, then—" Alex was lost. Zone 6 was gone. Zone 5 was far away, and the Hive would forever exist within the world's creases.

"Our focus should be on finding its heart. The Hive is some form of machinery at its core. It's the reason why EMPs kill it instantly."

He remained composed, but the unwelcome theory worried Alex. When they returned to the facility they found Takeo had bound Nero to a chair within the technology-fueled wing.

His wrists and legs were bound by sharpened silver wire, causing drops of blood to fall to the surface below, and his mouth was blocked by fabric.

David fiddled with the screen of the map that showed the image of the island while Takeo tightened Nero's restraints.

"What are you doing?" Takeo asked David.

"This computer will have a wealth of information."

"We have that right here," Takeo said while tapping Nero.

"We're going to talk. If you scream when we let you, I will kill—" Alex stopped speaking. He realized intimidation would not work. Nero stared at him with burning hatred. He was a man of the Hive, unafraid of death. Alex ripped the fabric from Nero's mouth.

"I was right about you Collectives being scum. You steal my first home. Then my second, but I've been here longer. Long enough to see fake Loyalists. I always knew."

"Then why not say anything?"

"I did. It didn't listen. It said you were interesting."

"Where's the Hive now?" Takeo demanded.

The room went black. A second later light was restored. David had gained access to the Hive's computer, and the screens within altered from showing just the island to various parts of the world where the Hive existed, its clusters shown through blinking green dots.

"Everywhere."

The bird's eye view of Zone 6 was the only map prominent in multiple screens. The outdated image showed a bustling society with an unending stream of cars, rushed people, and intact infrastructure. A city that breathed with the old world's spirit. The life Alex wished he could have. The people of the old world were arrogant, but within it they were happy in their frivolous pursuits. Overtaking the image was a cluttering of emerald circles, making Patton's escape a small miracle.

A realization clicked within Alex. The Hub's fall did not affect the bodies closest to it. Instead, they hit remote locale. The Collective's mission had done nothing. Even if they did manage to destroy the Hub it would not have ended the Hive completely.

"Where's its heart?" Alex asked.

"Where it all started," Nero spat.

"Details," Takeo demanded.

"Kill me already."

"Why?"

"Once the Hive sees me like this, he won't give me what I want."

Alex did not want Nero to die. He knew his story. He was a soldier no different from him, just born into a different path.

"We won't be seeing you for a long time," Takeo said. Without prompting he plunged Nero's skull. A hellish scream came from his mouth before death.

"Why do you always do that?"

The brutality of Nero's end made his face unrecognizable, but his body remained tied to the chair.

"He won't tell us. We have to find somebody who will."

"He said he," David said.

"The Hive's male. There's more that we need to discover."

David led Alex and Takeo to the undiscovered leg of the facility which was revealed to be a multipurpose lab. The front was harbored by weapons, some of which were unknown to Alex's eyes.

The second half was a Hub for research. Vials filled with colored liquids were scattered across lab tables and paper pads containing complex details of the Hive's physiology.

At the far end of the room was a control panel.

"Instead of leaving we can have people come to us," David said, pointing to a communication system. Extending from the board filled with colored buttons was a pair of muffs attached to the board, and a flat green screen that displayed coordinates.

"A radio," Alex realized.

Alex almost set the coordinates towards Zone 6, then reminded himself what it was. He set it for the Libertarians. No answer came when he called, but Alex allowed his words to flow.

"It's Alex. We have taken the island. It could be a potential new home."

Alex left to meet his followers when two men in jet packs streamed towards them. They moved in sync. It was the Hive.

The Loyalists immediately threw down their weapons and raced to the incoming perceived saviors. The Loyalist forces gathered on the beach quickly around the fresh Hive. `

"Who led you?" the Hive demanded calmly.

"It was Alex," the Loyalists echoed.

Within seconds Alex was surrounded by the Hive. As it closed in, Takeo and David placed their backs to one another in a circle of protection.

"Go," Alex ushered.

"No. We protect you," Takeo said.

"Now!" Alex commanded under his breath. They complied. As the Hive walked towards him he inhaled, ready for death.

"You rebelled against me."

"I—"

"I won't kill you. I will speak to you."

CHAPTER ELEVEN

THE ISLAND

Alex found himself back in the technology-fueled room next to Nero's deceased corpse, a presence that had not been mentioned.

"Taking over. Impressive," the Hive said through a quartet of bodies as it pushed forth a cup of steaming water, a white pouch drifting within it.

"What's in it?" Alex asked, tired of the games where every word from the Hive's mouth was nothing more than a covert attempt to scramble his mind.

"An old world delicacy."

"You're dying," Alex boldly accused. He sipped the liquid, indifferent to the chance that it might be poison. If the Hive wanted him dead it would be carried out as a brutal quick execution, not with the slow reach of toxins.

"Happens to everyone," the Hive responded.

"The truth will spread."

"So few in your position. So few have seen a Hub. I am a legend. A myth. The truth hides."

"What do you want with me?"

"I need Leaders. You betrayed me—"

"I—"

"No need to hide. You showed initiative. Exactly what I need."

"I'm just a former Commander in the Collective. Nothing special."

"You managed my forces. A great feat. Worthy of consideration."

"I'm already in your army. I am loyal."

"No, you will receive higher status. Before doing so I—"

The door opened, and a body bag was revealed, the person within it writhing around in a panic.

"Have brought a test," the Hive continued from its new recruits. It withdrew a knife and passed it to Alex.

"Kill him."

"I don't know what he did."

"Kill him."

Alex did not need more information. He remained still, refusing his offer.

"I won't hurt anybody unless I have a good reason to."

"A lie. You have killed many undeserving."

"So have you."

"I have. Do not hide it. You did not see the old world. A necessary action."

"Now we're beyond repair because you intervened with another species."

"No, old world souls had fates worse than death. Now man lives with passion."

Alex scoffed at the lie. He recognized the ploy to make itself seem layered. The same trick was used when Alex was offered false hospitality when he first became a Loyalist. Clever phrasing used to cover sinister motivations.

"You're a liar. You tricked us as to where your heart was."

"The Collective deceives. They claimed to know my heart. So arrogant. Many couldn't see how close I existed. My eyes everywhere."

Alex speculated that he was referring to one of his squad members, but he immediately pushed for rational thought.

"You had spies in Zone 6."

"Of course. More than spies."

The possibility that the Hive had gained the ability to take aspects of the environment made him think. He thought of odd places and legends, until he stopped speculating when he remembered the restricted area. Those who entered were subject to great sickness.

"You had a Hub in the restricted Zone."

"More. My true heart."

"Your—"

When living in Zone 6 he had been so close to the possibility of defeating it, but he had allowed it to slip from his fingers.

"Why admit it?" Alex asked, his voice shaking, unable to hide his anger.

"I have protection. Triple what you know. The knowledge is yours to command. Your next destination is clear. If I fall again."

"You want me to take these people there?"

"Do not falsify loyalty. You would mean to challenge me."

"I—"

"Eyes. Ears. Everywhere. I see, hear, everything. I welcome the challenge."

"You want to die?"

"No, but I am."

The admission gave Alex the only spark of joy that he had felt the entire conversation.

"My spirit will live. Maybe you. Maybe another, but Hive will live."

"How?"

"My replacement remains undecided. Defeat me. It is you."

"No!" Alex roared, his veneer of loyalty slipping.

"Anger. An emotion you must control."

The screen behind him flashed an image. Within the still picture was a woman of the old world wearing gray with black hair and blue eyes holding great beauty. Behind her was a trio of rockets intended for travel. The still photo propelled into motion. The woman spoke, her blank stare turning into a smile.

"On launch day the world could not be more excited."

"Our past," the Hive informed.

Between the rocket and the woman was a great crowd waving. They all wore gray. The height of the Collective's power. A time when citizens were happy to be a part of it.

"We have waited for years. Today we prevail. Today we will take what is ours."

The image shifted to an overhead snapshot of the vehicle. Silver triangles acted as the rockets' tips. Surrounding the vehicles was a gathering of green trees; at the edges of the landscape was sand where guards wearing the gray uniform of the Collective watched the borders.

"Under Collective leadership we have achieved great advancement. The best for us all. Today is the first step in bringing our guidance to the vast universe. We voted, and now the species that grovel in misery take our help."

"What is this?" Alex asked.

"A vote took place. Man choose genocide."

"Of us? That's your fault."

"Of them," the Hive stated, its hands pointing to the sky.

"The Web-200 is the same ship responsible for first landing on Planet 1, formally known as Mars."

"You're from Planet 1," Alex realized. "I know what you are. You were built by them. I'm sorry we attacked your creators. It was wrong, but the people now didn't make that choice. I don't know if you can think for yourself—"

"Largely responsible is the great Conrad Westwick. Our ambassador. One of our saviors," the woman on the screen babbled.

"Planet 1? No, I am of Earth origin," the Hive answered.

"Today we are given the gift of victory," the woman proclaimed.

"Planet 1. Truly peaceful. Unlike us. Planet 2,3,4,5. All peaceful."

"You're not from Earth," Alex decided.

"That's a lie."

"Conrad Westwick, owner and last son of the long running Westwick Enterprises, has been awarded the Collective peace prize," the woman stated. An image flashed on the screen of an elderly man. Handsome with tired green eyes, white hair, and determination etched into his face. Behind him was the symbol of a W: the same symbol that had claimed Alex's hand. The name was recognizable. The last time he had seen it was in the painting within Sheila's cabin.

"Conrad Westwick ... you're dead."

The Hive's heads turned towards the image on the screen.

"No, but dying."

Alex did not hide his reaction. He took a step backward. His stomach twisted. The Hive was Conrad—a human who had betrayed its own people for nothing.

"Invasion. Man's true nature revealed. Our world needed crippling before destruction of others."

"If you were Conrad then you ... you were one of the most famous men in the world. You could have stopped it. You ruined us."

"No—another would continue the cause. We always need more. Never satisfied."

On the screen the aircraft launched upward. Its fires beneath propelled it into space travel, an act that would not occur again. Its scream overtook the words of the woman while it jetted to its destination.

Alex did not respond. His entire life within the Collective, he had always gone along with their decisions since their movements were similar to the Hive's, Libertarians', Technicians', and the Amish.

A boom came from outside of the facility, creating an aura of mystery around the night.

"What was that?" Alex asked.

The Hive did not speak for many seconds. The faces of its bodies were in complete concentration. Eyes wide.

"Gather! Retreat! Take your weapons!" it yelled.

"What was that?" Alex asked again.

"A challenger," Conrad answered.

"Fight. Lead," the Hive commanded. The arm cannon of a singular body retracted to the size of a bracelet and was passed to Alex. Alex was bonded to the weapon the moment it contacted his skin, becoming aware of its capabilities while he willed it to its intended form: a shell of purple metal that captured his arm.

"I'm not fighting for you!"

"For survival."

Alex was given a second weapon. A PD-B8. It had the advantage of a pistol's compactness, and a shotgun's wide spread.

The silver revolver had one visible barrel which held two available others.

As Alex and the Hive's bodies departed, an overhead blast suddenly destroyed part of the roof, revealing the changed sky. The beauty of the twinkling stars was interrupted by a helicopter which dropped orange napalm that slowly devoured the roof. Shouts echoed in the distance, paired with trading bullet fire.

The last door to the facility was forced open before Alex could reach it. Five bodies stepped through. Takeo led Reese, David, Patton, and Gianna, ready to kill once it was seen that the Hive was present.

"Let him go! Fast!" Patton screamed as he raised an Uzi.

The entire team had upgraded their weapons. Takeo had a thick longsword, bordered with flashing green electricity, a metal sheath strapped to Takeo's back to hold the behemoth weapon. At his hilt was a BN-10: Nero's old weapon, a force destruction.

Reese was equipped with an SNH-21 sniper rifle, capable of detecting camouflage. David held an SK-BL shotgun, a weapon that could bend and was able to see what was coming round a corner on the small screen on top of the weapon.

"Quick. Explain," Conrad demanded through its concentrated faces.

"If we're going to survive, we'll need it," Alex said. His allies backed down.

The group stepped outside and saw pockets of the island burning, courtesy of a gathering of aircraft above which distributed destruction below. Shots extended upwards to end the invasion. A red streak smashed into the helicopter's side door which led the helicopter to spin downward and land in the water.

The Hive rushed forward. Its flying mutated beasts, of two different breeds, emerged from behind the facility: black flies and black crows. The crows each had four wings that propelled them with speed unnatural to their kind. Their talons were ingrained with gleaming metal. The flies shared formation, circling each crow in a ring of protection.

"Send your animals up to the helicopter!" Alex commanded.

The Hive complied with his request. Its creatures headed directly for the flying machines, attempting to black vision with a black swarm.

Shouting came from the forest. Aid would be needed.

"I'm going for it," Reese said.

"Conrad, look out!"

The animals parted from attacking the helicopter. The glass that protected the pilot had begun to crack, courtesy of the crows' steel claws.

Reese shot two bullets. The glass shattered, but the masked pilot remained. From his BN-10, a blue plasma sphere soared through the sky and hit the pilot, and control over the vehicle was lost. It sent the aircraft into a free-fall spin into the forest, causing an uproar of additional fire and wails.

From the forest the Hive's children ran alongside their mothers. Alex had seen the same terror and pleas of mercy before, when he had been a part in causing it.

"Gianna! Patton! Take whoever you can find! Bring them back to the facility! I'll draw the fight!"

Alex, Takeo, Reese, and David took the main road. They were flanked by Hive that ran at the same pace. Each passing group was urged to head towards the facility where he could only hope that Patton and Gianna had found a way to funnel them towards safety. He pushed doubt from his thoughts, reminding himself that Gianna had toughened up, Patton was trained, and Conrad was lurking to help.

The bombing of the island continued, but adding to the destruction was a wave of triangles that flew from the transports. After rushing through the trees they lodged themselves into the dirt, causing an eruption of dust at the moment of impact.

"Shit. Pinpoint lasers. We need to take them out!" David yelled.

Takeo wrapped his arms around one of the silver triangles, and heaved upwards. It did nothing. Claws extended themselves from the objects' sides and attached to the ground, further cementing its position.

"Keep going," Alex said.

Takeo tried two more lifts before abandoning the idea and continuing forward.

A sudden explosion lifted the group off the ground and threw them several feet apart from each other.

Alex smashed against a tree but, landing on his cannon, acted as a buffer for the pain. The straight edge of a pinpoint laser in front of him began to glow.

"Find cover," David screamed.

As Alex dashed behind the tree, red lasers beamed from the triangles' flat sides. The crimson beams threaded towards one another across the landscape, creating a deadly maze. As they crossed, some hit Loyalists, ending lives with their power. One cut through Alex's cover, nearly hitting his head.

"Destroy them!" Alex commanded.

"Destroy them!" all Hive bodies present copied.

As the lasers remained stagnant, the allies used their weapons to cut the triangles apart, dissipating the beams in a pace slower than ideal. Their rate of movement was based on the need to either jump above or crawl below the deadly lines carefully in avoidance of getting cut.

"We're going to be fine, right? This won't get worse," Reese guessed, his hands shaking. From his pocket he withdrew a small flask and took a sip as David appeared from behind. Alex did not say anything; a small amount would help soothe his fears.

"Let's keep going!" Takeo suggested.

The devastation coming from above had reduced, but so had the size of the Hive's swarm and the attacks that came towards the sky.

As they ran through the remaining field of red beams, the raging fire behind them pushed less emphasis on safety and more on speed. As they came close to reaching the center of the island they came across Raina who had crumbled to her knees, her eyes shining with tears. Her face was marked with black streaks.

"You need to kill me," she choked.

"What? No," Alex said, moving forward, not having time for a conversation.

"Do it," she demanded. "This is what I lived for!" she declared. Her desperate grip turned tight around Alex's wrist. "My children are gone! My husband is dead!"

Alex's arm cannon slowly burned, preparing for her request.

"No!" a Hive body yelled from behind. "You are chosen."

Raina looked to the Hive body with awe and stood with pride.

She retreated back towards the forest where others who were unwilling to fight fled.

Confused, Alex surged forward. He had thought that he was chosen. If Raina was too then it meant others were in the running.

The devastation of the island was almost complete, and if they did not find a way to escape, their lives would be lost to the flames. They maneuvered through whatever they could find based on wherever the growing flames did not burn. A physical toll struck. The rising heat killed the ability to breath. Alex's visual field blurred. Reese's pants caught fire, and he screamed. He frantically rolled in the dirt which killed the flames, but damage had been done. His skin was red raw.

Takeo picked him up, slung him over his shoulder, and aided in helping him limp through the landscape.

"Should have drank more," Reese said.

Alex did not smile nor scold. His energy was focused on escape as they reached the living space.

The huts had been licked by flames. The structures began to crumble, becoming ghosts of their past selves. Bodies from his new allies and the mysterious enemy clashed against one another. It appeared to be equal footing. The Hive was no longer an all- powerful enemy. The real war had just begun.

"Find cover," Alex commanded. The men left what little protection the trees provided, and entered the Loyalist living space: an altered environment engulfed in fire. The far end huts were torn to shreds courtesy of the destructive fires. The walls collapsed, taking whoever used it as cover along with the downfall of the structure.

The enemy had submerged themselves to the island's midpoint. The Hive's forces were lighter in numbers, but stronger with the technology they presented. The opposition catered to old world weapons containing little plasma within their ranks, but their numbers forced Loyalists back.

Struggling Loyalists made up the bulk of the defensive forces. The Hive was present but did not speak. Talking took effort, energy that the Hive did not have within the midst of sickness. Its low numbers meant that they could evade attacks, and unleash its own.

"Hold the line! Hide behind the huts! Not in them!" Alex demanded, fulfilling his purpose in battle. Conrad did not want him to be a soldier. He wanted him to be a leader.

The Loyalists looked to Alex with confusion, before recognition of who he was took hold and Conrad's bodies followed his commands.

"Partner up! One of you acts as cover while the other reloads!"

Alex's words were repeated by David, Takeo, and Reese. Then the Hive.

Alex followed his own advice. Alongside Takeo he sat behind an intact hut. It was not on fire, but it was being drilled by bullets. Alex flayed a stream of purple plasma towards the antagonists, hitting a man's chest. Critical damage was not done, but his intent was fulfilled. The enemy sent the bulk of their soldiers within the middle, leaving weak flanks.

Within the skies two enemy helicopters were circling. One dropped napalm. The other was a funnel for machine gun fire. Both caused destruction.

"Hit the center!" Alex commanded. His words echoed through the allies, manifesting in action. The enemy forces who had made a presence within the center were caught off guard by the sudden pelting, causing them to stagger, momentarily pushing the battle to a stalemate. Both sides had fighters occasionally rise from cover and attempt to advance, hoping to win an edge.

A change came when the aircraft dropping fire moved towards the living area.

"Get your animals on it!" Alex called to the Hive.

The Hive fighting alongside him all shook their heads.

"There's none left?"

"Busy," Conrad replied.

"Focus on the helicopter!" Alex called to the wider population.

The bulk of forces pounded bullets towards the flying machine. Shots of plasma blasted the machine and it crashed into the forest. An uproar came from its contact with the ground.

Alex surveyed his own forces to reevaluate. They stood strong, but the further deterioration of their cover made it so that a quick alteration of their position was necessary. If they went straight the group would be overtaken by the spreading fire, painting the dark skyline with gray smoke. Retreat was not an option as it would lead the enemy towards those they were trying to protect.

"Use everything that you have! Kill them!"

A great push from the allies created a cascade of distraction in the form of smoke, electricity, fire, ice. Elements of earth which left an opening.

"To the left!" Alex called.

They departed using the small gap of opportunity, managing to break into the forest without resistance. As the allies' feet reached the heavy tangle of trees the enemy attempted to climb through ice walls, billowing fires, and heavy smoke. Failing with death.

"Keep pivoting!" Alex turned and waved to Conrad. "Stay in the back!"

The allies swiftly moved left and right, preventing the enemy from making a clear shot, who foolishly ran straight. Untrained.

"Don't kill them, injure!" Alex called.

His forces shot at arms and legs, disabling the enemies, granting opportunity.

"Take their bodies!" Alex called with guilt.

Conrad withdrew hidden vials from the pockets of his bodies' clothing,. approaching the fallen bodies and plunging needles into precious skin. The enemies turned to allies as the formula took them. They slowly rose as Hive forces. Alex's forces.

"Let's win this!" Reese called with joy.

"Not over. They have the seas." Leadership switched as everybody followed the Hive. The new Hive bodies lagged behind as their movements faltered.

"Are the people safe?" Alex asked Conrad.

"Mostly. The boy succeeds."

The words gave Alex feelings of pride amongst chaos.

The Hive suddenly stopped after placing its bodies in a line, then stomped at the same time. A great rumble broke from the shadows paired with a trio of bright lights. Black tiles slowly unveiled themselves, peeling away the mystery of what stood before them. Three monstrous black forms with an unbroken line of wheels supporting the bottom. Their torsos held slim cabins with cylindrical guns.

"Remain silent," the Hive prompted. The trio of vehicles disappeared.

Alex walked with the others at the edge of the forest. The invisible tanks left tracks and had a threshold of sound so low that only standing right next to it would reveal its presence.

"Hidden tanks. If I had this shit earlier I wouldn't be stuck with you," Reese theorized.

"Focus on the mission," Takeo stated.

"For the record I never missed you."

"Are you on something?"

"I wish."

"This is why—"

"Wait a second," Reese interrupted, stopping the group from reaching the top point of an elevated hill. "Go back." The cohort remained still until Alex ushered them to make a small retreat. Afterwards he crouched and peeked to check the disturbance, discovering the origin of Reese's panic.

Spread across the forest the enemy had sent forth silent soldiers clad entirely in black. Their faces were covered by masks. A mini turret was strapped onto each of their bodies. They had chosen varied locations to implement them. A brown belt held them in place, wrapping around feet, arms, shoulders, and legs. The small barrels were constantly swaying in the search for an enemy. They all found one in the form of a scurrying rodent and pitched a red beam of plasma towards it. The mammal instantly exploded, showing the danger that those approaching possessed.

After the attack an oddity occurred within their bodies. They shifted away from clear visibility and slowly merged into the forest, camouflaging within the environment. The only marks that indicated their location were the footprints that embedded markings into the ground below.

"Let's kill 'em," Takeo said.

Reese shushed him again and lowered his body. He lifted his SNH-21 to his eye and twisted its vision both left and right.

"I've seen this shit before. It's old Technician technology."

Alex looked again and saw that the outlines of their bodies were gone. They had turned completely invisible.

"I'll take them out," Alex decided.

"I didn't know you could see things that were invisible," Reese mocked, shaking his rifle as a reminder that his was one of the few weapons that could detect camouflage.

In the moment Alex felt useless. He did not want to do nothing and wait for another to take glory for themselves, so he opted to use destructive power instead of simply waiting for them to approach. But then he realized that if they did attack, the origin of whoever led the assault would be tracked.

"Turret," Alex decided.

"We're prepared," David said as he approached with a rock in hand. A few others had followed his lead.

With his hand Alex indicated for the group to circle the invisible enemy. They began to edge away from one another, but Alex's original plan to circle the enemy ended when a twig snapped nearby.

"Now!" Alex was the first to toss a rock in the air. But the plasma lasers within the group penetrated the material, disintegrating the rock to dust.

Loyalists threw their material into the air, and with it came a shattering of rocks into it. Reese clamored up the hill and began to release bullets from his sniper rifle. Unable to see the layout of the battlefield without risking his life Alex kept on throwing whatever debris he could find around him. He crawled on his knees, desperately scouring the ground, tossing up rocks, sticks, leaves, and dirt, all in an attempt to draw the lasers away from Reese and towards the distraction.

Those around him did the same. As the lasers got closer, Reese continued his tirade until the shadowed enemy reached the edge, and the Loyalists discovered themselves dying based on red lasers that came only a mere few feet away from their starting points.

Reese stood and backed away. The Loyalists became chaotic while trying to defend themselves.

"Don't use your guns!" Alex warned. But the Loyalists had already foolishly fired at the invisible enemy and ended up hitting their own.

Reese continued to take shots. Each time one was hit, their body was revealed as the technology that allowed them to disappear was cut off.

Alex looked to the ground, and in the panic spotted that the footprints revealed the enemy's location.

Alex avoided a blast of plasma hitting his chest by lifting his canon upright and retaliated by shooting at the antagonist with his revolver.

Despite the Loyalists' misgivings, their high numbers made it so those running decided to retreat. It ended in a failed attempt, as Reese managed to gun them down through the use of his sniper rifle till the forest turned quiet again with the exception of the sounds of burning flames and desperate shouts at different distant points.

"Let's keep going," Alex said. He was surprised by the lack of help that the Hive had given them within the fight, but saw the reason for it.

The Hive wanted to see his prowess in battle, and regarding what had just happened Alex theorized that it was Reese who deserved the most credit.

"Wait a second," Reese said. He bent down to investigate a fallen enemy whose black mask was in the midst of slipping off as a result from the battle.

Reese peeled if off, and his eyes widened in surprise. "Holy shit."

"What?" Takeo asked.

"This is Tian."

Alex recognized the face upon closer investigation. It was one of the guards who had stopped them from entering Riverside without permission from Lonnie.

"Looks like I'm not the only one who left," he speculated.

"We don't have time to mull over the past," David stated. "We must go onward. The Hive has, and for the first time I believe it would be appropriate to match its movements."

Alex looked out to the sand on the border and saw that the Hive's tracks continued far ahead, forcing the group to move past where they stood and to continue their desperate journey.

The group eventually made it towards the edge of the island and discovered that the enemy had arrived by boats. The ground forces were in a state of celebration, confident that they had accomplished the Hive's defeat. Some had returned from the blazing forest injured with burns which they relieved with cool water, healing creams, and substances to ease pain.

Conrad released three non-stop plasma beams onto the lounging enemy. Many were vaporized from the impact. The lucky ones lived, but with separated limbs.

"Snipers. Forward," Alex instructed.

Those of Alex's forces with sniper rifles unleashed a hidden wave of bullet fire onto the chaotic beach. The tank's beams swept left to right, kicking up a yellow storm of sand.

"Co-Hive stop!" Alex called. The beams faltered. The snipers ended the lives of those who still remained.

"Keep going!" Alex demanded. Nothing happened. The enemy charged towards the tanks. Hive bodies lacked movement. They stood still. A malfunction. Conrad had failed him.

"Somebody go in the tank!" David called. They looked to David, confused.

"It appears that'll be me," David decided.

He grimaced, moved from cover and placed his hand on the back tank's passenger door, revealing the tank's interior. The inside had a single chair occupied by a passed out Hive body, a cascade of joysticks, and small screens showing all angles. Once inside, the tank slowly disappeared, blending into the environment. The plasma cannon activated, destroying those close to the vehicle.

The war boats took part in the battle. They shot at the deep forest while the Hive with him vomited green liquid. It turned to hardened gray quickly.

The bullets being fired towards David scratched the surface of the tank. Dents revealed the black markings of the vehicle, revealing its exact location.

Emerging from the forest came the few left in Patton and Gianna's group, barely making it out of the situation alive.

Alex spotted familiar faces. He recognized the boats which belonged to the Libertarians.

"Stop! We surrender!" Alex yelled. The group followed his instructions.

"Spare them!" a voice through a speaker said—a woman's voice. From a docked boat the outline of a slim woman appeared. Sheila.

CHAPTER TWELVE

THE RETURN

The opposing groups stood at a standstill, staring at each other with hatred, breathing heavily.

"Put down your weapons!" Sheila demanded.

Alex turned to the group. Less than twenty had made it through the hellfire.

"Disengage!" Alex requested as he retracted his cannon.

"Never!" a Loyalist retorted. She raised her gun towards Sheila, but was quickly shot down.

"Get on. You don't have much time," Sheila reminded him.

The burning moved closer. The safety that Sheila offered was all that they had to escape the fire's grip.

Most Loyalist bodies remained stagnant. "They can help us!" Alex said.

"You're all free to stay. Burn if that's what you want," Sheila stated.

Those who decided to have a longer life clambered towards the boats with Alex. Loyalists who cast doubt on Sheila's offer remained still, waiting for a slow death. Quick deaths came to those individuals who tried to attack the Libertarian forces.

Before climbing onto the boat Alex attempted to urge stubborn Loyalists towards salvation. Gianna was among them.

"Gianna, come on!" Alex yelled, and she shook her head in defiance.

"I'm not going back to them."

"There's nowhere else to go."

"I prefer that choice. I told you what they did to me. They can't be trusted."

"It's not about them. We're in this to work together and kill the Hive. Help us."

"It won't be done with Sheila. I didn't say everything about her in front of Raina, but she will never kill the Hive because she wants her kids to be safe before anybody else. I know that for a fact."

"Then we won't use them. We'll just use their army."

"Her other son used to be a Loyalist before he died," Gianna revealed. "She thinks he's still alive."

The flames came close enough to Alex so that Gianna's body was mere inches from being burned.

"Let's go!" Alex urged.

She slapped Alex's hand away and purged herself within the fire.

Alex climbed onto the boat, regretful that he couldn't save her. Her supposed theory left Alex bitter and tortured as he wondered if what she said was truth.

"Do you have any alcohol remaining?" David asked Reese.

Reese withdrew his flask. "Two sips for me," Reese said, taking two large swigs before passing the flask to David. "One for you."

David tipped the flask back, only a small amount of alcohol remaining. "It's about time we relax."

"The two of us need to talk," Sheila softly told Alex. She had undergone a physical transformation due to sheer exhaustion. Small fringes of brown hair were now gray. Additional wrinkles had formed within the skin on her face.

He followed her request and descended to the lower cabin. Before an additional exchange Sheila turned on the auto pilot, and the boat began to move. While it rocked Alex's thoughts lingered on how he was not able to save everyone on the island, taunting him with failure.

"You said there was no interest in attacking the Hive," Alex said.

"That's your greeting? No hello or thank you for saving me?" Sheila noted.

"Answer the question," Alex pushed.

"I said I wasn't picking sides."

"Why do it now?"

"I found out there was Hub here. We thought that it would destroy the Hive."

"You've made the right choice by fighting for man."

"Fighting for man? What were you just doing?"

"Fighting for survival."

"Oh. Was getting that marking on your skin required?"

"Your son did the same thing. He abandoned us," Alex said, surprised when the mention of Lonnie's unknown whereabouts did not seem to stir emotion within her.

"I know what happened."

"How? Spies?"

Sheila nodded. "In a sense."

"One of my team?"

"Of course not. My spies are good enough that you would never detect them. Good enough to go into Zone 6 and not get caught."

"Some of them did."

"They knew the things the Collective would do."

"Did they know what you are?"

"You're right. I'm not much different. I'm trying to be honest when I can be, and in complete honesty I want to see the Hive fall. I'm sure your men do too."

"I spent weeks under the Hive's control. Every moment that I had I was being watched. I'm not afraid of it anymore. Only people like you and your son."

"Don't talk about my son," Sheila hastily warned.

"You don't know where he is? Maybe he abandoned you too."

"Lonnie has done more than you think. He's the reason why you stand here."

"Yes, I know. He wanted to go retrieve the EMP."

"Did you know this island was hidden? Who do you think showed it to us? Be thankful for he saved you. He came straight to us. Wanted to destroy the island right away."

"Did he tell you what was on the island?"

"The Hive. Its Loyalists. Children. Their mothers. We knew."

"You almost killed us all."

"Yet you still remain breathing. A thank you would be appreciated."

A thud came from above, reminiscent of his battle with the Amish. Alex turned to see that Patton had entered the cabin.

"You've kept a child alive? Good job with this one," Sheila complimented.

Patton raised his head, revealing what battle had done to him. Scratches were etched across his face with dried blood turning into crusty scabs. His right eye was black. His hands were bruised.

"Did you get them all to safety?" Alex asked.

"I didn't get close. They're dead because of you," Patton spat at Sheila.

"You remind me of Lonnie when he was young. You're very headstrong."

"I don't care!" Patton screamed, rushing forward. Alex pulled him back, warning him to remember restraint. As Patton struggled Alex realized that his stay on the island meant more than he had anticipated. When he first saw him, he was interacting with others his same age, something he hardly ever saw happen within Zone 6.

"If you want the Hive dead they are going to be the ones who help us do it," Alex said. "I'm sorry that we lost Andy. Gianna too," he added.

"Andy was a nuisance," Sheila explained. "He wanted to undermine us. It's a good thing he's gone. Letting him go out in a blaze of glory was mercy."

"Alex, why with them?" Patton asked. "They kill their own."

The difficult question delayed Alex's answer. Not only did Patton's incomplete grammar make it hard to understand, but when he realized what the boy was asking justifying remaining with Sheila was something that he could barely comprehend himself.

"We all want to kill the Hive, and it won't be for long. If it's not with them, we would have to be with somebody just as bad."

"That's it?"

"You should be thankful we saved you. Even if you didn't deserve it," a recognizable voice called. A coward emerged downward. Lonnie.

"I'm not staying in Riverside," Alex decided.

"We're not going to Riverside."

"Where are we going then?"

"I wanted to offer you a position."

"What?"

"Vice President. Second-in-Command. General. Whatever you want to call it. When I die, it's yours."

Alex looked to Lonnie in confusion. "We don't have to like each other, but you're one of the best options that I have," Lonnie claimed.

"No," Alex answered.

"Why not?" Sheila asked.

"I'm not fighting beneath anyone again," he explained, leaving the tense environment with Patton.

"I hate them," Patton said.

"Get used to it."

The group docked at the mainland. Once they arrived Lonnie distributed orders. The Loyalists who had altered allegiances were given protein pills, a great departure from the island meals, and cloth wrappings to cover their markings.

"These suck," Reese complained.

"You should be grateful that you have some form of nourishment," David said.

"Not eating gives you a light head. It's fun."

"Maybe we shouldn't have saved you," Takeo stated. Lonnie and Sheila approached.

"What did you find on the island?" Sheila asked.

"Hasn't Lonnie told you?" Alex replied.

"First I was a prisoner. Then I was an adviser for a day. I did not have time to find anything," Lonnie revealed.

"How?"

"It knew who I was. It thought I was a threat when it found out how much I knew, like how Zone 6 fell. I actually knew before I met you."

"And you still forced us on that mission."

"Our agreement was that you could use our radio," Sheila reminded him.

"The Libertarians deserve people of higher merit than you," David accused.

"Our interests are now the same. It would benefit us both if we worked together."

"You need me more. I know the truth about the Hive. I know what it is. Where it came from and what it wants," Alex said.

"With your skin markings, who do you think will accept you?"

"I can talk my way into it," Reese suggested.

"Former Loyalists will always have a place with each other," Takeo said.

"You would fit better with proper allies. We are in talks with both the Technicians and the Amish," Lonnie stated.

"Those are enemies."

"Those factions are at a constant state of war," David said.

"Now they're at a standstill. We don't know why. I know you're interested in finding out," Lonnie mocked.

"It's a maybe for me," Reese stated.

"Are you going to run away again?" Lonnie accused.

"I was planning on jogging away this time," Reese jested.

Reese's plans tempted Alex, but he knew it was foolish. He had a responsibility to Earth, and he would spend the rest of his life finishing it.

"The Hive is not alien. It's a man. One of the elites in the old world. Conrad Westwick. He stopped us from taking over a peaceful planet."

Lonnie laughed at the prospect. The others were enamored by the idea.

"I'm going to need proof. What human stops other humans from proper ambition?" Lonnie mocked.

"A decent one," Takeo said, "but it can't be true. There is no such thing as peaceful planet."

"We know nothing about our universe. It's possible," David speculated.

"Conrad is dying. It's going to pick a new Hive. The moment that it chooses, the Hive will be strong again," Alex revealed.

"Really? Who would that be?" Lonnie asked.

"You," Sheila offered.

"The best time to attack is now," Alex proposed.

"Attacking Hubs. Now you're making sense," Lonnie stated. "The Hive's source Hub is in Zone 6."

The faces around him stared in shocked silence. "You lived there, you would have seen it."

"The restricted Zone," David realized.

As the critical information dawned on the others, Alex pondered how many within Zone 6 knew the truth. If the citizens who occupied it beforehand had kept it a secret. The chance that even Ives had known crossed his mind.

"All this to get your city back," Lonnie accused.

"I don't want to go back, but to defeat the Hive. It has to be done," Alex said.

Sheila and Lonnie locked eyes with each other. "We need to talk," Lonnie decided, departing from the group.

In the short break Alex approached Patton who sat at the shore.

"Do you wanna race?" Patton challenged.

"Try not to cry when I win."

Both men dove into the water. The cool liquid offered Alex a burst of refreshment. Alex did not put in full effort at first. He almost allowed Patton the glory of winning, but once he saw that Patton was faster than he thought, Alex increased his work ethic. During the chase Alex felt a sensation of inner joy that had not struck him since he first saw that Patton was alive.

"When you left Zone 6, did you ever get to the restricted area? Did it change?" Alex asked.

"I did forget to tell you. The radiation is not bad. Walking through is how I got out," Patton stated.

"It didn't affect you?" Alex asked.

"Nothing happened."

Alex clenched his fist in irritation over the Collective's lies. He came to guess that additional secrets lay within its depths other than the Hive's source.

"What did you see?"

"Mostly the same. Green smoke. I could only see because of goggles a guy gave me."

"I'm happy you were able to make it out."

"It was luck."

"It was skill."

Patton nodded. Listening. Learning. As he always did. "You think that?"

"You've survived two real battles. Surviving a third and fourth is likely."

"Thanks."

"If I die, keep going."

"Don't worry. I can keep us alive. I can kill a Mecha."

"You'll have to prove that to me."

Alex laughed, proud of Patton's newfound confidence, knowing that it would take him places.

Once they returned to shore Alex revealed his position. "I'm not going back to Riverside."

"It's not ours anymore," Sheila revealed. "Make sure Lonnie stays alive. I don't care how. My interest is that our family name carries on. For now, beating the Hive accomplishes that. We share the same goal."

The group departed, packing themselves into a vehicle of the old world. A brown car that lacked both armor and speed. As they bounced forward Alex looked to the team, worried for their future. He felt that Patton was growing too quickly, discovering additional horrors of the world. Reese slipped into his old ways, managing to refill his flask before departing. Takeo's bandanna gripped around his hand while the W marking on his forehead remained visible, highlighting his lack of foresight.

"Cover up your forehead," Alex requested.

"My past is a part of who I am," Takeo answered.

"If we're ambushed I don't want anybody thinking that we used to be Loyalists. Don't screw me over," Reese said.

"We were Loyalists."

"Not real ones," Alex reminded him.

"I need to get used to it. This is here for the rest of my life."

"Another time," Alex promised.

Takeo placed the wrapping around his forehead. A temporary solution to his permanent issue.

"It's a shame. In the old world markings like yours were a known sign of individuality," David said.

"You would know. You're old enough to have been there. What was it like?" Reese jested.

"I have read that they were happy."

"They better have been," Alex claimed.

"They weren't. People who are happy with what they own would not dream of taking the resources of another planet for their own."

"We're not bad," Patton said.

"At minimum we're constantly unfulfilled. The root of our demise."

"Our fall is from the Hive itself," Alex said.

"It was us first," Takeo reminded them.

"Can't wait till war's over," Patton said.

"Another one will replace it. Likely far grander than this one," David claimed. "In Zone 5 our armory only had one weapon that I didn't understand. It was like a cane, but it had crystals at its ends. I watched a man speak odd words and from it he managed to cut limbs. The cane certainly was not made by us, maybe the cosmos isn't as peaceful as we thought it was."

"There will be fights," Takeo suggested.

"Of course. Ancient texts have shown that wars between nations were sparked by problems much smaller than resource distribution, but most lived in luxury once the world united. Being forced to share the same language, policies, and government certainly helped."

"That sounds like hell," Lonnie said.

"I once read a journal from a Zone 5 resident. He had his entire day planned out for him. He hated it. I read from another man who loved his structured life."

"Still sounds like hell."

"I would have enjoyed that as long I got picked to do something easy," Reese added.

"I could have built something substantial," David proposed.

"What, like a children's toy? You would have been good at it."

"And you would have made an excellent homeless person."

"Maybe it was meant to happen this way," Takeo suggested.

"The belief in fate is a relic of the old world. Those who were religious had great faith. None of their holy books prepared them for what was to come. Some of them were lost to time. I discovered one called a Numen, full of stories about gods we have never heard of."

"If there is somebody in control, they left us to clean up its mess," Alex uttered.

"What an asshole," Lonnie echoed.

Their conversation about the old world carried them to nightfall. They traveled on both dirt and concrete roads, passing through dead towns which lacked valuable supplies, showing that they had already been ransacked.

As Lonnie warned that they were within Amish lands, Alex told the others to remain silent unless prompted to speak and to show aggressive intent only in terms of defense.

The first evidence of civilization was a tent only large enough for a single occupant. In front of the tent was a small fire pit, a pan for feeding, the hide of a small beaver that hung freely, and a horse tied to a pole.

"Weak defenses," Takeo noted. "They should be the ones who are afraid of us."

"It's a trick," Patton declared.

"The Amishmen don't use illusions," David said.

140

"Hiding bushes?" Patton guessed.

Alex watched the tent in anticipation as the front opened. A silver-tipped arrow emerged, followed by a bow, and a woman wielding it. Her hands were steady, her eyes suspicious.

"Stop the car," Alex demanded. The vehicle halted.

"We're killing her?" Patton asked.

"Only if she tries to do anything to us," Takeo clarified.

"Wait here," Alex instructed as he stepped from the car.

Upon a closer view Alex could see that her hands shook, revealing inexperience.

The bow she held was crudely made, clearly not manufactured within the old world's metal-based factories. It was instead a wooden invention crafted by her own hand. If she did attack, it would be her downfall.

"My name is Alexander King. I am here to speak with the Amish."

"I represent myself," she replied.

"Are you Amish?"

"Yes. What the fuck do you need?"

"I want to talk to your leader. I promise this is not an attack."

"Who's this?" Lonnie asked as he approached.

"I'm not sure yet."

"Who's your leader?" the bow-woman questioned.

"Put down your weapon," Lonnie threatened.

"I thought this wasn't an attack."

"It's not," Alex insisted.

"It could be," Lonnie added.

The woman did not lower her bow. "Make it clear what you want."

"The Hive has come back. We want to end it, but we need allies to take Zone 6," Alex said.

"We aren't warriors."

"We should go to the Technicians then," Lonnie proposed.

"They have taken a vow of peace. They won't be your friends."

"That won't last."

"I can take you to Eric. He might help you," she offered, mounting her horse.

Alex suspected that the beast might be an agent of Conrad, but when he saw its chestnut-brown eyes, he realized he was wrong.

"We can wait for the next lookout," Alex proposed.

"I'm not a lookout. I'm out here because it's quiet, and my things don't get stolen."

She spurned forth and the Alliance followed her down the winding path. Within a few minutes varied shelters appeared, all of which had differing aesthetics: small tents and wooden structures The individual bodies wore a vast pallet of clothing. Heavy armor, bare skin, and ancient threads were all on display while distinct reactions towards the convoy were made. Some withdrew weapons, some stared blankly; others did not bother to watch at all.

"Should we attack?" Patton asked.

"No," Alex clarified, unsurprised by his idea. Within the Collective any refugee was met with the same goal from Collective soldiers: to make them submit to their will.

The amount of weapons unfit for the upcoming battle became a recurring theme. They mostly wielded bows, swords, and spears. The occasional firearm was visible, crowded under an arsenal fit for the ancients.

The path ended when they met a clearing of unmaintained grassland. Within the center of it was a large tent where a long uneven line had cultivated for a seated elderly man. Two women had taken position in front of him. They pointed fingers at one another and waved with dramatics. Their anger was evident.

"That's Eric," their guide disclosed.

Behind the grassland two bridges crossed over to a rocky landscape on the other side. The left was metal. A promising crossing point. Its bottom appeared as a sturdy block that matched its rails. The right bridge was wooden, a dangerous path. Its sides contained frayed rope as a guard rail, and a bottom containing the occasional missing platform.

The men departed from the car and took themselves to the rear end of the line. The purpose of the gathering was discovered to be conflict resolution for petty inquiries. Land disputes and accusations of theft acted as the center for the arguments. Eric's role was to consider both sides until he came to a conclusion. His solutions resulted in giving a general idea of what to do, but he never directed orders. Many were unsatisfied and were encouraged to return.

The tent flap swayed, offering a chance to view the inside. Within its center was a bulky silver object, topped by an antenna. A blue path ignited within the silver shell. An EMP.

"Visitors! I personally welcome you!" Eric boomed before they could speak. "What are your names?"

"I'm Lonnie. The leader of the Libertarians and—"

"What about you, child?"

"Patton."

"And you?"

"David."

"Reese."

"Alexander. We're here for allies. To strike against the Hive. We have a chance to end it permanently. I'm sure that everybody here wants the same thing."

Eric's face remained warm while Alex spoke about humanity's enemy.

"Where are you from?"

"The Collective."

"In the Collective does everybody want the exact same thing?"

"Well, not always."

"It's the same here. Some will help you. They might see it as a chance for glory. Others won't be interested, but everybody will yield their own fate. Don't talk to me. Talk to them."

"Their own fate?" Takeo questioned. "You've banned advanced weapons."

"I see plenty of plasma among you. Our use of ancient technology is misconceived. It's a choice. Not forced."

"We're not here for backstory," Lonnie interrupted. "The Hive's heart is in the city of Zone 6. This might be our only chance."

"You'll need to explain how you're aware of this."

"We spent time as Loyalists," Takeo foolishly revealed.

"Former Loyalists," Alex quickly clarified. "We were prisoners."

"Don't explain to me," Eric retorted. "I will call a meeting for midday tomorrow. Anybody interested in your regime will be in attendance."

"How exciting," Reese sarcastically exclaimed.

"It will be. The last time we had an encounter with strangers is when our EMP was returned to us. Unfortunately, it turned out to not work."

"I'm open to fixing it," David offered.

"Be my guest."

David entered the tent; Lonnie, Reese, Takeo, and Patton walked towards the truck, but Alex remained still, the nagging images of the Amishmen who had died during their assault for the EMP taking hold of his memories.

"If there's anything else I'd be happy to hear it," Eric said.

"No … nothing," Lonnie claimed.

Alex swallowed, becoming wary of the repercussions that would pass by his reveal. Eric's chin tilted upward in interest.

"In the past we attacked Amishmen," Alex unveiled.

"Goddammit," Lonnie cursed.

Eric's demeanor changed. He leaned into his chair and inhaled deeply.

"May I ask why?" Eric inquired.

"They were taken by the Hive when we reached them," Lonnie lied.

Eric nodded. His arms folded. He looked to the living space of the Amishmen. "Consequences often come to those who leave us." Alex was surprised by Eric's underwhelming response to learning some of his own had been taken by the Hive, and perished in the aftermath.

"You're not angry?" Alex asked.

"I'm happy they were released. While under the Hive, one's mind still exists while their bodies are subjected to horrid acts."

Eric's speculation brought forth additional sorrow within Alex for all those under Conrad's control, for his time spent in Zone 6 completing tasks that he was not interested in was nothing compared to losing complete autonomy of one's life.

"How would you know?" Lonnie asked.

"I was under it once. It let us go," Eric revealed. "I know the feeling of doing another's bidding. It won't happen to another, not here."

"Why would you tell him that?" Lonnie asked Alex as they walked away from a pondering Eric.

"He had the right to know," Alex stated with a shrug.

"He could have been crazy and had us killed."

"It's a good thing that he's not like us."

"No, we're very different people," Lonnie insisted.

"How so?"

"I have people to take care of. People I care about."

"Don't tell me that you care now. You left them. That's why you're here."

"I left because I felt like they deserved better than what I could give them."

With the exception of David, the group returned to their truck and threaded through the camp. Reese requested that he be dropped off when he saw a circle of men exchanging odd cigars. Lonnie decided to join him.

"Don't do anything that's going to ruin you permanently," Alex warned.

"I'm watching him. That's not going to happen," Lonnie said. He leaned inward and whispered, "I'll gather intel. Make some contacts so that they're loyal if shit ever hits the fan."

"What?" Reese asked.

"Old world saying," Lonnie said.

"Nah ... old man saying."

Lonnie exhaled in annoyance and walked towards the circle of Amishmen.

"Drugs are going to be the death of you," Alex predicted.

145

"Please. You can't name one time that drugs have seriously affected my life."

"You got drunk. Couldn't escape a simple cave. Now you have to help kill the most powerful enemy that humans have ever fought," Takeo stated dryly.

"I'm still a war hero," Reese proclaimed.

"That means nothing."

"Talk to President Ye."

"I don't care about President Ye."

"I think you're the one who's drunk," Reese declared as he departed.

"You shouldn't have let them go," Takeo said. His arms were crossed, his tone short. "We should stick together."

"I want to do the opposite. I want you to take the car and go to the Technicians."

"I'm not interested."

"I'm asking you to do something—"

"We're not men of the Collective anymore."

"No, but we still need to work together. We're an Alliance," Alex proclaimed.

"You can't tell us what we can and can't do."

Taken aback by the sudden hostility, Alex opted to push further. "Do you want to take leadership?" he challenged.

"Not of anybody here."

"If you were given the choice back in Zone 6, would you have accepted the role of Commander?"

"I thought that it would make me feel powerful, but doing something that another tells you—that's not power."

"I still need you by my side."

Takeo frowned as he looked to Alex. "I'll be with you till the end."

"Do you really want to be around Reese till he's eighty?" Alex joked.

"He won't make it to eighty. I just know that I'm not going to spend my life watching citizens."

"I'm surprised that you of all people are going to live a life of peace."

"I never said anything about peace."

CHAPTER THIRTEEN

THE AMISHMEN

The Amishmen had more bodies than Alex expected. The cluster had gathered a minimum of two hundred men, women, and children. Members of the community were equipped with personal possessions. As Alex walked through, he was offered fishing rods, vain trinkets, and rare foods, as long as he had something valuable in exchange. The crowd spoke to one another while standing in circles, keeping themselves together, yet separated. He internally compared their operation to Zone 6 where, prior to a meeting, the crowd stood in stoic silence. The Amishmen acted on their human impulses by laughing, flirting, and arguing.

"Go ahead whenever you're ready," Eric urged as he stepped back. Alex took his position at the front-center of the tent before plunging into the prospect of turning a society who had lived mostly in peace into proponents of war. Many had their backs turned while engaged in conversation, and their attention needed gathering.

"Your flare," Alex demanded.

Alex expected David to pass him the flare, but instead he released the trail of purple smoke himself which captured the focus of those disengaged.

"I have a proposal for you that will be for your benefit!" Alex projected, hoping that his mysterious aura would keep voices quiet.

"Each of you makes your own living. It makes you vulnerable. To attacks, to famines, and to the Hive."

The mention of Conrad brought forth a downturn in the crowd's mood. Neutral faces turned to frowns. A scattering of whispered voices appeared. Alex ignored it.

"The Hive has returned, but it's dying. We are from the Alliance and our movement will shatter its return."

The presence of whispering grew. "We want your help."

As Alex spoke a few turned away from him, forcing him to consider holding interest through a different message.

"Afterwards the world will change. You won't have to worry about another great war. You won't be held by fear. If you're a farmer your crops will double. If you are an artist, your works will be seen to eyes that used to be inaccessible." Interest grew again. Silence took priority.

"The entire world will open, it will …"

Alex's words petered. He stumbled, unsure as to what to say that would be convincing, yet truthful.

"With the Hive gone you can travel to every inch of it. Cold snows and exotic oceans are within your grasp, but you have to reach out and get it yourself."

He received nods of approval.

"He's right," Lonnie unnecessarily added. "The chance to kill an alien will only come once in a lifetime. Don't waste it. Don't stay here as cowards because once the Hive dies, I will remember that it was the Amishmen who rejected us."

They received a mixed reaction of reluctance, joy, anger, and fear.

"You're liars!" a man from the crowd heckled. "We're happy here. Kind. Compassionate. Not interested. Eric, make them leave."

"I will not choose for the community," Eric decided. "Invasion is not our way."

"It's not your way."

"I'm talking about liberation," Alex replied.

As the congregation moved back Eric approached Alex. "War is not the way we know. You will need to lead them."

"When was the last time you were in a battle?"

Eric hesitated before speaking. "Not long ago we faced the Technicians. We have a peace treaty: don't attack them or their allies, they won't attack us."

"Then you can work together."

"You wouldn't want to. They've lined with The Hive."

Alex's eyes shifted to the crowd. Some had dispersed. Two who remained stood out with their shared similarities: faces with slight frowns, silent, identical. Alex realized that Conrad had slipped in with the Amishmen.

"Conrad!" Alex exclaimed.

The heads of Conrad's bodies tilted simultaneously, confirming their identity. One of them belonged to the heckling man.

"The Technicians are coming," Alex stated.

Conrad nodded his heads. "Soon. Very soon. No time for escape."

"We will end you."

Alex considered his threat flimsy. The Technicians had a substantial amount of power. Much higher than the Amishmen. The battle would result in many deaths, twisting Alex's thought with premature guilt.

"I welcome it," Conrad's bodies replied. "You welcomed war. You're reckless," the Hive accused. "A flaw."

"Joanna! Hector!" Eric called. He stood from his chair and approached Conrad's property, calling them by their former names, failing to return them to conscious existence.

"If you welcome a war then you shouldn't mind me having a few extra soldiers. Let them go," Alex coerced.

"They die. When let go."

"When your time is over, they'll all perish," Alex said.

"No. My replacement. Will take."

"What? They need to be brought back. These are people who had full lives. Please," Hector pleaded.

"They'll only die when removed. They have to be a part of the Hive forever," Alex said.

"There has to be a way. There has to be," Eric panicked. "One way. You take me. Your people saved," Conrad said.

"I'm not interested in taking others' lives, alien! Just give us these ones back."

"They fight for me."

"No!"

"Anger? A flaw. They watch. Feel all. Still alive, but no control." Alex mourned for those who had been taken, remaining conscious while their bodies were forced into either death or servitude of Conrad, and killed them with two bullets from his cannon. Red blood seeped from the wounds.

"Wait … that … this isn't Hive. Their blood …" Eric stuttered.

"It can mimic human blood," Alex explained to the returning crowd. "These were Hive bodies."

The Amishmen reacted slowly, which perplexed Alex as he had just killed one of their own. Instead, they looked to him for guidance. Two turned to leave. Takeo stood in their way. His eyes narrowed; his head shook.

"There is no running. The Hive will find you. It's more powerful than any of us," Takeo claimed.

"You brought it to us," a frightened woman accused.

"It was going to happen anyway. A new age is coming!" Takeo boomed.

Alex looked to the bodies that fell. The heckler was grasping onto life.

"Please, I don't want to die." His eyes filled with tears. He was free at his last moments. "Save us all."

"We need to create defenses!" Alex yelled.

"It appears we're off to a good start," David claimed as his eyes shifted to the EMP.

"What else do you have?" Alex asked.

"Whatever you can come up with." Unsurprised, Alex turned to the group.

"Get explosives on the bridges. Land mines only, no sensor bombs."

Alex looked to the landscape, searching for what could be of use to him.

"You," Alex called to the others, splitting the group with a wave of his hand. "Retreat to where you live. Hide behind the trees. We'll call for you later."

The bodies shuffled to their posts. Those who had been sent to the bridges layered explosive traps. Those sent to the rear manifested cover from scraps.

"It's a good thing the EMP's done," Alex said.

"It's partially functional. I'm still tinkering," David admitted as he dashed towards his goal.

"You should have kept one alive," Takeo argued while he fiddled with his BN-10, investigating its parts.

"He would have stalled us."

"We could have known exactly when it's coming. I want to be prepared."

"That's what we're doing."

"This won't win against the Technicians. We should try for another treaty."

"Alex, are you coming to the front with me?" Patton asked.

Alex looked at him and noticed that the boy had grown. His height and body mass had increased, his voice had deepened. He was mature enough now to achieve what he wanted: an experience at the front lines of a battle.

"I'll be at the bridge," Alex decided. "Those in the rear will need you."

"I want to be with you," Patton whined.

"We don't have time for bullshit," Takeo cut in. "Don't be blind. We both know the Hive's power. What if we made it think we're on its side again, and used—"

"I'm going on a scouting mission," Reese announced.

"Why?" Patton wondered.

"Making a discovery of how close the army is. Making a discovery and coming back a hero is my specialty," Reese announced.

"Come back alive. I'll stay here," Alex said.

"I'll help build the defenses," Takeo offered.

The trio traveled on horses provided by the Amishmen that Reese had become acquainted with. Alex's animal had a mini-gun mounted onto its rear. The weapon's neck extended above the heads of the men, and its shortened barrel was constructed to be a few feet long. The trigger to the weapon was threaded within the reigns, not with a button, but through a mental connection, a rarity of the old world.

Reese led them, his movements intentionally slowed, allowing time to investigate the atmosphere thoroughly. Alex followed closely behind, matching his intentions. Patton had joined the mission, telling Alex that he was going to search for the Technician army himself if Alex did not allow him to join, as his confidence showed he was prepared.

They were joined by the guide they'd met when first coming to the Amishmen. She held her bow, a cache of arrows, two spears, and a short sword. She introduced herself as Maria.

"I'm here to watch you," she revealed.

"Who sent you?" Alex asked.

"Myself."

"You people are so lucky. You get to do whatever you want when you want. That's like my dream," Reese said.

"How?"

"We're not so lucky," Maria claimed. "There's a reason why I stay on the outskirts."

"Why?" Patton asked.

"The long line to see Eric. That was a good day. When people do whatever they want without consequences, it leads to issues."

As they moved forward the terrain remained mostly the same, a maze of gray and red rocks acting as the surface. The only deviation from it was the discovery of statues within the landscape. Depictions of soldiers, citizens, and diplomats were scattered. They shared a theme of loyalty to the old Collective, for there was a faded blue circle on top of each one. One caught Alex's eye. A sculpture of Conrad Westwick. In his hands was a treaty with his signature scrawled across it. The promises of what the Collective would bring.

"We found them," Reese suddenly implored as his eyes detracted from the rifle's barrel. "Look."

Alex looked into the scope and saw what had caused Reese to falter. The weapon's ability to detect camouflage made a useful perk. Far ahead it appeared that a statue was moving forward slowly.

Alex cast suspicion towards it. Once his eyes were withdrawn from Reese's barrel, it became apparent that no moving statue was visible.

"Their army?" Patton asked.

Alex looked to his group with worry. Arrows and swords were nothing against plasma. Reese's weapon was useful for long distance assassinations, but not within the proximity of an enemy. Patton's pistol was weak. Alex looked at his own hand and manifested the purple cannon, adding a fatigue-inducing weight to his right arm. Despite the negative odds, it was possible to win.

The rifle was passed until each had seen the threat themselves. Once it returned to Alex, he saw that another change had been made. The scout revealed itself to be a green Mecha suit. It contained stumpy silver and clawed feet that sunk into the ground. Both arms had three cannon barrels each. When Alex looked with his naked eye the Mecha had transformed into the image of a boulder covered in moss.

"Now would be a great time to leave," Reese pleaded.

"If we interrogate their scout, we can find out exactly when they're coming."

"I meant a perfect time."

"Patton, take the horse. Go tell everybody what's happening," Alex commanded as he jumped off the horse that the two men had shared.

"No. I'm gonna fight."

"Patton, go."

"You can't make me."

Patton's defiance in this critical time sent Alex to his tipping point. His hand lightly contacted Patton's cheek.

"Go."

Alex had slight regret over his reaction, but the lives of others were more important than Patton's feelings.

"One of us needs to go to a higher elevation," Alex stated.

Maria shot an arrow attached to a rope upwards. It punctured the back of a statue's head. It propelled her upwards, ending with Maria perched on the sculpture's shoulder.

"Go for the joints," Alex commanded before each of them hid behind a statue.

The Mecha's mechanical nature made an impact across the land. From a distance one could hear it whirring with rage. As it stomped it shook the ground below. It matched the statue in size, extending upwards of fifteen feet tall.

"Go!"

Alex, Reese, and Maria all took a shot at its shoulder.

Maria struck first. The bow implemented itself into the joint, striking the tangle of visible wires. Each joint had the same image of wires prevalent at its knees, shoulders, and elbows. The arrow was quickly followed by a stream of blasts from Alex.

The enemy retaliated. From its right arm three rockets quickly detracted in three separate directions, one for each member of the Alliance. Alex braced and jumped from his position. His evasion coerced the rocket to hit the statue instead. The impact sent chunks of rock flying, a few of which pelted Alex. Maria managed to retreat by sliding down her established rope. Her smooth transition to the ground was interrupted once the missile contacted the statue, sending her crashing to the ground. The third rocket smashed into the rocks before Reese, denting the ground below and striking him with debris. The turning of events turned Alex's mindset, making him wish he had not risked the lives of his team against a nearly impossible enemy.

A countermeasure came when a stream of bullets contacted the Mecha's belly. It acted as a distraction as it did nothing to stop nor slow its advancement. Six rockets spewed from the Mecha, three from its left and three from its right, all of which headed towards the bullet streams' origins.

"Keep on the arm!" Alex pleaded. His plasma, Reese's bullets, and a streak of arrows hammered at the joint, eventually breaking through. The right arm suddenly dropped as steam rose from the wound, ending its use.

Three missiles came from the left which surged past the three of them towards the reinforcements. Alex turned to see how many had been brought. Only one; Patton had taken full control of the horse. It spurred forth with haste under his command, managing to dodge the explosions that surrounded him due to the sporadic nature of his movement.

Despite his anger for Patton's defiant nature, Alex swallowed the truth that it was Patton who had saved them and came to be thankful, for without his distraction they would not have been able to disable the right arm.

A sudden green shield of plasma acted as protection for the Mecha. The green sphere shimmered as the Alliance attacked it, slowly cracking, but not enough to end it, and the Mecha remained able to send its rockets outward, forcing the Alliance into constant movement.

"Save your bullets!" Alex commanded.

Patton did not listen, continuously using the turret, slowly draining its supply while making visible damage. The green began to flicker and the shield cracked, vanishing completely.

"Bullets all out!" Patton revealed.

"Go! Go! Left arm!" Alex exclaimed.

The left side proved itself more difficult, as the Mecha waved in a random pattern, managing to dodge the direct assault.

Maria withdrew her sword. She rushed forward until close enough to get to the Mecha. Once its arm was in a downturn she leapt into the air and plunged her weapon into the left shoulder blade. The Mecha's arm moved inward, crushing Maria's body in a horrid spray of blood. Her corpse fell, but the sword remained cemented.

Reese's accuracy allowed bullets to make their way into the Mecha's neck. A trickle of red blood left it. A human inside had been hit.

The Mecha's trio of cannons shifted by merging into one. From the process a laser swept across the land. Unavoidable, brutal, and inaccurate. To avoid it Alex leapt above; Patton dashed under it, but Reese had failed. The back of his shirt was shredded, leaving his back scarred with burning flesh.

With rage Alex allowed a blast to manifest within his Cannon for an extended period while moving dangerously close. Once released it hit the enemy's armor exposing its inner workings. A cascade of wires and motherboards, and underneath it all a sliver of skin was visible.

"Look out!" Patton called.

The beam stopped, and the Mecha's left arm swept towards Alex. It came rapidly. All he could do was embrace. He manifested a strong blast of plasma. The Mecha's arm was torn off, and Alex went tumbling with it. When he recovered he could sense that his cannon had reduced greatly in power, only containing enough juice for a few more maneuvers. He looked upward to see that the Mecha's left arm was raised, but unable to make movement. The sword within had drilled further, causing additional damage. The arm jerked with desperation, unable to move. The Mecha slowly turned and ran, intent on returning to the Technicians.

It was slow due to its heavy size, but ending its retreat would be tasking. Reese was decommissioned, Alex was close to losing ammo, and Patton had none. They would not end the Mecha's escape by traditional means.

Using the last of his power he anchored himself to the ground by manifesting a solid claw deep into the earth, and crafted a purple whip which wrapped against the Mecha's feet. Alex's body tore with pain as the suit crashed on his back.

"Reese!" Alex called.

Alex dashed to him. He was in a hunched position, rocking back and forth. Red splotches were prevalent within his back.

"We'll get you back right away."

"You better find out where they are first," Reese pleaded, "or this was for nothing."

Alex and Patton rushed towards the Mecha with caution.

"Thanks for listening," Alex told Patton.

"You mean not listening," Patton japed.

Alex used Maria's sword, and Patton had brought his own dagger. They ripped through the armor with brutal force while the remnants of a human body were slowly revealed.

"Can I try?" Patton requested, holding his palms out for the sword.

"You think you're good enough?"

"Ya. I just got a Mech—"

"Helped take down a Mecha," Alex corrected. "Be careful," he commanded.

The rise and fall of a heartbeat was revealed. Then a head. They hoisted the Technician free, who was gravely injured. The bullet had lodged its way into his stomach. His breath was ragged, he coughed harshly; death had almost taken him.

"How many Technicians are coming?" Alex demanded. The man shook his head.

"When are you going to strike?"

Patton raised his fist and struck the Technician. "Now!" the Technician stated.

From a ring on the man's finger, a blade emerged and plunged directly into Patton's heart.

Alex smashed his cannon against the already dead Technician, before tending to Patton's injury, knowing that through his persistence Patton would be able to survive. His body shook ferociously while blood streamed from his heart.

"We're getting you back!" Alex stated as he began to lift him.

"No!" Patton urged, "or boy dies!"

Alex's hands stopped. The odd dictation had a familiar cadence.

"Alex! Help!" Patton screamed.

Alex broke free of his flustered state and wrapped his arms around Patton's body.

"No touch! Or the boy will die!" Patton warned again. He calmed. His panicked expression stopped. His eyes cast down to his heart, an act that made Alex do the same. As the flow of red blood continued, a slow trickle of green came through.

Alex turned his eyes away. "I'll help—"

"Eyes everywhere," Patton claimed blankly, unhindered by emotion. His blood touched Alex's hand. It felt thick.

"Leave him!" Alex warned, allowing himself to face the harrowing fact that Patton had been partly taken at some point.

"Always mine," Conrad answered.

"Patton. You can fight it."

"A name given by another." Only green liquid left the wound.

"I'll do anything if you let him live."

"This is a test. Watch how you battle. Hindered by pain."

Alex tried shifting Patton's body. It had turned extraordinarily heavy. Green foam took over Patton's mouth, pushing Alex into submission.

"I'll take your place. Can you just give him back!" Alex attempted another overhaul of Patton's body which failed.

"I can. I won't."

The vile green blood that Alex was trying to swipe away changed to hardened gray, taking Patton's eyes, mouth, and ears. Patton turned still. His pulse had ended. Another one of Conrad's children had died.

CHAPTER FOURTEEN

THE BRIDGE

The early sun slowly crept upward, and the warmth clamoredon Alex's skin as he held Patton.

"They're coming," Reese pointed out, his pain evident through a restricted voice.

"Help me with this body."

"I really wish I could."

Alex shifted. Reese lay on his stomach, leaving his torn back exposed. His eye retracted, focusing on the scope, and shifted towards Patton.

Alex's eyes turned wet, his shallow breathing matching Reese's.

"He was a great kid," Reese continued.

As Alex mourned, he lamented the previous indicators of Patton's true form. He realized that Patton's residence within the island was not based on courage, but instead an act of Conrad keeping his family together. Memories bolted into Alex's thoughts. The epiphany came that when Patton had fainted, it was not due to the effects of alcohol, but instead the genetics within his blood stream that made him susceptible to David's invention. His short speech patterns were not the result of a child learning grammar, but instead an inherited flaw. Alex felt violated. Every word that he had shared was being listened to. It was part of the reason why Conrad was interested in him.

"He was one of the Hive's children," Alex realized.

Patton's body had not reduced in weight; it remained at a crushing mass that Alex was unable to lift. The hard gray remained still, mocking him with its presence.

"Take Patton. I'm old enough to walk myself." As Reese struggled to stand, his arms shook sporadically, until he collapsed.

"The body's too heavy."

Alex's hands slipped from the corpse as he recalled his own advice to Patton, citing that if he were ever to fall that he must continue. The guidance felt foolish as Alex struggled to follow his own words. He missed everything about him. His voice, his curious nature, his spirit, all never to be seen again. Alex wanted nothing more than to reverse time to prevent further deaths.

Alex looked to the Technician body with hatred. From its hands Alex spotted a purple wristband on each side. He stole them both and they bonded to his body.

Alex turned away from the grim image, slung Reese over his shoulder, and staggered forward. Patton's horse had departed, forcing them to travel by foot. They moved in silence, advancing quickly as Reese winced with each step.

Once they returned the Amish defenses had been completed. Various pieces of cover had been implemented onto both bridges. Nets that had the illusion of being a plain surface were placed between the bridge and Eric's field, used to plunge one into danger once a foot collapsed onto it. Alex's request for sensor bombs had been honored.

Reese stumbled ahead, coming into contact with both David and Takeo before Alex. The way that he spoke made it clear that he was speaking about the death of Patton. Reese was led back to the housing area, as a woman had offered to take care of his wounds.

Takeo approached Alex. David gave him a nod and returned to the tent.

"Alex, I'm sorry."

"I know."

"We can't let emotions—"

"Stop," Alex warned.

Takeo was not taken aback by the command, as he looked past Alex into the horizon. "They're here!"

A formation of Technicians jetted forward through the airspace. Metal wings propelled by blue fire blessed them with flight. The defensive measures on the ground would be useless.

Once the enemy was close enough the Amishmen made their first stand. Many of the aerial warriors were shot down by a concoction of gunfire, arrows, spears, and thrown knives. They spiraled downward both onto the bridges and to the river underneath. The Technicians above worked to destroy what was below. Their guns were able to make considerable damage to the bridges and the soldiers who fought on it. Many of them moved past the main battlefield altogether and instead moved towards housing.

Alex activated both his cannons, instantly sensing that they were different from what he had previously owned, for he now had the ability to craft weapons based on personal handiwork being no longer restricted by simple plasma blasts.

Technician ground forces arrived. They matched the Amishmen in their choice of weapons, wielding swords and shields with the exception that their own were bordered by the superior plasma.

Within minutes the Amishmen defensive line began to crack. Many had fallen, others began to flee from the inevitable enemy hoping to preserve their own lives.

"Hold the line!" Alex repeatedly screamed. His words shifted morale. Those considering running cemented themselves in the skirmish.

Alex projected plasma blasts in the air against the reduced aerial forces, most of which had either died, flew past the skirmish, or stopped attacking due to the presence of their own within the structure.

Alex pushed his way to the front of the metal bridge where a trading of intense swordplay took place. The Technicians cut through the Amishmen with efficiency. Alex vowed to change that.

"Step back!"

The Amishmen heeded his words. They stopped attacking, and Alex used both of his arms to produce a flat shield in front of them. Multiple Technician weapons embedded themselves within the shield.

"Now!"

Alex released his shield, and with it came a counter from the Amish, their metal weapons producing vital strikes against the Technicians.

"Now!"

The same maneuver worked for a second time. Alex differentiated the third.

He used his canons to form a block wide enough to push those in its way off the edge. He released it, and with it came the downfall of many Technicians.

"Screw the Hive's rules!" a Technician decided. He tossed aside his sword and from his hilt withdrew a pistol. The enemy's arm was dismembered, but soon many Technicians began to trade ancient weapons for plasma.

"Retreat! I have an idea!" Alex demanded.

During the departure the Amishmen were able to make small indents into the enemy's forces. Once back onto the surface, cover was provided for them. One of them being the large blue spheres of a BN-10 from Takeo that tore into clumps of the enemy.

The Amishmen took the position of being in constant movement. They would shoot then scurry to a different location, ensuring difficulty in hitting them. Alex did the same as his rage boiled. Each Technician he killed was deemed as a direct insult to Conrad's will. Revenge for Patton's life as a prisoner.

The antagonists eventually slaughtered all Amishmen on the bridge and poured forth onto the ground.

"Sensory bombs, now!" With Alex's call the entire bridge detonated at various points. The Technicians that had filled the bridge perished, either evaporated by the explosion, or from falling below.

As a countermeasure the Technician flyers hovered to the ground in order to counteract the Amishmen's avoidant nature.

"The EMP!" Alex called to Takeo.

"Down!" Takeo tacked Alex while bullets pelted the earth near them. Takeo sent a sphere towards the failed orchestrator of Alex's death. The flyer was blasted and his body flayed. Alex returned the favor by willing a triangle shield around the duo, forcing a rocket that was headed directly towards them to be averted.

"Get it! I'll command the front!" Takeo offered.

Alex took off, while Takeo screamed orders that rallied the Amishmen towards cohesion, advising two Amishmen to focus on one flyer at once.

Alex sprinted in an uneven pattern of breaking left and right, throwing off those in pursuit while his arms were raised to craft a sphere around himself. Each shot that ricocheted off his shield rattled Alex's being, making it increasingly difficult to maintain his sphere of protection.

Alex tore open the tent to find David shirtless with tools of the old world scattered around him. Sweat dripped from his body and he had a look of sheer concentration on his face.

In the time that he had been with it, David had managed to radically change the EMP's appearance. Its dim blue had turned radiant, illuminating the darkened tent. Instead of a low hum, a boisterous crackle of energy emerged from the machine.

"I'm finished, but I need to increase the blast radius," David explained.

"How much longer?" Alex asked.

A blast from above shattered through the tent's top and almost hit the EMP.

"There's no more time. We'll need to move it outward."

"Get your weapon," Alex said.

"This is all that's required."

David picked up three impulse crystals that lay on the table below, placed them within his pocket, and wrapped his hand around the metal ring that surrounded the base of the EMP.

"Keep those on," David said. "You can craft a beam of energy for support."

Alex created a small hook and shackled it to the bottom. His attempt failed as the crushing weight of the EMP made it difficult to concentrate, and his creation broke.

"You have to focus, forget the illusion that it's impossible," David encouraged.

Alex placed a rectangle underneath the object. It lifted off the ground, slightly releasing strain, allowing the duo to move with minuscule steps. Once they reached the door, bullet fire hit right where the EMP previously was.

Once outside they discovered the battlefield's scope had changed.

Both sides had been cut deeply. The Technicians who had made it over the bridge were snagged by brutal traps that ensnared their legs with metal spikes, blown away by sensory bombs, and cut down by Amish cover fire. The Amishmen were bombarded by the flyers who matched the Amishmen's strategy of constantly moving, giving them the agency to avoid death, and distribute it to others.

"Quicker!" Alex demanded.

The pace of their movement increased until a nearby explosion destabilized their path, resulting in the EMP toppling to the ground.

"No!" Alex shouted.

"Protect us," David requested.

Alex created a dual shield around them while David crouched to his knees to inspect the fallen titan. Alex remained centered on maintaining the sphere as bullets came towards them from two different directions.

"Remain strong, it's all in your head," David encouraged.

The words were taken lightly by Alex as pain shredded through his body. During his last seconds of resistance, a flat blue circle jumped from behind him which encircled the entire area.

Alex collapsed as the harassment from his weapons ended. His cannons lost power without his consent. Their connection had been cut. His fear bounded as he considered the prospect of having to face the Technicians without a weapon to counter them, until he saw that the EMP had worked.

The flyers plunged to the ground. The fire from their jet packs had been extinguished. They screamed while flailing downward. Many curled in defensive positions hoping to break the severity of their fall into both harsh rock and soft grass. Both gave them the same result. Blood flew from those impacted, violently ending their lives. The survivors stared in horror as their allies died in brutality against the backdrop of the orange sunset.

"The rest will be hostages," Alex informed David.

"Kill them!" Takeo yelled from ahead.

The Technicians pleaded for mercy. The Amishmen were non-compliant. They cut down the defenses of Technicians whose weapons of plasma were not viable against the onslaught.

Alex's cannons made it difficult to move, forcing him to move slowly.

"Wait, you can be hostages!" Alex called. His words went unheard.

He was forced to fight when a dethroned flyer approached him with a blade in hand, screaming for revenge. Alex bashed his right arm against the enemy's face.

A weaponless Technician surprised Alex with a sudden tackle. He used his fist to produce damage, and Alex found himself defenseless as the enemy had placed his entire body weight against Alex's arms.

Alex shifted his body to avoid strikes, an unsuccessful endeavor until he altered tactics and lobbed a vial of spit that landed on the enemy's eye.

"You're filth!" the man screeched.

Alex crunched upward and clenched his teeth around the enemy's ear.

The flyer screamed and quickly withdrew from his position, his hands wildly coming to his ear in pain. Alex lightly brought the metal cannon down to his heart when a sudden surge pushed it harder than Alex had expected, unintentionally ending the man's life. The power disappeared as fast as it had come.

Alex arrived at the bridge and spotted Takeo leading the Amish. The BN-10 swung at his hilt while his longsword tore through enemies. It lacked the crackle of electrical energy, but the blunt metal edge contained enough power to slice through the bodies of various fleeing foes.

"That's enough!" Alex said as he gripped Takeo's shoulder. "They can be taken as prisoners. They're useful."

Takeo stopped moving as his sword was near the neck of his next victim who shook with surrender.

"You know that I'm right," Alex urged, tired of the senseless killing.

Takeo agreed with Alex's message. As he lowered his weapon the other Amishmen did the same.

"Take them as hostages!" Alex commanded. "Where's your camp?" Takeo asked.

"We don't have anything here, but there is a Hub—"

"The Hive's there?"

The woman nodded.

"That's what I'm looking for. Where is it?"

Alex's cannon returned with full power. The flames on the woman's shoulder ignited. She rose in an attempted escape, but Takeo cut both her wings with swift strikes, aided by the green current that surrounded his sword.

"I'm sorry, please …"

"What would the Hive do if you betrayed it?"

"I-I don't really know. I imagine that it would—"

"Does it ever show mercy for betrayal?"

"We-I—"

"Tell me."

"I-I've seen it show mercy."

Alex turned to the battlefield and at multiple points small streaks of the Technicians' weaponry returned. The power of his cannons had returned. The EMP had failed to leave a lasting impact. Only a few flyers managed to escape.

"To who?"

"T-to you first. The Hive wanted us to only use our jet packs and our melee weapons. It said it wanted you alive," the woman stuttered.

"Me?" Takeo asked with interest.

"I never got a name or anything, but the Hive does believe in mercy. Preserving human life."

"Well, I don't." Takeo drilled his sword into the woman's chest, ending her life.

The escape of the flyers was underwhelming. Alex's misconception of the Technicians' power left him with momentary relief, as it was famed that they had hidden technologies unseen by the world, but the skirmish showed that it was a manufactured lie to inspire fear. He decided those remaining alive could still be used within the Alliance.

The Amishmen reacted to victory in different ways. Some shared boisterous laughter and drank pints of beer, others shed tears for those who had perished; a select few became reclusive.

"I can interrogate Conrad myself," Takeo insisted. "What would you even say?" Alex replied.

"I'm going to ask how many soldiers it has in Zone 6 up front."

"It will kill you on the spot. If you're with me, he won't touch us."

"You don't know that."

"I was chosen. The reason why the Technicians were not supposed to use guns was because of me."

"Could have been others too."

"Who else?"

"Maybe Eric. Lonnie. Maybe even one of the Amishmen that we don't even know about. You need to rest."

"That can come later. I want to hear from Conrad himself."

Alex and Takeo departed quickly afterward. They only told David where they were going. With the metal bridge gone they were forced to travel across the wooden platform. Once on the other end they found and subsequently decided to use two of the abandoned motorcycles that allowed the Technicians to travel swiftly.

Having to head back to the path where Patton had died threaded Alex with pain. He stopped once they reached the Mecha suit wreckage. Patton's body was gone.

"Why are we stopping?" Takeo asked.

"That's the man who killed Patton," Alex revealed.

"You got your revenge."

"His death was senseless. So was Patton's."

"He attacked first?"

"Of course."

"Good thing we ended them," Takeo claimed.

"Why would you kill that woman? She could have been part of the Alliance," Alex asked.

"She tried to escape. She's just like everybody else, wanting to take more then she deserved."

"She would have changed."

"By what? Joining the Alliance? She would turn the moment something better came across here. They are all the same."

"The Technicians are—"

"I mean humans," Takeo clarified. "You and I are far from selfish."

"You held information that Conrad was a human back against the Amishmen. I did not say anything because I was weak. They don't even know that we attacked and killed some of their people. You said there would be peace after war. That is a lie."

The chance that they would win was already low. Having his closest confidant unable to foresee their success cast Alex into rethinking his entire purpose.

Takeo stared at the body within the wreckage. Its internal organs spilled onto the rock below.

"He died harshly."

"It was necessary."

"If this is necessary, I don't want to be a part of this. Look at what I have done with my life."

Takeo's fighting skills were unmatched by any other companion. He had the traits of a great Commander, making it so Alex could not afford to lose his support as their final confrontation with Conrad drew closer.

"I found out what the Collective used to be. Humans wanted to take an alien planet."

Alex did not ask why he was told, for he already knew the answer. The Hive had seen within Takeo the ability to lead. To become one with its army. Worthy of vital information.

"I know. It's a good thing we were stopped."

"We never stopped. We stole Zone 6."

"Our Alliance won't be anything like the Collective."

"We're exactly like them," Takeo stated as he investigated the Mecha.

"He killed Patton," Alex clarified.

"And you killed him. This cycle is all I'm good for."

"Once we beat Conrad we can end it."

"It won't ever stop. I won't either."

Alex kept his solace submerged so that Takeo would continue to fight for the Alliance, but his distress in having to do so worried Alex.

"You don't have to be on the front lines."

"I killed Andy."

"A grappling hook did that."

Takeo shook his head in disagreement. "That was the final blow. I held his head down when I saw it heading up. Sheila gave me the mission. She could see the type of person I was the moment that I came up. Somebody used to carrying out evil acts. A human."

"But why would you say yes?"

"If I didn't, we would not be allowed to use the radio. He wasn't even a threat to us. Only to their legacy. He had the support of many Libertarians and he would have better for them. I cut that down."

Alex paused before responding. Andy was kindhearted, calm, and aged. Unlike Lonnie who was a reckless figure endangering those around him with his foolish antics.

"The family has lied to us before," Alex admitted. "There may have been more to the story."

"If you want to survive they can't be on your side."

"She has pledged to our Alliance."

"She has no reason to stay loyal."

"Her son is with us."

"He left the island. He will probably leave here too."

The suggestion pushed Alex's desire to check on Lonnie, but he pushed it away in order to console his friend.

"You could stay with her and watch—"

"This is not about her. It's about who I am. Who we all are. If the Hive falls, more leaders like Sheila and Lonnie will replace them. Not just now, but forever. Your Alliance will fall. We will go back to fighting each other. It won't ever stop. Not until somebody brings it to an end."

"We can do it together. We can have a peaceful life."

"I never said anything about a peaceful life."

Takeo's fists clenched around his longsword. Its electrical shell around it returned.

Alex activated his weapons and turned to face the incoming threat. Nothing was present.

Alex's attention shifted back to Reese, as there was no valid reason to withdraw the weapon. The battle with the Technicians was over and the Amish were allies.

"I have to fight for what I believe in," Takeo revealed.

Alex turned to him with heavy concern. Takeo withdrew his headband; Conrad's marking on his forehead became clear.

"What would that be?" Alex accused.

"If you want to bring peace you need power. Power that the Hive has."

"He is the thing that destroyed the old world!"

"It chose you. Nobody else is worthy. The world that you want. It's possible with Conrad's power."

"I will never join him!"

"You won't join him. You could become him—"

"That's enough!"

"Conrad is evil, but not the Hive. You are not the only chosen one. If the wrong person takes it this war could drag on forever."

"We can end Conrad together," Alex proposed.

"Good."

"Complete peace will never happen, but we can try our best," Alex admitted.

"Man has to end … completely."

"You're being insane! Just stop and—"

Alex recalculated his words, making sure that he did not treat his partner as beneath him. "Think about what that would look like."

"Species other than us would never be bothered again."

Alex struggled to find words that would alter Takeo's madness.

"That would mean David would have to die. Reese. Raina, everybody that you have ever known … You would have to be killed."

Takeo lowered his head. His sword rested within the earth. "This is not an easy choice."

"You're a fool!" Alex screamed, discarding his personal vow to remain stoic. The stakes were too high to remain in a neutral state. With Takeo sharing his true feelings, Alex decided he could do so with his own. "You are worse than Conrad. You would cause more pain than he ever had."

"And less in the long run."

"You brought me here to kill me," Alex guessed.

"No, I wanted to convince you."

"You failed."

Alex lifted his cannons, prepared to fire. A necessary sinful act. His heart twisted. The death of Patton, the realization that the world would never receive peace, and the betrayal from Takeo converged, pushing Alex into an agonizing state.

Takeo dashed towards Alex. His sword came down with a heavy clash against the shield that Alex projected around himself. The hit of the sword caused excessive pain, but did not cut through. His mind wandered towards pure hatred. Hatred towards Takeo. Hatred towards Conrad who had turned him. Hatred towards man for their nature.

When Takeo attempted to push downward, Alex subtracted his shield and crafted a block which separated them, bargaining a few feet of leeway, slowing the aggressive intent of his ally.

Alex shot a plasma bullet and he dashed left into avoid it, leaving him vulnerable. He expected death. Instead a patch of black smoke exploded from the ground and Alex faded to slumber.

Alex rose from the ground with tenacity. He found that the day had settled. The sunrise had risen.

"Takeo!"

He heard nothing back.

Alex cursed with a scream that echoed through the terrain. He investigated to discover that both of his weapons remained intact. His body had no new wounds. Takeo had left Alex alone when he could have murdered him one hundred times over.

The only change within the landscape was the remnants of the smoke grenade scattered across the floor. The object had ensured the survival of both men. Without it one of them would have killed the other. When Takeo's sword clashed against Alex's shield, the purpose was to bring forth death. Alex's shot was powerful enough to rip through Takeo's abdomen.

Alex shuffled back towards the Amish, entranced by both thankfulness that he breathed, and a desire to sleep forever. His mistakes that lead to losing both Patton and Takeo within the same day pounded at him, barring him from other thoughts.

His ability to defeat his new enemy came into question. If Takeo was deemed a chosen one by Conrad the war would not end until all humans were dead. It would force Alex into a never-ending harsh war backed by whatever allies that he could muster. It was a necessary act. Takeo would have to die.

CHAPTER FIFTEEN

THE AFTERMATH

"He left, just like that?" Reese inquired. David sat beside him on the cot, both in disbelief as they processed the information that Takeo had departed.

The three of them sat under a tan canopy that had been transmuted into a small center for medical services. There were three cots inside. The other two were occupied. One by a man whose hand was wrapped in gauze due to injury by a blade. The other was a woman who moaned in the distance. She clenched her stomach. Large red splotches seeped through the bandage that covered her lower torso.

Reese's shirt was withdrawn. Along his back was a gathering of bandages placed on the most severe sections of his injury, leaving an incoherent pattern. In some areas he was given nothing where pink scabs infected his body.

"I can see right through what this is. They're trying to make a joke, if you're going to try make it funny," Reese suggested.

"It's not," Alex clarified. "I tried to stop him."

"Takeo! I know that you can hear me! Get in here so we can talk about what to do next!"

No response came from the outside. "You need to take this seriously."

"Here's why I know this is bullshit. The two of you went out, and you came back without a scratch on you. If he left that means you let him leave. Something I know you wouldn't do."

"He used a smoke grenade to get away."

"So?"

"It makes one faint," David flatly presented.

"If Takeo wants to kill everybody, it wouldn't be a problem to kill his Commander."

The former title coerced Alex to wince. "I'm not a Commander anymore."

"Conrad may have evolved to make his speech patterns fluent. Before its return, the Hive took hours to infect somebody. Its blood was an obvious indicator of host bodies. Those both changed ... Takeo could have been taken," David suggested

"He chose to go," Alex asserted. "I should have tried harder. I knew he was changing, and I did nothing about it."

"Takeo can be brought back. He spent his whole life among humans, but we're not going to be able to do it by sitting in a tent," David theorized.

"It's a little hard for me to stand right now," Reese said.

"Then stay here. Eric will allow you to enjoy a life of leisure."

"Don't get me wrong. I will, but I want to see what else is out there."

"Let's trail him. The three of us."

"No," Alex decided. "We can't waste time. We need to take Zone 6."

Before either David or Reese could react the caretaker barged inside, ending the conversation.

"These will help you feel better," the caretaker claimed. She held three white pills. Reese took one.

"You can have all three," she offered with a sympathetic smile.

"I'm good with one for now, but thank you," Reese said with a wink.

"Are you both ready to leave?" Alex asked.

"First I'll need to bargain for some supplies. I have some tinkering to do," David stated.

"I also have some tinkering to do. You know what I mean," Reese quipped.

"It's not going to happen," Alex joked.

"I've heard women don't enjoy injured men," David added.

"You've heard wrong," Reese claimed.

"I'm going to kill him!" a familiar voice claimed. Lonnie aggressively strode into the tent, trailed by the caretaker whose guilty eyes gravitated to the floor. "You let a traitor live. It's obvious that mark on your hand shows who you really are. You're still a Loyalist!" Lonnie stopped when he was just a few inches away from Alex. His screech was used as intimidation, but it did nothing to falter. After watching two loved ones depart, Lonnie's displaced rage was meaningless.

"I can tell you what happened, all I need from you is that you remain calm," Alex suggested.

"You left to plot with him! Everything that has happened is your fault! This place is surrounded by Amishmen who will kill you the moment that I say the word!"

Alex saw a shuffling of feet alongside the bottom edges of the tent. Above them were the shadows of Amishmen, prepared to kill under the false accusation that Alex was a traitor.

"What would your mother say about this?" Reese insinuated.

"Stop with the jokes," Alex warned.

"You don't know anything about the layout of Zone 6. That's information you'll need. Plus your mom likes us. I'm pretty sure she really likes me."

As a response Lonnie pushed Reese to the floor. Reese landed on his back and screamed in pain. His pestering insults ended.

"We'll figure it out. We have drones."

"Which the Hive will be able to detect," David clarified. "Everything that flies within Zone 6 airspace will be shot down."

"What is Takeo going to do?"

"The Hive saw something in him. The same thing it saw in me. The ability to lead. He never saw it in you," Alex claimed.

"It would have if I'd stayed!" Lonnie defended.

"Stayed where?" David asked.

Lonnie bit his lip.

"When the Hive falls I will support you," Alex offered.

"I don't need it."

"If I was with the Hive I would have left by now!" Alex screamed, loud enough for those outside to hear.

"I'm the man who activated the EMP," David recalled as he fearlessly stepped away from the tent, coming to face an arrow pointed towards him.

"They are trying to corrupt you!" Lonnie accused while his face flushed red with anger.

"Without the EMP every individual within here would be dead."

Lonnie turned to leave, but he was too late. The Amishmen supporters had slipped from his flimsy grip. They were ready to kill their former master.

"Maybe you're a part of a Hive," a gunman accused.

"He's not. He recently lost some people important to him and is looking for somebody to blame," Alex justified.

"He has my full support," Reese added. He placed his hand on Lonnie's shoulder as a false symbol of friendship. Lonnie rapidly shrugged it away. "Okay, half support."

"But we all have the same goal."

"That's not true," Eric said as he entered. "I told that to all of you when we first met."

"Where the hell were you?" Lonnie asked.

"You almost killed the ally that you came with. I don't want any more dead. I'm surprised that seeing all the corpses doesn't make you feel the same."

"They chose to defend their land."

"I'm not faulting them, but you are trying to use these people as pawns, trying to spark another fight."

"Takeo—"

"I know about him. It doesn't bother me," Eric revealed. "You all need to leave. Do not come back. Don't bring your war here."

176

"It's not my war," Alex defended. "Whoever the next Hive is, they might destroy everything."

"You're making choices for your people," Lonnie accused.

"I'm not stopping them from going with you. Be gone by the night."

Eric turned away, leaving the men alone.

"This is going to be an awkward ride back," Reese stated.

"I want nothing to do with you," Lonnie proclaimed.

"I meant what I said. If we kill Conrad, I won't oppose you as long as you promise peace. I don't want another war," Alex remarked.

"I still don't trust you."

"You don't have to, but for now we need one another," David stated.

Alex opened the tent flap. The warm passing sun projected a reminder that time was running short.

David went first, deciding to speak to a circle ready for travel. Their horses carried bags of essential food, medical supplies, and weapons.

"I need another promise," Lonnie said. "If I die the Libertarians need somebody to lead them."

"Your mother."

"She's old."

"There has to be somebody else."

"Andy was the only one who could have taken the mantle. I'm sure Takeo told you why he's gone. If I die I deserve it. It's a sign that our family has led long enough."

Alex agreed to mull over Lonnie's terms, and the duo set out to take the day for recruitment. They spoke with large groups and individuals. Those in mourning had a desire for revenge. Some came to their aid right away, some refused, terrified of the prospect of having to face Conrad again.

Those who sat in the middle ground asked for terms regarding them joining the cause. Many wanted to scavenge the treasures within Zone 6. Others asked to be let out of future battles. Alex promised them he would try his best, not that he could bring an end to war, losing him some possible recruits, but allowing him to live with dignity.

David and Reese acted in the same way. It did not take long for the quartet to speak to each of the Amish, and with each one that he spoke to they were bombarded with different questions. The results of Takeo's betrayal made it impossible for some of the group to put their faith in Alex, citing that Alex and the others remained Loyalists and it was in their best interest to leave. Alex was forced to explain his entire story to the others, telling them how he got the mark, and what it meant to him. During the entirety of the recruitment process Alex was forced to focus on the fact that Eric loomed over. He spread his influence over the campground, reminding others that there was no pressure to fight if it was not needed. He did not speak with anger, nor sadness; it was a neutral presentation of fact.

As the night wrapped its influence around the campground, the new recruits had left their positions, traveling by horse and car, all at a similar speed so that one individual did not find themselves miles ahead of the others. Those who were left behind were left with the job of cleaning the remainder of the campground, taking bodies and burying them, granting small services of respect to those who had been lost due to the effects of the battle. The remnants from the Technicians that had been scattered were stripped of their original use, no longer being used for weapons and instead finding new purpose, such as research.

As a parting gift Eric awarded David with what Alex considered a useless endeavor: empty metal shells which were used to produce detonators of the old world. An artifact that Alex thought would only be used as a novelty item.

Alex kept his promise, leaving by the time the night had fallen, his new allies by his side, but the same goal remained. The Hive's death or his own would occur soon.

The road to the Libertarians was torturous. Alex spent long moments wondering if he would disappoint those who followed him; the loss of Patton and Takeo gave little upward mobility to his confidence. It hindered his ability to face the three great confrontations that stood before him. The first two were of allies. He would need to ensure that Sheila let him go free once Conrad was defeated, for Alex was a threat to their imminent reign. The second was having to meet Ives again. The third was needing to face the Hive.

Lonnie directed the group to their new encampment which stole a day's journey away from the Amishmen. The Libertarians had chosen to live on a coast. Their remaining fleet lined the waters, pressed tightly amongst one another. The land contained houses that had been structured by designs of the old world. Each of them shared the similarities of being a withering asset and having enough space to fit twenty men. The differences existed within each of their exteriors. Dark structures lived next to those with eccentric color. None of it mattered.

The Amishmen kept their independent spirit. Some opted to explore the beach. Others mingled with the Libertarians. A select few stayed with their own. The Libertarians were alert with distrust until it was seen that Lonnie led the group. Many approached, asking him for tales of his adventures. A request that he denied.

Lonnie led Alex to a home similar to what he lived in at Riverside. It was made entirely of brown. Its walls had the illusion of being made from trees. He did not knock and entered without courtesy, for their schedule required directness.

The inside was grandiose and mostly bare. A shred of light poured in through windows allowing them to see that in the open space was a sofa, and a left wall comprised of dead black screens. Whoever had once owned it had evacuated. Cardboard boxes were patterned across the floor, full of items of the old world that had no use in the new.

"She's here somewhere," Lonnie suggested.

Alex and Lonnie forked in their directions, urging a small gathering of rats within the entrance to scurry away. As Alex searched for Sheila the theme of old-world wastefulness came into view. He discovered a child's room. Its small bed was surrounded by toys and gadgets.

The other rooms that Alex discovered held his interest. He found a bedroom where storage for clothing was in a separate section. Dust seeped onto dresses and shoes. Alex picked one up and jumped when he saw a rat hidden underneath. Its stature was the size of Alex's forearm. A mixture of green and gray at its lips. An unnatural occurrence.

"What do you want, Conrad?" Alex asked.

It scurried away, leading Alex to the bedroom and saw that the floor had over two dozen rats of the same caliber. They had organized themselves to form the words hello Alex.

"I asked what do you want?"

The rats bound to create a new formation. The minimal sound that came from them was the pattering of feet against the carpeted floor. Some stumbled as they walked. Some moved away in a frantic direction. Some died, filling with gray.

Takeo with me, the words formed. Alex's fists clenched at the reminder of his failure, and Takeo's success to reach his desired point. He held back rage to present calmness.

"Is that all?" Alex asked.

The message changed: *a chosen one.*

It did not surprise him; Conrad had taken a liking to Takeo within the island, and his tenacity made him a potential candidate.

I choose now. Come.

The message gave Alex enough motivation to propel him forward.

As he walked away the animals screeched. He looked back and saw that the letter S had been created before the rodents' usefulness expired. They died with red, green, and gray slowly exiting their mouths. Their quick deaths after little use made it clear that Conrad's degenerative state had increased, pushing his need for an immediate successor.

He rushed towards Lonnie as the idea of arguing with Sheila turned petty. The fate of the world was at stake.

He looked through the structure and found him on the back porch standing with David. On the wooded area was an empty washing tub; within it were many white circles, their purpose unknown. Sheila was nowhere.

"Nobody has spotted her in two days," David said.

"Then we go without her."

"She is the only family I have left." Lonnie paused. "I'll find her after the battle. We need a strategy. More recruits too."

"The Collective has a rendezvous point for Commanders. If we get there they'll fight against the Hive."

"The Collective is only interested in weak enemies," David reminded him.

"I know," Alex said as he realized that the false "heart" was only attacked because of its supposed vulnerable position. "We'll make them think it will be an easy kill."

Reese stumbled outside the room. His eyes were wide, his forehead was dotted with sweat. Exhaustion was evident.

"Great," Lonnie said.

"It will pass," David claimed.

Reese bent over and vomited into the tub. Alex bent down and placed his hand on Reese's back.

For their journey David opted as navigator. A map on the dash contained a few marked red dots symbolizing areas of importance for the vehicle's former owners. David set a new route based on the rendezvous point coordinates, and the internal systems tracked the best way to arrive at their destination. Doing so revealed the vehicle's flaws as it stated that it would take three days' of travel to reach Peddlers Lake. In reality it took two.

The entire truck shared the same fate of old age. When Reese first swung the gun its movements were clunky, lacking proper swivel that would provide accuracy in tight moments. Alex took control of the wheel until the group reached the outskirts of Peddlers Lake. Alex halted the convoy and stepped outside to speak to Lonnie.

"I can only go to the rendezvous point with Reese and Takeo," Alex revealed.

"You better not be trying to escape us," Lonnie commented. "If they see me with the Collective they will think it's an invasion."

"If there's only a few of them, we could take them as hostages."

"It would be a fool's gambit. I'm not planning on dying today," David said.

"Do you seriously think anyone ever is?" Reese jabbed.

"Have you heard of suicide?"

"That's not fair."

"Make sure you get them quickly," Lonnie said. "I'll give our Alliance a real pep talk."

"What are you going to say?" Alex asked.

"You may have told them the truth about the Hive, but I can top that. I'll say that we're a family. People want to feel like they're a part of something."

"That's corny. Let me try," Reese proposed.

"We need to go," Alex said as he chuckled, imagining the disaster that would result in allowing Reese to speak on higher matters.

"You can stay here if you want," Alex suggested to David, his eyes casting back towards the Alliance where audible snippets of Lonnie's speech were within earshot.

"To ensure we beat Conrad I must join you," David decided.

"Is this your way of being special? Because we both feel the same way," Reese pointed out.

"But we didn't do the same things. I should have died as an alternative to aid in increasing Conrad's abilities."

"Don't take all the credit."

"Your time on the island … what was it like?" Alex asked, realizing that he hadn't ever divulged into what they had done.

"Horrible," Reese revealed.

"Likewise," David added.

"At least you got to do something you liked."

"And I need to atone for it … I've found a way."

"It's all of our faults," Alex said.

"Just us three? You're overreacting," Reese explained.

"Not us three. Every human. Every man. Every woman. Past and present. We let Conrad grow into what he is."

"For the sake of our young … genocide can't happen again," David proposed.

"How are you gonna stop it?" Reese asked.

"If it's not us, it'll be someone else," Alex confidently theorized.

"Be a little hopeful we're all going to make it," Reese suggested. "Even without Takeo ... we can still at least survive, even if he hasn't."

"He was the best fighter out of all of us," Alex admitted. "Wherever he is, he's fine."

The ravine was shallow, making it easy to wade through it. As the three of them turned a corner they came to face a cave. Emerging from it was man in a gray suit.

"Alex?" Ives boomed. His beard had grown long, and there were dark circles underneath the man's eyes.

The men embraced without speaking, relieved that the other was still alive.

"Why didn't you come?" Ives inquired with concern.

"After the attack we went to the Libertarians to use their radio. We couldn't use it until we finished a mission. That's when we were ambushed again ... Joining the Hive for a short time was necessary."

"It would have killed you on the spot if you'd refused."

"We found out that it's dying and—"

"Dying?"

"It's weaker than before, but not for long. It's going to choose somebody to follow him. We have an Alliance that can stop it."

"From where?"

"The Amish. Libertarians. Former Loyalists and Technicians."

"How?"

"We asked nicely," Reese commented.

"You should have come back to us instead, but you're safe now."

"We didn't arrive asking for safety," David revealed.

"We're here to end the war," Alex stated.

Ives frowned.

"The Hive's true heart is within the restricted area. The radiation was produced so nobody dared to enter," David explained.

"You've been traveling too much."

"I was told so by the Hive itself."

"You three are men of the Collective, you ..." Ives's string of words ended briefly. "Takeo's dead," he observed.

"No, he left us."

"He betrayed you."

"I'd like to remind you that with each passing second the Hive continues to build its defense," David cautioned.

"I thought the Hive was getting weaker?" Ives countered.

"He actually has a name—"

"No, he doesn't!" Ives denied. "We don't pursue useless wars. We protect the vision of the old world, and shove man forward. Not back to old conflicts ... The two of us need to talk."

Once inside a silver rectangle cast downward from the entrance, sealing the duo from the outside world. The roof was illuminated by a string of white light above. Ahead was a second metal door.

"Are they keeping you as a hostage?" Ives asked. He withdrew a knife that glowed with a blue tint. "We can end them now."

"No. Of course not."

"Then why spread lies?"

"These aren't—this might be our only chance to beat the Hive."

Ives's eyes narrowed. Then he swung a knife at Alex's throat, narrowly missing his target. "Give him back!"

Alex jumped away and formed his dual cannons in defense, restricting their power within the barrel.

"Ives, it's me!" Alex insisted.

Alex parried Ives's second blow with a raise of his right arm. The plasma blade eased into the cannon's exterior shell. Alex crouched and projected an oval forward with his left arm. The bubble pushed Ives away.

"Free his body or I will!"

Ives aimed for Alex's stomach. The elder was side swept by a solid block in the form of a crafted hammer, slamming him into the granite wall, shattering hope of a peaceful outcome.

"I can tell you anything about me!" Alex offered.

Ives pitched his knife towards Alex's head. After it was avoided, Ives revealed a silver band strapped onto his hand. Alex's knowledge of its purpose forced him to the floor, making it so the knife missed as it returned to Ives.

Ives withdrew a second knife and brought it downward. Alex countered by applying blasts from his guns. Both struck Ives's chest but had no effect. A surge of metal expanded from his upper body and spread until his entire frame was protected by a Mecha suit. Engaged onto his back were three silver pipes occupied by purple fire. Twin swords extended Ives's hands, granting him the advantage for the close quarters battle.

Ives pointed his blades forward and advanced rapidly. Alex clumsily conjured his own duo of blades which came close to dissipation once it clashed with Ives. Ives flew upward, and sliced in the same direction, seeking Alex's arms. His failure in doing so allowed Alex to slip past Ives and send a blast directly into the metal door behind them. A ray of sunlight cast through it.

Ives rose and turned downward while spinning his blades in an intimidating whirlwind.

Alex could sense that he was losing power. A shield would not be able to withstand the enemy's blades. A crafted sword would be overpowered, and a bullet stream would be blocked.

"Stop!" Alex demanded as he summoned a short plasma whip from his right arm and dashed forward, missing the downward strike. Ives continued his pursuit, forcing a brash swing from Alex's weapon. The whip ensnared Ives's body, but he managed to cleanly disembody the top layer of Alex's cannon, destroying its serviceability. Alex deflected by blasting Ives's facial coverage. Ives's jet pack ignited and he blasted into the air, evading the majority of the shot.

The damage delivered to both men was prominent. Alex's right arm burned in agony. The inner components of the cannon trickled to the ground in a mixture of wires, metal rings, motherboards, and sparks. The left half of Ives's mask had fallen. The skin underneath was covered with blood.

"Ives," Alex pleaded. "It's me. I met you for the first time by the wicker tree."

Ives spat blood downward and screamed. His purple flames increased. Alex ended it by creating a continued beam that was initially blocked by Ives's swords, but within seconds penetrated, shredding into Ives's armor, reaching his skin. As Ives crashed to the ground, he left a trail of blood.

Alex ran to him and saw that his wounds were deeper than expected. His stomach had been cut through completely. Alex cradled the body with great regret. He wanted nothing more than to reverse his action.

"I'm sorry-I-I need help to lead them."

The door to the inner cave rose. A pattering of feet slowly poured upwards, prepared to kill. Alex stood, ready to take his last stand.

CHAPTER SIXTEEN

THE COLLECTIVE

Alex spotted many feet within close proximity to one another. An impressive blockade.

"Stay back!" he warned.

From behind booms echoed, urging Alex to turn his head. A group of openings behind a cloud of smoke had been created. David emerged first, followed by Reese.

The rising wall on the cave's inner end revealed Collective soldiers in an identical stance to the Alliance: weapons raised upwards, prepared to kill.

"Don't attack! We're not here to invade!" Alex shouted.

"I know, we saw the battle," a voice replied. The identities of the Collective line remained hidden by masks of a Commander. Hiding their faces and distorting their voices.

"You saw that Ives attacked me first?" Alex asked.

The masked figure dissipated his covering, revealing that Commander Green was alive.

"Good to see you," Alex responded.

"Likewise," Commander Green said.

The other figure removed their covering to reveal Hazel was also alive.

Alex spotted fresh corpses dotted across the floor behind the Collective line. The walls were riddled with bullet holes.

"I want to make it clear that I'm not with the Hive," Alex declared.

"If you were we would be dead," Green guessed. "We heard your story. You're right about the Hive changing. Hazel and I both saw it personally. Ives wanted to have us killed after that. Even in a time like this we're still fighting with each other."

"The way of man," David said.

"Or just Ives was a prick," Reese said.

"He's the reason you remain breathing."

"Still a prick."

"We're not with the Hive either," Hazel said.

"I would know if you were," Alex stated. "You're with us then. Our Alliance."

Commander Green nodded in agreement. "Do you mind sharing weapons?"

"We do have some spares," Hazel offered, her eyes cast backwards to the bodies, "especially now."

Alex kept his remaining cannon on a low frequency in preparation for a sudden attack, while thrusting himself back into the lead of Collective soldiers who walked him towards the base.

The large open room was multifaceted. At the back end was a gathering of sleeping rolls packed tightly together. On the right side, an influx of old world weapons hung from gun racks, some of them being idle Mecha suits.

Those within the Collective began the process of moving their deceased comrades. As they were transferred, turmoil gripped Alex. He speculated that through faster movement he would have been able to stop the civil skirmish and convince them to join his cause in the upcoming battle.

"Who's the leader of this Alliance?" Green asked.

"Me," Alex replied.

"Then come take your pick. I'll get mine ready," Green offered, sending Alex towards the Mecha suits. There were only a few left to take;

each held an allure. The most common one comprised of fading red and blue. The red was striped. One line ran down the middle, the only two extended throughout the arms, leaving the rest of the Mecha to be painted by a frosted blue.

Alex hastily picked a suit within the center, for time burned away. It was golden in color. Its left arm was donned by a trio of silver barrels.

Once within it, the armor closed onto his body allowing him to experience the full power of a Mecha for the first time. His previous experiences with them were punctured with glitches, diminishing their potential. Once connected, his limp right arm jumped with life. He could sense that it gave him the same abilities as his previous cannon, allowing him to craft differentiating melee weapons. The left barrels had distinct purposes. One would stream plasma; the second held a magnetic pull; the third could spark fire and ice.

Underneath its great power Alex sensed a limitation, for it had the ability to make large unnatural jumps, but didn't have enough strength to sustain flight.

"It's going to be weird going back to the city," Hazel mentioned whilst Alex adjusted to his suit.

Alex froze, remembering his promise that Zone 6 would not belong to any single faction in the battle's aftermath.

"The Collective shouldn't expect to stay long," Alex warned.

"Zone 6 was ours," Hazel said.

"The citizens come first," Alex sternly decided. "But we deserve it."

"They do more than us."

"We're supposed to stick together."

"I'm not from the Collective anymore."

"But where is there to go?"

"The world is much bigger than a few Zones."

"Well, wherever you go, the Collective will eventually take it."

"I know. That's the problem," Alex admitted both to Hazel and himself. Behind Conrad's defeat a second obstacle would present itself: factions fighting endlessly over leadership. Human lives would be taken vainly. Alex looked to the Collective faces, wondering how quickly they would turn from ally to foe.

"It's not a problem. It's what we do," Hazel declared.

"After this battle you have the choice to go anywhere. Don't get stuck," Alex suggested.

"I wouldn't just leave like that. I got to be a Private because they saw me winning a few fights as a citizen. It took too much hard work."

"Who taught you to fight?"

"My family."

"At some point they were killed," Alex speculated.

"Yes."

"Then we have the same story."

"Did Amishmen kill your parents too?"

"No. I barely even remember it. All I know is they certainly were a part of something much bigger than us."

"Whoever it is the Collective will stand by your side. I'll stand by your side. I already hate them almost as much as I hate Amishmen."

"You'll have to get used to them," Alex stated.

"Why?"

"They're a part of the Alliance."

Hazel crossed her arms. "I haven't seen one since my parents died."

"It will be hard. Your mind and body will tell you to lash out, but it isn't their fault. The Collective, we did the same to them. Plus Libertarians, Technicians, Loyalists. Other groups who we didn't even know had a name. They have forgiven us because we are bound by our true enemy."

"The Hive didn't force them," Hazel defended.

"If it had, would you have forgiven them? What if it was the Collective then, would you hate us? We were just as awful as the people who killed your family. Everybody has it in them. Don't be mad at the Amishmen. Be angry at what we all are. Use it as fuel in battle to protect the people who guide you."

"The Collective isn't like that," Hazel rapidly sputtered. "If we were at full strength then we would have been peaceful."

"We were once the center of the world ... we were worse than the Hive."

The young Hazel frowned as she pondered his words.

"What's it like out there?"

"Terrifying," Alex admitted. "But worth it."

Hazel nodded in interest. "Do I have to be friends with Amishmen?"

"Not friends," Alex said. "But have some courtesy. I understand that you feel alone. I did when my family died, but you're not. The Alliance is on your side."

"Let's get this done," Green said. The Collective soldiers stood in a still formation, patiently waiting for a catalyst that would instigate movement.

The group left the cave and marched in a strict formation in silence, driven to save the world from tyranny. The loudest aspect of their procession was the few vehicles that they brought forth which purred, bellowing a low vibration.

The Collective were brought to the Alliance. Lonnie had found a rallying point in the form of a building meant for educating Collective citizens. The structure was abandoned and ripe for residence. The small army gathered within the grass field next to it. The greenery had oddly not grown in the aftermath of neglect, for the false blades stretched to a few inches high. Their location was off the main road. At various points large signs sprang from the earth, projecting messages of Collective vitality through pictured depictions. One showed the treaty that brought the world together as one. Another gave the impression that Collective citizens lived with over-robust happiness as they navigated within Zone 6.

Lonnie was elevated above the gathered army on a middle section amongst a diagonal ascendancy of silver benches.

"How have they been getting along?" Alex asked.

"A few fights here and there," Lonnie revealed.

Alex nodded. "Is there anything you want to say?"

Lonnie shrugged. "It's your Alliance. I'm just a part of it."

"A speech would be wise," David suggested as he trudged upwards with Reese. "I have heard whispers from all sides that they want to take Zone 6 for themselves. Guide your people so a skirmish does not break out."

"And a few of them are getting drunk," Reese accused.

"Possibly you're their role model."

"What about the Amishmen? The Technicians? The Loyalists? They have nobody telling them to stay calm," Lonnie said.

"I'll make sure they do," Alex promised.

"Just make sure my people end up okay. They'll need a new leader," Lonnie stated.

"What about your mommy?" Reese poked.

"She's gone," Lonnie decided. "It's time for somebody new."

"I will if your people behave themselves. I'm going to make Zone 6 a place of peace," Alex decided.

"Stop being dramatic, Lonnie. You won't die," Reese claimed.

"I didn't say I will, but my family has taken ownership of the Libertarians for too long."

"I'll do it," Alex promised.

"Unfortunately, I won't be joining you," David revealed. "I have seen so little of this world. Greatness as an inventor will only be accomplished when I venture to places I have never been and discover textures that are unknown, but I'll always bring my findings back."

"I better see it first," Reese warned.

"Don't waste your life, Reese," Alex requested.

"I want to come with you. After what we've done, relaxing doesn't feel the same," Reese stated, his eyes drifting to two beautiful women many feet away. "Besides, the possibilities are endless."

The Alliance had grown impatient. The small fights that Lonnie referred to were beginning to expand. Alex stood; it was time.

Alex's failures gnawed at him as he prepared to speak, making him apprehensive. He doubted if he would be able to take full command of what stood before him. Whether he was worthy of making the correct decisions not only in battle, but in the aftermath. All that brought him down, Alex pushed aside. It was time to end Conrad's reign.

"The Hive is a human!" Alex revealed. His words caused the crowd to give him their full attention. "He went by the name of Conrad Westwick. A legend of the old world. Part of the reason why it came together as one. He lives within the city. He is the Hive and he terrorizes us because human beings were going to take alien planets for their own. He thought we couldn't coexist with them. He was right, but we need to prove him wrong. Be better than our past. The people who you're standing beside right now, consider them to be your brothers and sisters. Not just now, but forever. Treat every human that way. Even Loyalists. Even those who are taken."

Alex raised his hand and slowly peeled off his glove, revealing the W that marked him as former property of Conrad.

"I spent time with Conrad. I was forced to work under his regime. It's a part of my past. I'm not ashamed of it. From it I learned that he's dying, but it wants a new host. If it picks wrong, our world will fall. If the right people rise, man will ascend into something greater."

Alex stepped back from his position, terrified that his words would result in nothing but laughter and interruptions. Instead, the force of over two hundred nodded in agreement, ready for battle. Ready to be led.

Alex expanded his golden Mecha, covering his body. "Let's move out!" Alex commanded as his helmet crashed downward, shrouding his head with a golden crown.

The front line consisted of formidable power. It was where the majority of vehicles chose to linger alongside wielders of Mecha suits, flamethrowers, RPGs, and plasma weapons. David and Lonnie were amongst them, roles that they had chosen for themselves.

They were backed by a mixture of characters. The right flank were outcasts, former Loyalists, Technicians, and Amishmen who had only a few of their own within the Alliance. The left was a collection of Libertarians and Collective soldiers who remained with their squads, which were designated long before the Alliance's formation.

A few Amishmen scouts were sent ahead, riding beasts and two-wheeled vehicles making Alex decide on a direct attack.

There had been changes made to the Zone 6 outskirts. The trenches had been completed. Additional troughs had been added. The guard towers that were once empty husks had been filled. The front gate remained with the same bars of purple plasma.

"Section one," Alex called. The entire communication system of the Alliance had been set to one untapped frequency courtesy of David. "Attack the towers."

Before moving Alex reminded himself of Patton, a boy who did not deserve his ending; Takeo, a man corrupted; and Ives, an elder made a coward, and how their fates were orchestrated by Conrad.

Alex lifted his hand and brought it downward. The action propelled the front lines forward onto the outskirts.

Those within the guard towers made the first attack with inaccurate bullets towards the assault. The first wave broke off in different directions, making sharp turns, scattering the enemy's fire. The Alliance's first reaction was to cause the fall of the towers through threaded attacks on the tower's legs, forcing them to crumble onto the ground, pushing the guardsmen from their elevated positions.

Alex used his suit to jump high onto the tower's platforms. On his first attempt he blasted cool ice to make the enemy's body unmovable. He moved to a second tower and magnetically pushed on its steel legs, forcing the guardsmen to jump from the tumbling structure.

Through his actions Alex was able to get a closer look at the defenders. They had fresh W markings on their malnourished bodies. Alex did not recognize their faces as citizens he had seen, confirming their status as refugees to the city. A group untrained for war who had spent their lives searching for a cause, finding it eventually in defending the Hive. They gave up quickly by running towards the trenches. When close to death they begged for forgiveness. Dropping to their knees, throwing their weapons aside, and pledging loyalty to the Alliance. The skirmish was too fast paced for their requests to be considered. Most were either shot down from the crossfire between those within the trenches and the Alliance, or were brutally crushed by a pursuing vehicle.

From the trenches, turrets released a strike of revenge. A truck in front of Alex had its tires penetrated, forcing it to flip, killing those inside. Additional vehicles soon shared the same result.

The retaliation from the Alliance was swift. They jumped into the first trench and cut down those who opposed them. Alex joined in, primarily using his magnetic cannon not to kill, but to injure. Within the trough he spotted a tuft of back hair, and at first, he thought it was Takeo. The man turned and showed his unknown face. He'd become a helpless victim of war. His body was ripped in half by the steel claws of an Amishman. The citizen beside him fell through a purple portal generated by a former Technician, disappearing forever.

A bullet bounced off Alex's steel back, unable to reach his skin. He turned to face the perpetrator and saw that before him a refugee screamed for revenge. Alex pushed the man without touching him, his magnet sending the enemy deep into the ground.

The defenders within the first trench were quickly killed by steel, lead, and plasma. The Alliance advanced.

Those in the further trenches peeked from their cover to investigate the carnage. In defense they used pistols. The shots rattled the dirt but did not hit the Alliance. Many climbed out from the pits below. They ran to the Zone 6 entrance and screamed for help. Their pleas went unheard.

From the top of the concrete wall, snipers and turrets pelted below.

"Mecha suits! Take out the turrets on the wall!"

The Technicians and Collectives flew into the air and destroyed the turrets above. The brick crumbled. The bodies on top of the wall fell either back inside the city or plummeted outside it.

Those in the second trench were murdered. The occupiers of the third searched for a savior. Alex chose to take the role.

"Hold your fire!"

Alex's message went unheard. The Alliance violently continued their crusade, painting the dirt red.

"They can be hostages!"

The refugees curled on the ground, tearfully accepting their end.

"They can be property!"

His third offering broke through to the group. The killing mostly stopped. The unsettling nature of his own troops sickened Alex.

Before he could say another word the plasma bars dissipated and the steel door rose. The refugees turned towards it and extended their hands. From a sliver within the door a claw emerged and sliced through the closest refugee. Additional talons slithered through the opening and killed them. Not by the hand of the Alliance, but of modified animals. Conrad.

He sent forth a cohort of the same bear that Alex had faced off against on the island. They all had six limbs, six eyes, and claws that cut through human bodies with ease. From above the concrete wall a group of both small bees and hefty vultures sprang into the sky. A black swarm of danger.

"Don't shoot yet!" David called. On a motorcycle he advanced forward, moving past the Alliance, making himself the first to face Conrad. His hand held a hand grenade.

"Hold your fire!" Alex shouted.

David lobbed the explosive at the approaching animals. Once it landed, an explosion of blue light came from the ground. The bears submitted to its power. They froze in place, hard gray spilling from their lips.

David retreated back to the Alliance. "EMP bomb. An invention of mine."

The Hive's flying mammals descended in a swarm. The bullets that came for it were ineffective.

The bees ate away at Alliance bodies. Once a stinger was implemented, the insects regrew another. Alex was protected by his metal skin, and when a swarm came towards him, he pushed it away, sending the insects flying in an alternative direction. Once blown upwards he used a blast of ice to freeze their flight pattern.

"Handicap them!" Alex called, as he learned that the insects were too small for bullets. He set an example by continuing to utilize his cool air. His lead was followed. The animals were killed by the use of electrical currents, firestorms, and rays of ice.

The bears reached the Alliance. One vaulted through the air and crashed within Alex's vicinity. It used its left claws to swipe at him. An attack he avoided by sending his magnet to the ground and propelling himself backwards. In the process he tripped and as the bear thrust towards him Alex shot a beam of plasma at the animal's head. Green blood exploded from the hole.

A second charged directly towards Alex. Its speed was unmatched by any human opponent that Alex had faced. While charging it lifted its mouth, and a wave of supersonic energy burst from its mouth so powerful that it knocked Alex onto his back. He fell through the trench and tumbled backwards, but his recovery was quick, and as the beast slashed downwards, Alex fell once again as he jumped backwards, narrowly missing the deadly tips of its claws. Alex blew cool air towards the animal, hoping to stop it in its place, but his attempt failed as the beast responded with a second scream. The sound waves broke though Alex's blast of winds and forced him deeper into the ground.

He could not move. The unfamiliar feeling of being unable to move anything left Alex screaming.

As the bear screamed it slowly stalked closer. Alex refused to use any of his long-range defense mechanisms, for they would only backfire within his own skin.

The bear was a mere foot away from him. The pounding screech brought great irritation to Alex's ears. He refused to close his eyes, staring at the animal, into Conrad, as death descended upon him.

Alex embraced death, its cool touch itching upon his skin, The bear raised his claws but its screeching ended, due to a close-range laser blast. The bear turned towards its originator and pierced their flesh with two of its available arms. A scream tore through the air. Alex rose and saw that it was Private Hazel who had saved his life, sacrificing her own in the process.

In a bid for revenge Alex struck upwards at the animal's right arms, managing a clean strike with his sword. The animal screamed as its arms were decapitated from its body. Its electronic innards were exposed, meshed with natural organs, flesh, and blood, leaving it with its two legs, and unnatural left arms.

It slashed towards Alex. He backed away, his anger over Hazel's death fueling his movement. She was young and innocent. Having suffered a fate that Alex knew he would have to deliver to Conrad himself.

The animal followed his flow of movement. It remained on its hind legs, unable to descend downwards, but even with its great injury it did not slow down, constantly slashing at Alex, not allowing him to make any accurate shots against it.

An opportunity arose when the beast tried to force Alex into the ground with another supersonic scream. Learning from Takeo, Alex used the attack to move forward while the enemy was engaged with its rage. He pushed it away with his magnet. The heaviness of the animal brought forth a great strain, but eventually the beast tumbled backwards, defenseless against him. Alex detracted his sword and slashed the animal's remaining arms.

Alex jumped forward and stabbed its mouth, then its legs. The bear fell to the ground, rendering it useless in battle. Alex climbed on top of it, whispering into the bear's ear.

"I'm the best you could have had," Alex said, knowing that the message would reach Conrad.

CHAPTER SEVENTEEN

THE CITY

The Alliance quickly set explosives to the wall, opening entry into the market which was guarded by Conrad's third wave of defense: citizens. They froze as the Alliance revealed their great numbers. Alex recognized some of their faces, for they held an expression of fear that he had seen while formally supervising their lives. Their bodies were placed behind the flimsy structures of wood and metal stands.

As the Alliance moved closer, the citizens broke from their cemented state. Their resistance was far more advanced than the refugees had created, but not enough to break the Alliance's advancement.

Alex barged through a wooden stand before him. The lumber smashed against the man who crouched underneath it, submerging his body under a timber avalanche.

"Join us. Help us beat Conrad!" Alex offered, extending his hand.

The man scoffed and turned to using his pistol. Before doing so Alex struck him to the point of unconsciousness.

Alex proceeded and ducked behind a second stand. Above him a rack of clothing swayed from the earth's winds. A barrel peeked through them. With his right arm Alex manifested a sword and slashed upward. The guns quickly retreated back. A second later Alex's back was pelted with dots of pain. He turned and sent the perpetrator flying backwards. The onslaught on his back stole his ability to jump great distances.

As citizens were rapidly cut down, the Alliance stole their cover, giving a small crevice of breathing room within the skirmish.

"Get them to surrender!" Alex shouted.

His call was echoed by the Alliance, who mocked the citizens with imminent death if they refused to submit. The citizens ignored the proposal.

The citizens continued with their raw style of attack, leaving themselves open to be killed while they aggressively advanced in an attempt to get close to the Alliance. Alex watched as the boy who had offered a truce continued to navigate the battlefield. Bullets did not hit him, and he was able to avoid the onslaught that the others around him faced. The signs of the battle ending were nowhere near a grasping point, and Alex instantly regretted his decision to not push for stronger diplomatic means.

Those on both sides retaliated from the action. The citizens attempted an assault, but it was ended by the sheer force of the united invaders. Their bodies were blown to the mud within seconds while the flesh and blood tore from their bodies. Their body count piled high while the Alliance lost few.

Alex was enraged; he wanted nothing more than to strike down each and every citizen, ending their lives for their defiance. He felt trapped, wanting to kill the others, but Alex found himself turning away from the idea. It was not viable. They were not evil, just a group of people who had been treated unfairly by the Collective, and now searched for revenge in the form of following Conrad's orders. The thought quenched Alex's anger, putting him in a position where he could see the enemy's side.

"Join us!" Alex requested.

The Alliance soldiers continued to seep into the city. The citizen forces were quickly surrounded.

"You've been wronged! I can make it right. Our Alliance can stop the fighting!" Alex told the captured civilians.

"The Hive is better than you!" an adolescent boy heckled. His skin was tan. His hair curly. Alex recognized him. His parents had been killed by himself and Takeo together during an investigation. His anger was justified.

"It lies to you. It's not an alien—"

"We know. Conrad showed us the truth right away. We were happy. Then you came. The Collective killed my parents like it was nothing!" the adolescent claimed as he slammed his fist against the dirt.

"We were wrong, and I hope to make it right."

"You can't get into the restricted area."

"Nothing's impenetrable," David said.

"There had to be more citizens than this," Lonnie said. "Where are they?"

"Conrad told them that a fight was coming, and if they didn't want to join they were allowed to leave. If you get chosen you better be like that."

"You can leave too. Find a water supply, take any weapons or food you need. Just be safe. It's a dangerous world."

"What?"

"All of you who don't want to fight with us, go!" Alex commanded.

The captured citizens turned from the battle and fled into the forest.

"In the city, the Hive is everywhere," the boy warned.

Alex considered the possibility that the curly haired boy was nothing more than a distraction to stop the Alliance from further proceeding. A brief thought of Conrad's nature killed the idea, for he had welcomed Alex's challenge.

"Is this force large enough to challenge him?" David asked the boy.

"I don't really think so," he answered.

"Why are we taking advice from a six-year-old?" Reese pondered.

"I'm thirteen."

"You look nine."

"When we get into the city, move from building to building!" Alex commanded.

"That won't be viable. If it's everywhere Conrad will be in each skyscraper. There won't be opportunity," David theorized.

"Not unless we create it," Alex said.

"You'll need a distraction," Lonnie said as he willed himself into an M-ATV. "Where can I place a second attack?"

"The far right," Alex said. "We'll go from the left. Once we get close to the restricted section I can radio you, and we'll meet in the middle."

"A few of you need to come with me." A few bodies marched forward, ready to join.

"You better take care of my people," Lonnie warned.

"I will," Alex said with a nod.

"The Collective should have made you an Officer."

The bodies that volunteered remained with Lonnie and surged to the right.

As Alex's battalion surged forward the landscape slowly shifted. The heart of the city was defended by Loyalists. Their skin markings showed intent to kill for Conrad. They had the will to do so, for their battle abilities were stronger than the citizens that came before.

The Loyalists screamed at the Alliance to stop. They complied, deciding to remain at a standstill while staring at an added gate. Alex refused to shoot, and the Loyalists matching his actions ignited the idea that they not only could be turned to join the Alliance, but that they actually wanted to.

"We want to see who you all are! Walk forward slowly!" a Loyalist demanded.

"Do it, but keep your weapons up," Alex said.

Those ahead of him listened; a few steps were taken.

"Wait! Look to the ground!" David suggested.

Alex cast his eyes downward. Deep within the dirt he spotted blinking red lights embedded within the surface: land mines. Ahead of him a few bodies exploded in a mountain of fire, cutting off hope of a diplomatic discussion.

The opposing sides traded bullets. The Loyalists had set up plasma barriers to hide behind. The Alliance end had the protection of abandoned vehicles and unoccupied tents. The flimsy material found itself torn once bullets blasted through it.

"Find cover!" Alex called.

The Alliance rapidly lost both people and ground. Alex took instant action to combat it.

"The animals! Send them forward down the center!" Alex demanded. The Amishmen gathered their horses and released them directly through the middle. As the beasts converged, their lives were ended by the explosives, clearing a path for the Alliance. Death seeped into the atmosphere. Horse body parts and debris were thrown in differing directions, trailed by smoke and shrapnel. The beasts cried in protest, becoming weary of their masters' demands.

Following the sacrifice, the Alliance refused to cower. They stepped onto the path, moving close enough to harbor an attack.

"Explosives, now!" Alex called.

A lobbying of detonators came from the Alliance. The burst of energy scattered the Loyalist forces. The silver gate toppled, becoming a piece of twisted metal.

As the last of the Alliance's beasts attempted to continue they were killed before completing their mission. Both dog and horse collapsed before reaching their destination.

The gap between the Alliance and Loyalist was almost nothing. The two groups stood on equal footing. Both groups had snipers who picked one another off with slow but consistent accuracy.

Bravery came from each side. Neither had members retreating. The Alliance jumped over the mammal bodies, becoming careful not to step foot on the ground. David was one of the few who led the charge. His masterful footwork was copied.

"Aim for the ground!" David suggested.

Once bullets hit the ground it was found that they were able to discharge the remaining mines.

"Mechas in the air!" Alex commanded.

The Loyalists' attention diverted to the sky, allowing the ground troops to experience a shred of relief. The Mechas desperately maneuvered in avoidance of bullets. They were only able to do so for a short time. They fell to the earth as their wings were clipped quickly.

"Down! Down!" Alex called. From his cannon he continuously blew cool ice and spread blazing fire, maiming Loyalist defenses.

The Loyalists began to break. Their backs were shot while trying to retreat, their slaughtered bodies crashing to the ground.

"Keep going!" Alex heeded. He placed his hand forward and sent a cool blast of air towards an approaching enemy. He followed the act by pulling a Loyalist towards him, knocking him unconscious with his metal arm.

Alex took multiple hits. His golden metal armor had been carved with dents. Marks that would have killed him without his shell. The damage forced him into slower movements, as his symbiosis with the Mecha had lowered in quality.

A harsh force collided with Alex's back, sending him stumbling forward.

"Great," Alex complained.

He wheeled around and swept a continuous circular beam behind him.

"Look out!" a voice shouted. The call was too late. Alex's beam struck the enemy's hand. They screeched in pain as their body was revealed. The previously invisible Loyalist was draped in the same outfit that Alex had seen within the island, an all-black covering with the exception of a glowing blue glove wrapped around their right hand.

While observing Alex was kicked in the ribs. The injured man disappeared, bit the drippings of blood from its wrist, his agonizing whimper revealing his location.

Alex released a push from his magnet. The tumbling outline of a body imprinted itself within the earth three times. Alex was punched again. He aimlessly slashed his sword and hit a body. It had etched itself into the Loyalist's skin. They flashed between visibility as the Loyalist perished.

Alex released the corpse and returned his attention east. A great weight descended onto his neck. The familiar sensation of being pinned down rapidly came upon him. To escape Alex thrust his magnet to the earth, allowing him to divert left. The foot that crushed him slipped. He released two shots of plasma. The first missed, the second hit, ripping through the Loyalist's heart. Its feet matched the weapon of its brother. Blue dots appeared where its toes ended.

Alex rose and the Loyalists decimated those who refused an offer of ceasefire, fighting until their last breaths.

Alex killed the last one. A Loyalist whose Mecha suit had various small holes on his back, arms, torso and legs. The circles projected small jets, allowing him to navigate the field with tenacity.

Alex attempted to pull the enemy inward. The enemy's body did not comply. Alex could feel that his magnet lacked the power to shift the heavy metal.

He forced himself near Alex. As a countermeasure Alex shot his plasma stream forth. The enemy dodged with ease, and as he got close lifted his hand and spat fire. Alex exerted cool air. The forces of nature clashed. The flames licked past Alex's defense, dwindling his cache.

Alex dove to the right. Once he did the flames engulfed his former position, some of them managing to burn his arm.

He crashed to the ground, hauled his suit upright, and sent a blast of plasma directly into the fire-bearer's heart.

Alex's arm taunted him with pain. His connection had been severed. Not only had he been damaged, but when he glanced at his forces it was clear that they had been reduced to half.

"Alex. Stand up. Zone 6 is ours for the taking," David encouraged.

"It'll take five minutes, tops," Reese said.

His eyes turned towards Zone 6. It looked barren, but Alex knew in reality it crawled with enemies, placing fear within him that they would be reduced from half of their original Alliance to nothing.

"Forward," Alex commanded.

Between the ranks of perished Loyalists, a small group of vehicles was left unattended. Reese took command of an M-ATV. Alex sat within the passenger seat. David placed himself as gunner.

Prior to departing Alex sifted through the fallen, searching for Takeo's hulking figure amongst the deceased. Across the field both Loyalist and Alliance looked the same. Their bodies remained still on the ground, never to speak again. Alex found nothing.

The group moved forward with caution. Their eyes often darted to the ground in search of land mines. They spread thin and entered each building with careful observation on what was within it. Those within vehicles trailed behind, only opting to move forward when the area ahead had been confirmed clear. The force moved with a slowed pace as rushing would leave them sloppy.

Conrad's dying essence spread throughout the urban scenery. His vile insides had gathered on the ground and low points of walls. Much of it existed in the form of hardened gray; a small amount was slimy green. Some areas were in the midst of its crystallization.

Through his paranoia Alex called for an extra incentive once they reached the former military residency. As a response the Alliance picked up rubble and chucked it outward. A rock thrown farther than the others skirted a few bounces and deflected backwards once it hit the illusion of open space. A hexagon panel suddenly appeared, then vanished as quick as it came.

"Throw others!" Alex requested. The group halted and threw a cascade of rubble towards the invisible wall. Additional sparks revealed themselves, paired with the emergence of more hexagons. As the debris continuously smashed against the invisible wall, brief glimpses of what lay ahead slowly revealed itself. The shapes of Conrad's forces stood together in waiting. They were of the Hive. Controlled, and unmoving. Then they advanced.

To the right side a large portion was in the midst of departure, leaving to meet with Lonnie's distraction, giving the Alliance a slight chance.

A sudden burst of both plasma and lead bullets came from the empty space that refused to fully reveal the other side.

"Behind the buildings! Go!" Alex guided. The rapidness of enemy fire emitted incredible strength, slaughtering the members of the Alliance who ran behind the structures in a desperate bid for cover.

Alex dashed off his passenger seat and forced himself left, followed by a small group of Alliance members alongside David.

"Back! Keep going back!" Alex called through his radio signal.

Alex followed his own orders. As he ran he was crushed under a great pile of metal. His slow loss of connection to the Mecha forced him to move using brute strength.

The interior of the darkened building he ran through was illuminated through a thin sliver of light from an Alliance member ahead. The flashlight attachment strapped onto his weapon allowed small areas of the building to be seen. On both sides of the building was a long desk. The desk glass remained intact. The floor was made of checkered tile. Most of it was broken, rusted, and littered with dirt.

The assault from Conrad stopped, but the advancement of his feet continued.

"Fight! Fight against me. Find a way. Don't disappoint," Conrad's voices called.

"Stop!" Alex commanded as he froze his retreat. "Break the glass!"

Those within the building ran to both sides, shattered the glass, and hopped over the elongated wooden desks.

It was revealed that on the other side of the material black monitors had been placed underneath. Screens which had once been used to watch the remainder of the building had been relegated to uselessness.

The shuffle of feet stopped from all ends of the battle. Alex knew what it meant. Conrad's technology was failing him, giving an opening to act.

Cheers rained from the Alliance soldiers outside. They were cut short by gunfire. Conrad had quickly recovered.

"Keep under your cover!"

"You're reckless. Disappointment. Unworthy," Conrad mocked. His legion was growing closer. Their shadows took a sudden presence within the entrance way then dripped into the building with a lethal supply. "I am near choosing. You are no longer one. Forgotten. Exterminated. A failure," Conrad informed. His voices echoed against one another as opposed to being in perfect synchrony.

Conrad's forces brought a heaping of white light across the room which made the white visible. On it was the Collective's blue circle. Within the middle Conrad's W marking was etched in gold.

"My City. My People. Not be yours."

The message came not only from inside, but distant voices within the exterior.

"Hey," David whispered. From his hand he withdrew a second EMP grenade. David stood and smashed the weapon into the middle of the Hive's forces. While he did so Alex pulled the Hive forces inward.

Conrad yelped. Then screamed. His bodies met the tiles below. An influx of hardened gray burst from them. The lights that he provided shut off, turning the room back to its dark origins.

"How many did you make?"

"There's two left. Reese is equipped with the other," David revealed.

"Hit the entrances!"

The Hive bodies on the outskirts of the initial burst stiffened. Unable to reach for their weapons, the Alliance made their attack.

"Good! Use your soldiers!" Conrad said while he sent forth additional bodies into the building.

"Keep fighting!" Alex called into his radio as a path to boost morale. He blasted ice towards the approaching Hive. His desired result was not met, his arm only projecting chilling wind. Weakness brushed within him as the connection to his Mecha suit vanished. He collapsed onto the ground under the metal weight. He groveled with regret as he realized the cause of his sickness came from David's invention.

As the Hive jumped over the desks Alex's connection to his suit reignited, allowing him to cross his arms in defense as a Hive fist crawled its way towards his helmet.

"Kill it!" Alex called. Those who remained inside followed his will and sent shots towards Conrad's failing bodies.

"Join me. The south. My building," Conrad's bodies called weakly. Those that crawled inward were killed by outside turret fire.

Alex's eyes ravaged past the entrance and met with the origin of Conrad's fall. Reese remained in his M-ATV. He remained in expert control over the vehicle. His right hand was stiff on the wheel while his left was in constant movement shifting between gears. In the backseat an Amishman spread turret fire. The car was subject to attack, but due to evasive handling the bullets missed their target.

"Yes!" Alex called. Then, seeing streams of plasma heading in his direction, he screamed, "Reese, back!"

Reese opted to listen.

"Stay slow!" Alex cautioned, making sure that he did not repeat the same mistake of approaching Conrad too swiftly.

"I have chosen! My replacement will arrive!" Conrad revealed.

As Alex emerged from his building Reese's car stopped next to him after it crafted an impressive skid across the concrete, forming a cloud of dust. The Amishmen that controlled the turret had been killed.

The Alliance tried to move forward, but once they got close enough to the wall they found that they were unable to get past it and perished as a result. The skirmish quieted.

"Nope," Reese told David as he attempted to hop inside the car.

"Excuse me?" David asked.

"Sorry, manners. May you please take your feet and entire body out of my car."

"You require a gunner."

"Not where I'm going."

"Where would that be?" Alex asked.

"The restricted Zone. It's here now," he said.

"I can't believe you figured that out before I did," David groaned.

"How do you know?" Alex asked.

"These things called eyes," Reese stated, pointing to the right where a silver dome with a long antenna resided. An object that was not within the city when Alex was last there.

"If we take it out what does it mean?" Alex asked.

"The true nature of the city will be revealed," David said.

"We're too late," Alex said as his ears became attuned to Conrad's message.

"Not yet. That's Conrad's pattern of speech," David said.

The Alliance had been dwindled down to less than fifty voices. A head-on assault would be their downfall. A change in strategy was necessary.

"It's along this line?" Alex asked.

"Of course it is," Reese said.

"I was asking David."

"For one of the first times he's right," David said.

"You mean the sixth time," Reese shot back. "I was right about where the Hub was."

"That was a false Hub," Alex corrected.

"Okay, five times."

"What's your plan?" Alex asked.

"Just watch and learn," Reese said.

David attempted to open the car door, finding that it was stuck.

"After this, both of you go get a life," Reese said as the car surged forward, breaking free from the restraints on conversation. The car rammed forward. Conrad's forces shot at the vehicle.

The car dashed both left and right with power only one with a clear mind could possess. Within seconds it forced itself into the shield generator. An explosion came from it. The invisible tiles ahead collapsed. The camouflage disappeared and a blue beam found its footing within the grave of Reese's sacrifice.

CHAPTER EIGHTEEN

THE KING

Reese's direct contact with the stealth seeker caused the blue wave from the EMP to stretch across the land. Before it hit, Alex dispatched his Mecha suit so that it wouldn't be bonded to him forever. The golden plates fell from his body leaving him armor- less.

The scenery ahead showed that Conrad's sickness had reached far beyond the restricted Zone. Large gray clumps of his residue sat across the ground alongside buildings.

"Attack!" Alex shouted, attempting to shove Reese's death away from his mind, but it ate away at him and he forced tears down. Despite the adrenaline of combat, it was all he could think about.

The Alliance took priority of killing the Hive which lay decommissioned on the ground and the newly arrived Technicians who remained still unable to move, unable to fight. Amishmen showed their mastery in combat by using weapons to pierce through the weak points of enemy armor using bows from afar, and swords once in close quarters.

In a bid for revenge Alex picked up a sword nearby. He stabbed it into the flesh of fallen Technicians. Those who did not remove their armor remained trapped in metal cages. They were in the same position as the Hive, only able to defend themselves with their fists. After a great slaughter of the Hive bodies Alex commanded that some Technicians be left alive. After doing so the Alliance threaded through the buildings, but due to the last attack a great difference had been made in their numbers. They only had twenty left. They had lost too many to keep advancing in their current manner.

"Wait!" Alex said as they ran inside a building. "Follow me." Alex led them up a stairwell.

Once at a higher level Alex looked out a window and saw that both Loyalists and Technicians were no longer being used as an offensive force. They instead carried fallen Hive bodies back to the restricted area. Their numbers were too many.

"We don't have enough," David realized.

"I know I failed, but I won't let that happen anymore."

"We remain breathing. It is not a failure."

"It's only success once this city is without war. I need you to lead the others."

"Are you abandoning us?" an Amishman asked.

The challenge did not bother Alex. He remained calm and understanding of the Amishman's worries. "No, I'm going to kill Conrad."

"You can't just walk through the city."

"I can," Alex stated as he lifted his hand upward showing the W marking etched into his skin. "David, take them out of the city. If Conrad passes his power onto another before I end him, the Hive will reignite. You won't be able to escape them."

"You'll require more than that tattoo to survive, considering what you're wearing," David criticized as he pointed to Alex's Collective uniform.

From the Amishman Alex receive a beige hooded shirt. A Libertarian gave him black pants. The last Technician gave him a knife for protection. A former Loyalist hung a W chain around his neck. David withdrew his last EMP grenade.

"My inventions are coming to be useful after all."

"I was wrong when I told you they aren't," Alex admitted.

"So was I. Everything I made was originally just for me."

212

The two men embraced, and without another word Alex slipped downstairs. Once he arrived at ground level, he picked up one of Conrad's cast-aside useless bodies. Its eye looked up towards him and nodded, knowing who he was.

"Why not kill me?" Alex asked.

"Proved yourself again," Conrad weakly revealed.

Alex gripped the body, angered by Conrad's indecisiveness, while he walked with haste. The edge of the restricted area appeared the same as it always had. A swirling of green smoke, deadly, incompatible with human lungs.

Next to Alex Loyalists and Technicians alike entered the smoke without any form of restraint. Once a body passed through it a hexagon appeared around its form, matching the camouflage technology of the island.

"It is fine," Conrad stated.

Alex held his breath and stepped forward. The swirling green mist clashed against his skin with a light brush, yet it did not do enough to cause him any pain. Alex kept his eyes closed while he walked, terrified that he would be used as a way for the Hive to steal his eyesight.

The wind against his skin suddenly stopped and Alex opened his eyes. What stood ahead of him appeared to be a dream. An image that he had only seen in photographs of the old world. The glass of the city's skyscrapers was intact. The concrete was without cracks. Solar electricity remained active.

"What is this?"

"My palace."

"It couldn't have always been like this."

"It has."

"But … the Collective that came here. They died, or came back sick."

"No. Some stayed. Those that did not. Memories stolen," Conrad revealed.

Alex felt like a fool for never entering the restricted Zone himself, to see what lay beyond its depths.

Huge signs were dotted around the city displaying the happiness of old world people. One showed a family sharing a meal; a second pictured an island where a rocket-ship lay dormant. A third showed Conrad. He was older in the photo. His arms were outstretched. He stared ahead with an inviting smile, his eyes brimming with life, his body athletic. His clothing was of the Collective's gray. On each of them Alex spotted the words Westwick Enterprises alongside his trademark W.

Seeing him from a different time period was enough to dishearten Alex about his own chosen path. Conrad had once owned so much. In return the well-known man had destroyed the world.

"This is old world. Will be new world," Conrad stated.

"I'm not interested in doing what you did."

"Can do better," Conrad proposed.

After a few minutes Alex came across his intended destination: Westwick Enterprises. The building was surrounded by Loyalist soldiers. Conrad's defunct bodies were piled within the gates; deterioration was clear across all, but their time spent dead varied. Skeletons were at the bottom of the pile and on top of them corpses lay in the midst of liquidation. Capping the pile was a few bloated figures turning blue. The cohort reminded Alex that the Hive was comprised from evil, but lost souls were used to perpetrate a cycle of war.

"To door," Conrad commanded.

The entrance to Westwick Enterprises mirrored the outside gates of Zone 6. It differentiated in the cultivation of green plasma bars instead of purple, which dissipated as Alex moved nearer.

Alex sighed and pushed his way through, embracing the fates of the deceased as motivation to enact revenge.

The inside of the building was painted gray. It was illuminated by solar powered white light. Three hallways stood before him. Signs indicated the purpose of each. To his left was a path to research and development; the middle to offices, and the right led to finances.

"Left," Conrad said.

As he progressed Alex looked into each of the rooms that he passed. They were all nearly identical. Each contained a silver sink embedded within a long black table. Brown cabinets were propped on the walls where labels revealed the material inside.

"Where it starts," Conrad revealed.

Alex realized that he was walking within the labs where the first experiments to manifest the Hive took place. He spotted jars both small and large brimming with Conrad's inner liquid. Photographs of the human anatomy were plastered onto walls. A notable image showed the inside of a human brain where flecks of green invaded the pink matter.

"Stop," Conrad's body said. It was its final word before it died.

Alex dropped the body and saw that the room he stood next to differed from the others. A hexagon table was erected at its midpoint.

Once Alex entered, the table shook and slowly lifted off the ground. Steam emerged from it, and as it cleared three metal pillars helped the object move. Underneath it all a staircase was revealed.

Alex was thankful for his decision to leave the others behind. With the remaining Alliance they would not have been able to arrive at Westwick Enterprises by brute force, and would not have known that the Hive's true heart was underground. It would have left them stranded for answers, wandering the facility in a long-form search for a location that would remain out of reach.

He stepped through it and after a short trip he was underground in darkness, but not alone. There were children of Conrad to his left and right. Alex reached for his sword and once his hand made contact with the weapon, he could sense that it now had the potential to be bordered by plasma which had been briefly killed by the EMP. Alex moved forward with suppressed fear. His last resort of the EMP grenade gave him the confidence to take quick steps. Once he reached the end of the tunnel the Hive's heart was revealed.

Directly ahead of Alex, a man sat in an elevated golden chair. Stairs made of metal led up to it.

He appeared past any age that Alex had seen. Wrinkles dominated his pale skin and willowy body. On top of his head was a circular ring. Thin wires stemmed from it. They threaded towards the ceiling, crossing over one another in a battle for airspace, pumped full of what was the Hive's signature liquid: a green stream infected with particles of gray.

Alex knew that it was Conrad who sat before him. His breath was weak. His dying aura matched the Hive that he controlled. Circling him in the room, standing far away from one another, were those who he had chosen.

The first he saw was an individual in a Mecha suit. It was white and thin, fitted to the tall body that owned it. The occupant's identity was covered by a mask. Its eyes were illuminated by a cold blue light. It did not have any visible weapons attached, but Alex was not fooled, for plastered onto it were blue dots that ran along its arms and legs. Alex knew that they would be used in an offensive maneuver.

Alex recognized the rest. A weaponless Raina stood next to him. She stared at Alex then glanced away, barely acknowledging his entrance. He wanted to go to her in comfort, knowing that everything she had loved had been stolen without an explanation as to why.

The others shocked Alex. A woman stood. Her braided gray hair remained still. It was Sheila who looked to Alex with a harsh frown. By her expression he was unable to tell if she knew about her son's fate. He almost withdrew his sword and cut her down where she stood for her betrayal. He figured he would have if it weren't for the final member of Conrad's chosen. Takeo.

Takeo and Alex looked into one another's eyes, in shock that the other still remained standing. Alex's instinct was that Takeo was a hostage, being held against his will through the Hive's grip on his blood. But Takeo's physical appearance dispelled the theory. He had been covered by Conrad's markings. The forehead stain that he had received on the island was small compared to what else he had received. The markings of Conrad had been placed all over his skin, leaving no body part untouched by permanent black ink. Takeo refused to break eye contact, unashamed of his state.

Compared to Takeo, Alex felt bare. He had nothing but his sword and the grenade that sat in his pocket. Takeo held onto his sheathed longsword strapped across his back, and the BN-10 cradled in his hand. Weapons that had potential to cause Alex's destruction.

"I will choose," Conrad announced. His primary body did not speak. Instead, it was from two Hive that resided at the bottom of the stairs.

"You already did! My son!" Sheila stated with desperation.

"You chose Lonnie?" Alex asked, stepping forward.

"Stop there!" the Technician warned. His hands raised, and from his palm a sliver of blue plasma made an appearance.

"He did, Alex," Sheila stated. "Don't ruin this. My son will—"

"Where is he?" Alex asked. The fact that Lonnie and Sheila had lied to him once again made him ball up his fist in disappointment, resulting in Lonnie's supposed death as a ploy to get him away from the Alliance.

"He was with you. Call him here."

What had occurred registered with Alex. "He didn't know what you were doing."

"Call him."

"If he doesn't want it, he shouldn't be considered," the Technician said.

"He can't be. He's dead," Alex announced, not knowing if it were true or not.

"Not good successor," Conrad decided.

"Stop lying to save yourself. After this we can work together," Sheila offered as her voice became brim with desperation. "Tell Conrad how capable Lonnie is."

"What I said was the truth."

"Is he in the city?"

Alex nodded.

"He's on the far left." From Sheila's pockets she withdrew a photograph. On it was not just Lonnie but another who shared his appearance. Not just one family that he had wiped from existence, but two.

"Stay back!" the Technician warned. "I'll bring it."

"Good try," Sheila said, ignoring his warning.

"I'll kill you."

"No," Conrad argued.

"I'll bring it," Takeo said, breaking his silence.

Takeo approached Sheila and she handed him the photo with reluctance. He then walked up to the Hive bodyguards and revealed the image.

"I search."

"You're not going to argue for yourself?" Alex challenged Takeo.

"I did," Takeo replied, ignoring Alex's plea.

"Dead," Conrad stated. "I will pick anew."

"No," Sheila whispered, falling to the floor.

"You're not here for Conrad's power," the Technician said. "Leave or die."

"I left my people for you."

"That was a choice that you made. Reginald here is the leader of the Technicians. He left them to be here, and he makes no complaints," Raina reminded.

"None of you understand! None of you have children!" Sheila shouted.

"Several," Conrad revealed to her.

"Fuck you," Sheila said blankly.

"You'll die for that!" Reginald claimed.

"Takeo. Go ahead. Do what you love."

Takeo withdrew his longsword. Its edges cackled with green energy. He approached Sheila and thrust.

Sheila's body fell and in that moment he understood why she had been so wary to join his cause. He wondered if he'd have known about Patton's fate, whether he would be so eager to kill the Hive, or if he would have done anything in his power to save it. Alex thought about the countless human lives that had been taken due to Conrad's selfishness. How they had the potential to live a full life if Conrad had descendants. A family together once again.

"Alex, why do you deserve this power?" Raina asked.

Alex froze, unsure what to say. He was not there to take Conrad's place. He only stood among them for the purpose of ending him, but achieving his goal would require the deaths of all those around him. A nearly impossible task without an ally.

"You chose me because I was able to take leadership of the island. I was able to unite different groups—"

"You failed," the Technician interrupted. "You would be dead if Conrad was not merciful towards you."

"Let him speak," Raina warned.

"I started as a Commander. A person who took orders. Then I turned into somebody who gave them with the short amount of time I had. What would I be if I had more?"

"He's here to kill you," Takeo said.

"Killing sounds like you," Alex accused.

"Conrad, I have been by your side for years!" the Technician growled in anger. "The people here. They are nothing!"

"Another comes," Conrad whispered through its final guard. From the entrance an additional body entered the room:

President Ye.

"Conrad, I apologize for my tardiness."

"Why should you have the Hive's power?" Raina said.

"I am the president of the Collective. I have led them to victory on multiple occasions, joining them in battle."

"You were never in battle," Takeo accused.

"I kept my people loyal."

"No, you didn't."

Conrad's primary body coughed and a gray trickle came from his mouth.

"You have to choose now," Raina suggested.

"I … Reginald," Conrad decided.

"You made the right choice," the Technician declared, revealing his true name as he walked towards the stairs.

"No!"

"The choice is made," Raina uttered, cutting off Takeo's pleas. Alex and Takeo looked to one another. Alex's eyes shifted towards Reginald and he subtly indicated that the Technician would be Takeo's target while Alex challenged Ye. Takeo nodded, showing his understanding.

Alex withdrew his grenade and smashed it onto the ground. It crafted the expected blue wave that took over the room. Reginald's suit turned black. His body fell due to technological failure.

Takeo pressed the trigger of his BN-10. Nothing came from it.

"Use your sword!" Alex commanded.

Takeo heeded his words, dropped his BN-10 and withdrew the blade from his back while Alex sprinted towards a helpless Ye.

"Leave!" Alex warned.

"I came to speak with Conrad," Ye declared. Alex raised his sword in response. "Please, this is all I have!"

"Go back to the Collective."

"I can't. The Zones have been stolen."

"By the Hive?" Alex asked. Ye shook his head.

"Other factions, but they're unlike anything I've ever seen, they—"

Alex grabbed Ye by his collar and threw him to the ground.

"You lied to us!"

"Us? You're a citizen?"

"Commander," Alex corrected. "Now go." Ye's focus turned towards Conrad's chair.

"Then remember your vows and help me. That's an order."

"I said leave."

Ye frowned with confusion. He then scoffed and tried to stand up.

Alex forced his sword into his former leader, killing him. When Alex turned, he discovered that Reginald's suit had somehow reactivated. Takeo moved against him with harsh strikes from his broadsword that were consistently blocked by a blue sphere that projected around Reginald's arms. His blue eyes flicked, signifying that the machine was in the midst of being reignited.

Alex ran forth to join him as Takeo took a swing at Reginald's right arm. Alex used the opportunity to strike his ribs. Reginald anticipated the strike and blocked it.

"What was that thing?" Takeo asked while the duo tirelessly slashed at Reginald's body, only to be parried.

"EMP grenade. David made it," Alex said.

"He's dead?"

"He's fine."

"EMP? I thought so," Reginald interjected. "A backup generator was a good idea."

"Drop!" Alex yelled.

Takeo ducked and swung for Reginald's legs. The maneuver forced the Technician upward, and Alex lodged his blade within the enemy's neck. Takeo delivered the killing blow by stabbing his own sword in Reginald's chest. The only enemy that existed was Conrad himself.

Both men turned to see that Conrad's mouth began to fill with gray. The EMP had taken a great effect. The two bodyguards that stood under him collapsed to the floor.

"Pick," Raina instructed. Conrad coughed again and his hands gripped Raina's wrist.

"How I feel. It hasn't changed at all," Takeo revealed.

"I know it hasn't, because you can't kill me. Most people are like us. They don't deserve to die."

"Look at the people here. Sheila betrayed you because she wanted her family to stay in power. Ye left us. Citizens turned on him. All of it was for stupid reasons."

"The world's pain will be because of you."

"Pick already!" Raina shouted.

"The Hive is dead! We won! We can walk away!" Alex begged.

"My mission is not over."

"Then neither is mine."

Alex lunged. Takeo sideswept and implemented an overhead strike. Alex blocked, but the driving force sent his sword clattering towards the ground. Takeo's secondary swing was cut short when Alex dove into him, forcing both men onto the ground.

Despite the setback Takeo managed to recover quickly, shoving Alex away.

Alex backed away weaponless, until he realized within his back pocket was the knife gifted to him by the Libertarian. As Alex's hand slipped to the hilt Takeo broke the silence.

"You had the chance to leave!" Takeo roared in anger.

"So did you."

Takeo charged. His blade remained ahead, blocking Alex from moving forward. As an alternative he pitched the dagger. The weapon plunged into Takeo's ribs, but it did not stop his movement. His red innards dripped onto the floor.

Behind him was the BN-10, its blue tint flickering behind Takeo's sprint. Alex matched his movements.

Takeo swung and Alex dashed underneath the assault. He rushed towards the BN-10. It rattled with power and within seconds Alex generated a sphere that hit Takeo's chest. His torso burst with blood and he collapsed to his knees.

Alex caught the body and Takeo's expression turned blank.

"Take the position. Rebuild," Takeo commanded with his final breath.

"I'm … yours," Raina said.

Alex turned to see that it was Conrad speaking through Raina's body. It was in the midst of dying; a trickle of green left her tear duct.

"Did you always have her, Conrad?" Alex asked. Conrad shook Raina's head.

"The EMP did this. Now you can't take anyone fully," Alex realized.

Alex walked past a dying Raina as he retrieved Takeo's sword from the ground.

"Why me?"

"Potential. The island. This city. Seen it everywhere. Others. Not fast enough," Conrad answered.

"Good to know I'm not your first choice."

"What about your children?" Alex asked.

"Unworthy."

"You trained them."

"Failed them."

"Because you didn't care," Alex accused. He thought of Patton who had been abandoned by his apathetic father.

"I gave them an island and mothers. Kept them safe. Protected them."

"When you die, do they die?" Alex asked.

"No. Only when the Hive dies."

He looked to the corpses that surrounded him. All of them being humans who would have desired peace, only able to achieve it through carnage.

"They gave up everything for you," Alex accused. "Raina. Takeo. Reginald!"

"Be better," Conrad said weakly.

Alex ripped the crown from Conrad's head and cast his body down the stairs. As he fell the ancient Conrad's flesh peeled, spilling blood of both a human and Hive. Within seconds it turned gray.

Alex decided to allow Zone 6 to fulfill its original promise. To do so he would need power. Alex took Conrad's crown and placed it onto his head, succeeding the Hive. Becoming an Alliance.

CHAPTER NINETEEN

THE PORTAL

On his motorized bike David rode alone. It was an object of the old world comprised of rusted metals, a thirst for gasoline, and a roar as it moved. At first David rode with caution, but once he understood its limits he became relaxed, moving across the land with intensity, for the bright day made for a peaceful ride and easy navigation.

His helmet allowed him to see through the night with clarity, gifting his eyes with information about both the surrounding terrain's temperature and time zone.

Having ridden far away from Zone 6 he began to wonder how Alex was holding out. He chuckled, recalling the many times he had called him by his first name. To David he would always be Commander Alexander King. Others deemed him to be God, even after it had been spread wide that the Hive was just a man, same as its replacement.

In the time that had passed since his transformation, David, alongside a few select others, were in the midst of making modifications to Alex's body, granting Alex the ability to move freely without the restrictions set in place by Conrad.

His journey had led him to Zone 4, a long-abandoned wasteland where whispers spoke of technology hidden by the Collective. David's confidence remained high for his previous expedition had reaped successes, bringing forth a great deal of resources to the Collective.

As David lamented on the past a black figure soared through the air. Its appearance caused David to stop suddenly as he stared, at first believing his eyes were failing him. He willed his helmet to look deeper, confirming that what he saw was not false. He had spotted a man covered in a black veneer that contained the occasional twinkle of bright light, somehow flying without a Mecha suit, nor jet pack.

David's immediate hypothesis was that the individual was wrapped within the technology of Zone 4 that he had pined for. Creations that were not seen in the world, written about in any books, or spoken through the mouths of shared myths, confirming that Zone 4 contained secrets ripe for discovery.

The man that he had seen had launched himself into the upper atmosphere of the earth, snaking its way through the clouds, moving past the point where David could see him.

David quickly reignited his bike and propelled himself forward. The option to follow the mysterious man with his eyes was gone, leaving him to search whatever he had left behind.

While navigating with his bike his drone followed closely, granting David an opportunity.

"Search the middle of the city," David commanded.

The drone took a few seconds to process his request, but eventually heeded his call, rising high above David and jetting itself into the empty city.

Having not received a warning from the drone, he stopped for a short moment, switching his helmet's priority so that he could view what the drone saw. His view of the drone suddenly faded, the reason of which was unknown. Many ideas popped within his head. He theorized that it may have been shot, but he did not hear any bullets dispel through the silent city, yet it remained a possibility that a silencer could have been used. His considered the chance that an EMP may have been activated, killing both the drone and his wireless connection to it. For a brief moment he regretted being alone, wishing that Alex were with him, or even Takeo, or Reese.

Guilt consumed him when he thought of their names, for he knew if a different set of actions had been taken they would still be alive. Their memories haunted him each day. He often lamented about how he would have given up his entire set of weaponry to have Reese hurl another insult at him, or for Takeo to speak about the future in his pessimistic terms, but his wishes were never granted.

David's arms were suddenly brought down to his sides, but not by his own doing. The rest of his body followed, coming to cement itself in one position. He quickly came to accept that he was facing some form of an attack, the origin of which became visible when a human figure wrapped in obsidian landed in front of him. It floated without either a Mecha or jetpack, implying that its flight came from the individual itself. As David came to face it directly he became unsure if it was human at all, for it lacked a nose and mouth, held the frame of a human, but had no skin. Instead it was surrounded by an inky blackness, where shining white lights rapidly dashed across its body. Some brighter than the others, each of them moving at a different pace. Both of its eyes were spheres of burning orange fire, and it stood without clothing.

"I am one. Meti, The Conqueror of the Cosmos. I am a steed of Demi. The true god of this land, and all others. I can already see your past. David Merlin. An inventor of sorts. One piece of what we need."

The being opened its fists, releasing David from his tough grip. The instinct to attempt an assault alluded him, for he did not know the bounds of his power.

"I will bring you to a different world."

David was suddenly pushed back to the earth where he stumbled through a beaming purple circle, making an appearance behind his feet.

"One with gods."

Manufactured by Amazon.ca
Bolton, ON

26996299R00129